FINAL DEMAND

Deborah Moggach

CHIVERS PRESS
BATH

First published 2001
by
Willian Heinemann
This Large Print edition published by
Chivers Press
by arrangement with
Random House Group Ltd
2001

ISBN 0 7540 1599 8

British Library Cataloguing in Publication Data available

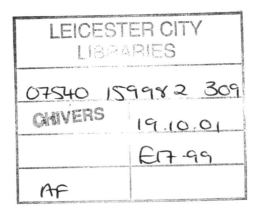
Printed and bound in Great Britain by
BOOKCRAFT, Midsomer Norton, Somerset

FINAL DEMAND

Natalie is a girl who should be going somewhere. Beautiful, bright and ambitious, she's stuck in a dead end job in the accounts departments of NuLine Telecommunications. Living her life through wild weekends, yearning for something more. When she sees a chance to change her life, she takes it. After all, it's only a minor crime. Nobody will be hurt, will they? But Colin gets hurt. He's the man Natalie marries. And other people's lives are changed, terribly and irrevocably. Because Natalie's actions do have consequences—tragic consequences for Chloe and her parents.

To Gerry W-F, with love

PART ONE

CHAPTER ONE

They blamed it on global warming. *It's a wake-up call*, they said. *It's a sign of what's to come.* All that November it rained. Britain was flooded, great swathes of it. On the news, the quaint names of rivers became as familiar as those of the latest celebrities. Day after day gales blew, buffeting Natalie's car when she drove to work, rocking it at traffic lights. Perhaps that had something to do with it, with her restlessness, with a feeling of *Is this all there is?*

The future of the planet held no interest for her; she seldom read newspapers. The rain, however, affected her. It trapped her in the present tense, the clouds blocking any vista beyond, any possibilities. She was trapped at work, perspiring under the strip lights. Back home she felt unsettled yet torpid, sitting on the edge of the bath and then realizing, with a jolt, that an hour had passed.

Something should be happening. The next big thing in her life should be happening but though time was speeding up, the days whisking past, a breathlessness to them now, Natalie's life remained doggedly the same. She was thirty-two. When she paused to consider this, the accumulation of years startled her. She found it hard to apply *thirty-two* to herself. Until recently she had been carried heedlessly in the current but now she found herself stilled in the bathroom, gazing at the fogged-up mirror, thinking: what next?

She rubbed herself dry whilst Kieran sat in the next room, channel-hopping. He should be a part of the *what next?* but when she went into the lounge there he sprawled, in a fug of smoke, and words failed her. They had lived together for three years. She adored him. She adored the way his finger traced her skin, under her dressing gown, with his eyes still fixed on the screen. She adored his fine profile, his mouth twitching as he smiled. His hair, pulled back in a ponytail, was tied with a band he had nicked from her bag.

Words failed her because he seemed content, and until recently, so had she. This new desire to shunt things forward made her shy with him. It revealed her to be like the girls at work, like large plain Stacey who had the hots for Derek in Dispatch and who dreamed of marriage and babies, doodling his surname on her jotter, MRS STACEY WINDSOR . . . MRS S. WINDSOR . . . Natalie pitied this; the naked need seemed humiliating. And then the desire would grip her, so strongly it stopped her breath.

She had no illusions about Kieran. He was a flirt. He sponged off her and stayed out late, supposedly with his mates. He worked when the mood took him, as a motorbike courier, roaring round Leeds on his Kawasaki 500 and chatting up receptionists. One day he might roar off and never return. She had a shameful desire to keep him to herself. He was like a deer, captured and kept in domesticity; one day he would grow restless and make a break for the wild.

This was how she felt, those dark autumn weeks with their turbulent, un-British storms. *It's a warning*, they said.

The next thing should be happening. And it did, but not the thing she had imagined.

4

*　　*　　*

It was a Saturday night, and they went down to the Club Danube in Chapel Street. O-Zone were playing. They were her favourite band and she had been a fan for years, long before their biggest hits ('Dog Days', 'Give It To Me'). She felt a proprietorial tenderness towards them, having had a one-night stand, back in 1995, with their lead singer Damon. Travelling down to London to hear them play, she had ended up in Room 316 of the Kensington Hilton (curling hospitality sandwiches, two lines of coke). When she had left, flushed and rumpled, in the small hours, Damon had given her a publicity photo with her name spelt 'Natlie' but she didn't mind. The guy might be dyslexic.

So now they were dancing, jammed up front near the stage, and Natalie was trying to catch the singer's eye whilst also watching Kieran, who was pressed up behind her friend Farida, his arms waving like hers and then dropping down around her shoulders when he shouted something in her ear and made her laugh.

Natalie edged closer. 'I wouldn't bother,' she yelled. 'Farida's getting married next month.'

'Anyone I know?' he asked.

'She hardly knows him herself. She's only met him twice.'

'You kidding?'

Farida nodded. Though Natalie was fond of her—they worked side by side—this arranged marriage revealed Farida as foreign, an Indian girl with her future an Indian one. Soon Natalie would lose her; Farida would step into the next room of

5

her life and close the door. Maureen, too, who worked in the same office: she was leaving to have a baby and Sioban was moving to Scarborough to be near her boyfriend, a married security guard at the Seaspray Caravan Park. Natalie's life felt flimsy, no foundation to it. Up on stage Damon's eye passed over her without a flicker; it was as if she had never crept from his hotel room, her knickers damp with all those unborn songs. In January this very building was to be demolished for redevelopment.

And when they stumbled out into the damp night, ears ringing from the music, she found that somebody had smashed the window of her car and stolen the radio.

Kieran picked up a cassette. 'Seems they didn't fancy your *Best of Moby*.' He kicked the glass away. 'Should get an alarm fitted.'

'Know how much they cost?'

'Yeah, but—'

'Why don't you pay half then?'

'Listen, babe, it's your car.'

She glared at him. 'Oh, so you'll be wanting to walk home then.'

This had happened before, several times. The neighbourhood where they lived had the highest crime rate in Leeds. Natalie, however, was still upset. She loved her car. It was a silver Honda Civic with sunroof and—before it was ripped out— quadrophonic sound system. Humans were not to be trusted—she had learnt this at an early age—but her car could be relied upon to remain where she had left it, awaiting her return like the most faithful of lovers. When she pressed her foot down, it surged in response. When she changed up to fifth,

6

it sighed like somebody settling back in an armchair. She cared for it too—she, who had cared for little in her life—probing its interior with her dipstick, daintily wiping her fingers with a moistened towelette. Each day it released her from work, from the numbing repetition, swallowing the motorway under its wheels as she sped across the moors, the huddled sheep caught in the headlights as she swung left towards Leeds (South).

And now it had been violated. On Monday morning, when she drove to work, Natalie seethed. The wind blew through the empty window, freezing her shoulder. What turned a human being into a criminal? The moment they smashed the glass? Or did they consider themselves a normal person who occasionally took advantage of other people's stupidity or inattention? Driving to work, that fateful Monday morning, crime was on her mind. She parked and slammed the door shut, hearing the fragments of glass settle into the lining.

Her insurance had expired. She had discovered this the night before, whilst rummaging through the unpaid bills wedged behind the toaster. She would have to find a garage and spend her precious Saturday getting it fixed. This nameless window-smasher, did he consider the time he had stolen from her life, apart from the money? And her O-Zone compilation tape was missing.

So it was hardly surprising that Natalie was in a mutinous mood that morning. It was a dank, foggy day. NuLine Telecommunications, where she worked, was a large office building stuck in the middle of an industrial estate, out on the moors, miles from anywhere. Around it loomed warehouses, Midas Wholesale, K.M.M. Refrigerated

Meats. Today they were shrouded in mist. There seemed no reason for the existence of these buildings in this particular place; like Farida's arranged marriage, it was just a matter of chance. 'This way's as good as any,' she said. A random choice, a pin on the map.

Accounts was open-plan. Natalie sat down at her desk. They were mostly women who worked there; they were blurs to each other through the frosted partitions. These were stuck with holiday postcards—beaches at dawn, Seattle at sunset, anywhere but here—and blurred Polaroids of Salsa Nite at Club X-Press. Photos of boyfriends and fiancés too. Soon these girls would disappear into other lives, for nobody stayed at NT for long.

For eight hours a day Natalie's life was suspended. Only her hands were busy, and a small portion of her brain, the part that ticked over like a car engine, for she was good at sums and could do them in her sleep. There were nine of them sitting there, lost in their daydreams. Cheques arrived, customers' cheques, payments for phone bills. They tapped them into their computers, registering them as paid. In the next office, Processing, the money was transferred from the customers' accounts to the one belonging to NuLine Telecommunications plc, a rapidly expanding company that prided itself on being, in the dizzy world of communications, the most aggressive competitor to BT. Natalie didn't give a fuck. She never stayed anywhere long. She was restless, waiting for the next thing, whatever that would be.

And the next thing arrived at ten twenty that morning. She slit open the envelope and pulled it out. It was just a cheque, like all the others.

The sum startled her for a moment, it looked so familiar. Then she realized.

Leaning back in her chair, so she could see Farida, she held out the cheque. 'Five hundred and fifty pounds,' she said. 'That's what a car alarm costs. Wouldn't life be simple if I could just pay this into my account?'

Farida took the cheque and looked at it. 'Will they never learn?'

'What do you mean?'

'They've written it out to *N.T.*, the wallies. They should've written the whole name, NuLine Telecommunications, otherwise it could get tampered with.' Her voice went syrupy. 'Bashir told me, the first time we met. He knows, being an accountant.'

At the time this meant nothing to Natalie. She didn't even ask how somebody could tamper with the cheques. She was more fascinated by Farida's voice, the way it softened when she mentioned Bashir's name. Was she already investing this man with love-at-first-sight in retrospect—a sort of backwards rosy glow? And how on earth could they have talked about something so boring?

*   *   *

Later they stood in the smokers' doorway, the two of them. Beside them, the extractor fan whirred out curry smells from the canteen. The fog had cleared; sunlight gleamed on the rows of parked cars. A white dog sat between a Range Rover (Management) and the rusting van belonging to Derek (Dispatch), the object of Stacey's lust.

'What did you mean about the cheques?' Natalie

9

asked. The dog stared at them with a fixed expression, as if remembering them for later.

'It's dead simple,' replied Farida. 'Like, there used to be a dental suppliers called C. Ash. What dentists did was write out a cheque, leaving out the full stop. Then they withdrew the cash, claiming it was business. Pathetic really, but it mounted up.'

'So what about here?'

'Easy. If your initials were N.T. you could write in the rest of your name and pocket the cheque.'

'That easy?'

'Have to have the right initials, of course. You and I couldn't—well, you could with the Natalie bit, I suppose.' She flicked away her butt. 'That's why people should pay by direct debit. That's what Bashir says.'

Farida went indoors. Natalie ground out her cigarette with the toe of her boot. The curtains of cloud had lifted; beneath them, between the buildings, the moors glowed with a lemony light. They looked like a stage set, like a show ready to begin.

Natalie couldn't move. She felt the blood draining from her body, down to her feet, leaving her weightless.

She looked at the dog. It held her gaze. Then it turned its head away and licked its balls.

*   *   *

The block of flats where she lived was called Meadowview. Somebody had a sense of humour. In the barricaded shop across the street, Natalie bought a bottle of wine. When she took the change, her hand was trembling.

10

She stepped outside. It was all strange to her—the heavy brick buildings, bathed in sodium light; the plastic seats at the bus stop. It was as if she was seeing them for the first time. Her own unfamiliarity filled her with panic. Heart thudding, she crossed the street, let herself in and walked up to their flat on the third floor. Soon I'll be out of here, she thought. Stay calm, it can happen.

Natalie went into the kitchen. A lone man had moved in next door; through the wall she heard his kettle whistling. She fetched a bowl and filled it with Bombay Mix. She was no home-maker—nor in fact was Kieran, they were similar in this respect—but tonight she plumped up the cushions like a housewife. She lit a candle and set out the wine glasses.

Hours seemed to pass before Kieran arrived home. He unzipped his leathers. She always loved this moment when he sloughed off the outside world.

He kissed her, slumped down in the armchair and felt for his Rizlas. There was something wrong with his bike, he said; she didn't catch what, she couldn't concentrate. His mate Keith tried to fix it but apparently it needed a whole new something.

She watched him as he licked the papers and laid them on his knee. 'It's OK,' she said. 'You won't have to worry about that.'

He bared his gums. 'Got my teeth cleaned today, just for you. Like 'em?'

'Soon you could buy a whole new bike.'

He looked at her, puzzled.

'A whole new set of teeth,' she said.

She started speaking. He was assembling the spliff. As she told him her plan his hands came to a standstill.

'You what?'

'It'd be so simple, see. I'd only do small sums, a hundred pounds here, a hundred pounds there. Not enough to notice.'

'But that's stealing.'

'What do *you* do each week?'

'That's different—'

'Signing on, claiming benefits?'

'But you'll get found out.'

Natalie ignored his tone. Her voice rose in excitement. 'No—see, I'd process their bills as paid, I've worked it out, it's bloody brilliant.'

He lit the joint and, with a hiss, sucked in the smoke. 'How have you worked it out?' His pale, bony face looked at her. With his hair scraped back like that he looked Slavic, a horseman of the Steppes.

'I'd log into the Processing program . . .' She explained how she would do it. As she spoke, the white dog flashed in front of her—sitting motionless, watching her face.

'You're bonkers,' Kieran said.

'I'd open building society accounts and pay in the money. And we could go on holiday. We could move somewhere nicer, somewhere with bus shelters that aren't smashed.' She smiled at him. 'You could buy a 1,000-cc Harley with a nice new whatever.'

Kieran didn't offer her the joint. She didn't dare reach for it; she didn't dare move.

'I can't believe you're saying this.'

'It's just an idea,' she said. 'I thought you'd be up for it, all the stuff you've told me, about what you did when you were a kid—'

12

'So how're you going to change your surname? Look a bit suspicious, wouldn't it? Just suddenly calling yourself something different.'

There was a silence.

'We could get married,' she said.

He stared at her. 'What?'

'Then I would be Natalie Turner. N.T.'

In the kitchen the tap dripped—plunk, plunk—on to the heaped-up plates in the sink. She didn't look at Kieran. Out of the corner of her eye she could see him leaning forward, his shoulders hunched, gazing at the carpet.

'I mean, I'm thirty-two,' she said casually. 'Other people do it . . . Maureen and Farida and your brother and, well . . . people *do* get married . . .'

'Yeah.'

'I mean, we've lived together for three years . . .' A little laugh. 'It's not such an odd thought, is it? I mean, we've never talked about it, but, you know . . .'

Kieran didn't speak. She felt heat spreading into her face. He cleared his throat. She couldn't look at him, not now, not ever.

'Forget it,' she muttered.

'Look, Nat—'

'Who wants to get married anyway? It's only a bit of paper.'

'Didn't know you were thinking about it—'

'I wasn't. Not really.'

'I mean, if you really want—'

'Forget it. I didn't mean it.'

Oh, the embarrassment, the horror of it. Natalie got up and went into the kitchen. Clattering and banging, in a fury of mortification, she washed up last night's dishes.

*   *   *

They didn't speak of it again. All week the conversation lay between them like a dead weight. I thought I knew him, Natalie reflected bitterly. How could I have got him so terribly wrong? She told none of her girlfriends about that humiliating night; their pity, their contempt for Kieran, and their rallying female solidarity would have been too much to bear.

To an outsider they carried on as before. Kieran was out most evenings. He was helping his dad, who was an electrician, refurbish a bar. This sudden interest in work was obviously an avoidance tactic. Back home they were polite with each other, as if they had recently met; Kieran was uncharacteristically solicitous—no flare-ups, no irritability. He even took their washing to the launderette. Natalie had no idea what was going on in his mind, none at all.

She had forgotten the conversation that had prompted this whole business. Tampering with cheques . . . how ludicrous it seemed now! How could she have entertained such a thought? Maybe it had spooked him. She tried to convince herself of this: that her plan had shaken him to the core and it would take him a while to recover. She tried to justify it this way, but it didn't work. The truth was simpler: he didn't love her the way she loved him.

On Friday her wages were smaller than usual. She took the pay slip to Mrs Roe, her supervisor, a woman with a mole on her chin, a woman who, until this week, Natalie had considered past it. But things were different now. Mrs Roe was a woman

14

somebody had loved enough to marry; no doubt there was a Mr Roe around, oiling his lawnmower ready for spring. No doubt there were Roe children, grown-up now, who dropped in for Sunday lunch. Natalie gazed at Mrs Roe with venom.

'There must be some mistake,' she said.

'Ah yes,' said her supervisor. 'I presume you were informed. It only affects the smokers.' She gazed out of the window, at the rain-lashed car park. 'You should have received a letter.'

Natalie shoved official-looking letters behind her toaster. 'I never got a letter,' she said.

'Those who smoke, and choose to do so in the designated areas, are from this month onwards subject to a mandatory time penalty.'

'A what?'

'The equivalent minutes are deducted from their wages—seven minutes, to be precise, mid-morning and mid-afternoon. Fourteen minutes in total.'

Natalie stared at her. 'You must be joking.' Mrs Roe was unmoved. She didn't care; in a month she would be retired and living on Lundy.

*   *   *

'It's so unfair!' said Natalie. 'They don't give a toss, not about us. You know how much profit they made last year?'

She was sitting with Kieran in a Slug and Lettuce. Though outraged, a small part of her was secretly gratified by NT's behaviour. It would draw Kieran closer to her, in sympathy.

Friday night, and the place was heaving with people. Natalie had to shout to make herself heard.

'They don't give a toss, what a dump! Monday morning I'm going to give in my notice.'

Things were easier between them; she felt it. A good moan put things back to normal. Happiness swept through her. So what if her boyfriend didn't want to marry her? Until recently she had felt exactly the same.

'Fuck 'em,' she said. 'Fuck them all.'

Natalie was a spirited young woman, toughened by life, for she had learnt resilience at an early age. It had been a humiliating week but all that was over now. She had an adorable boyfriend; he might be feckless, but in his own way he loved her. He just wasn't the marrying kind.

Kieran traced a puddle of beer with his finger. She gazed at his bent head, his hair scraped back from a centre parting. To tell the truth she didn't like his long hair, it made him look girlie, but what the hell. He was the best lover she had ever had. He could make her come just by touching her nipple with his finger.

He hadn't spoken, but then he had never been overly interested in her work. It was beyond his comprehension, how people could work at office jobs, nine to six, day in day out. So she just thought that his mind had drifted. They were going to a Michael Douglas film later.

He looked up. 'Natalie, we've got to talk.'

'What?'

'This is kind of hard, sweetheart . . .' He stood up. 'Let's get out of here.'

*   *   *

His mate Dexter arrived with the van he drove, for

kids with learning disabilities. Natalie, sitting on the bed, heard the thuds in the hallway as they removed Kieran's belongings.

After a while the thuds ceased. Down in the street the van drove away. The engine rattled; there was something wrong with the exhaust.

Kieran tapped on the door, already a visitor. He put his set of keys on the bed. Under the leather jacket he wore the green sweater she had given him for his birthday, back in August. This was the first time she had seen him wearing it.

'Let's stay in touch.' He hesitated, then he kissed her forehead. 'You going to be OK?'

What reply could she give to this? She took the piece of paper he gave her. A phone number was written on it. Dex had apparently found him a room; maybe they had spent all week looking for one. She didn't have the energy to speculate.

Kieran gazed around the walls. Maybe he was checking he hadn't forgotten something; maybe he was remembering this bedroom for later. She doubted this; he lived simply, in the present. He had already disappeared from this place.

'Take care,' he said, and then he was gone. A moment later she heard the roar of his motorbike, for the last time.

*   *   *

Natalie, who seldom phoned her mother, tried the last number she had been given. It was somewhere in the Dundee area.

'Nobody of that name here,' said a voice and rang off.

Later, after a spell of inaction sitting in the

17

kitchen, she went to collect her car from the garage. It was already dark; Saturday's meagre spell of daylight seemed to have come and gone without her noticing it.

The garage was up an alleyway, under a bridge. The cobbles shone greasily in the lamplight.

'Thursday last, a girl was stabbed along there,' said the mechanic. 'She was a Hungarian.'

Natalie leaned against her car. She had drunk the best part of a bottle of wine—maybe all of it, she couldn't remember.

'Can't take no chances,' he said. 'You're a wise girl, getting an alarm fitted.' He moved closer. 'This here activates it . . . series of beeps, listen . . . you press this, here, it immobilizes the engine.'

She tried to concentrate. They were alone. Outside, a train rattled past; the tins on the shelves trembled.

'And I fitted you a nice new radio.'

She said: 'Looks like I've bought back my old one.'

'Naughty naughty.' The mechanic wiped his hands on a rag. His nose was red and spongy, as if made from different material to the rest of his face. Yesterday, when she had brought in the car, it had been another man here. The garage seemed changed too—more cramped and lurid, with girlie calendars on the wall. Overnight her old life had gone, and been replaced by things that were entirely unfamiliar. She wouldn't have been surprised to find, when she returned home, that her flat had disappeared.

The man took her credit card and swiped it through his machine. 'Oh oh,' he said, 'who's been a bad girl then?'

'What?'

'Won't take it. You've exceeded your limit.'

She paused. 'Can I pay by instalments?'

He passed her the card. 'Only if I can look at your tits.'

Natalie's head swam. *I'm drunk.*

'Let's take a look at those boobies.' He moved to the door. It was one of those up-and-over ones. Grasping the lever, he started to slide it down.

'Don't close it,' she said. 'There's nobody around.'

It was freezing. Her fingers fumbled as she unbuttoned her coat. It seemed to take ages. She pulled up her sweater and T-shirt; then she pushed up her bra around her throat.

A moment passed. 'They do you proud,' he said, and turned away.

The concrete floor was stained, as if an ox had been slaughtered there. His face averted, the man blew his nose.

She readjusted her clothing and wrote him a cheque for the first instalment. He opened the car door for her.

'My wife lost her hand,' he said.

*   *   *

Gales blew across the moors, those dark November days. Sheep were battered by the rain. Trees cracked and split, exposing their wounds. Natalie was adrift, an ice floe broken loose. Oh, her friends were sympathetic. *I never liked him,* they said. *Typical bloke,* they said, *afraid of commitment. You can do better than him,* they said. But they were preoccupied, flat-hunting in the evenings, absorbed by their own futures. Nobody wanted to go out any more, drinking and clubbing, staving off the darkness. They were becoming too old for that. They had found their own pockets of light and had disappeared into them, one by one. Even Farida, her closest ally at that time, was preoccupied by her wedding preparations.

Natalie returned at night to an empty flat she could no longer afford. Bills silted up behind the toaster; the landlord had left a message on her answerphone. Outside, whoops echoed from the multistorey car park. She missed Kieran, desperately. That a man is worthless, in the eyes of the world, fails to ease the pain. In fact it makes it keener. How could she have been such a fool?

And then, two weeks after Kieran's departure, she came home to find the lights fused. Blundering around in the darkness, her lighter flickering, she suddenly burst into tears. She sat down heavily on a kitchen chair. Where was her father, now she needed him? The last she had heard, he was living on a beach in Thailand, with a girl called Phoo Long. She was alone in the world, lost, her breasts exposed to men with handless wives.

Through the wall, a woman shrieked with laughter. Kieran knew about electrics; it was he who had found them this rotten flat in the first place. How she longed to hear his voice. He would come round and fix the lights. He would gaze at her, in a blaze of illumination, and realize what a mistake he had made.

Natalie found the piece of paper and dialled his number. A machine answered. It was a woman's voice.

'Hi. Angie and Kieran aren't at home but please

leave a message . . .'

*   *   *

Revenge, like love, is a driving force, blind to
consequences. Like love, too, it is a form of
madness. Looking back, later, Natalie realized that
she was possessed by something beyond her
control. She had done some wild things in the past,
but nothing as bold as the plan that began to form
in her head.

Maybe it was triggered by Stacey's doodlings . . .
MRS S. WINDSOR . . . STACEY WINDSOR . . .
the married names that existed in a dream,
holograms of hope superimposed over a reality that
lay beneath, stubbornly problematical. Natalie had
done this herself, when she was a teenager.

She could remember the moment, however,
when it all fell into place. They were huddled in the
smokers' doorway, three of them, shifting like
cattle in the cold. It was four o'clock and already
dark. Up on the roof of the building, amongst the
masts and satellite dishes, glowed the sign: NT:
IT'S YOUR CALL. They stood there, smoking
their way through seven minutes of wages. The top-
floor windows were lit; those were the management
offices and the corporate hospitality suites.
Needless to say, none of them had been invited up
there to nibble canapés.

They were talking about love, and for a while
Natalie didn't listen. For the hundredth time, she
was picturing Kieran and Angie in their love nest.
He hadn't wasted any time, had he? How long had
he been seeing her, on the sly? Had he been
planning it for weeks? Natalie had met this Angie

21

once in the pub; she was his friend Dexter's ex-wife, a mousy woman whose features Natalie could scarcely recall. Kieran had left no address, only a phone number. His new life existed in limbo, but the images were horribly real. Was he pinioning Angie against the kitchen units as she tried to dish up dinner? Was he nuzzling her ear, the way that made Natalie swoon, and sliding his hand between her thighs? The setting for these excruciating tableaux was, for some reason, a dated, soap-opera domesticity that was entirely alien to the life she and Kieran had shared. It pained her, to make it too real. Besides, try as she might, she couldn't picture Angie and Kieran together. She was not his type. One's successor, however, always gives one a jolt, it reveals the unknowableness of the man one had thought so familiar.

Natalie suddenly realized: it was for Angie's benefit that he had cleaned his teeth. In their three years together he had never once visited the dentist.

Belinda, the other smoker, was cross-questioning Farida about her impending wedding. The girls at work kept returning to the subject of Bashir, it fascinated them.

'He might be a mass-murderer for all you know,' said Belinda. 'How can you do it?'

'It worked all right for my mum and dad,' said Farida. 'I mean, marriage, it's all a matter of chance, isn't it?'

'What about love?'

'Love comes later,' said Farida. 'You have to work at it. It's all a lottery anyway . . .'

Headlights swung across the car park; far away, Natalie heard the hum of traffic on the slip road that led to the motorway. The warehouses were bathed in a sodium glow. She had never seen a sign of life there but people must be working in those pointless places, just as she did.

'It's all luck. You never really know what you're going to get, even if you think you know somebody.' Farida flicked her butt into the darkness. 'My mum says it's like raw ingredients.'

Natalie inhaled a lungful of smoke. Something stirred in her brain.

' . . . they don't mean anything till you start to cook them . . .'

Like the white dog, Natalie's earlier plan had long since disappeared. The one that replaced it was so staggeringly bold that it took her breath away.

She leaned against the doorway. She wanted to burst into laughter and grab the others. *Guess what I've just thought of!* She wanted to see their faces.

Why not give it a try? After all, she had nothing to lose.

The wind blew down from the moors. It blew, with it, the faint sound of sheep bleating. Such a flustered, female noise; so silly. They sounded more nervous than she did.

*   *   *

Back at her desk, Natalie remained calm. She told herself: it's just a game, just a lark. Casually, she downloaded the NT staff list. Bella in Personnel had opened the file for her. Natalie scrolled down the surnames and stopped at T. She gazed at it.

After all, she had made some stupid choices in the past. Why not try pot-luck this time? It seemed as good a way as any. And if it didn't work, nobody would be the loser. Nobody would even know.

'Nat!'

She jumped. Beside her, through the partition, Farida burst into laughter.

'Nat, come and look at this.'

On her screen was a woman's face. *Hi, I'm Tiffany. Come and lick me for a fiver!*

'Surely your tongue would stick to the screen.'

Natalie laughed. Suddenly, what she was doing struck her as ridiculous. Worse than that, as mad. Touching the Print key, she already felt like a criminal. The paper slid like a tongue out of the machine.

She only printed up the T page, of course. There were nineteen of them, of whom six were men. *Tring, Mr P.: Product Development, Room 812 . . . Talbot, Mr L.: Office Services . . .* She scanned the list as if the names would tell her something, as if she could learn some detail about these men simply by inspecting their initials. Few of them looked familiar; NT was a large organization, over two hundred people worked in the building and there was little fraternizing, not in that godforsaken place; after work everybody simply got the hell out of there.

She held the sheet. The room drained away from her, like waves retreating hissingly from the shore, and she sat there alone in the echoing space. She thought: I've done nothing yet. I need do nothing. Across the partition, Sioban told Farida: 'They did it in his Datsun.'

Time passed. Natalie sat there. Her pile of envelopes remained unopened, but nobody noticed. Mrs Roe was in a meeting. At five thirty people started leaving for home.

'Know that girl in Huddersfield, the one who was raped? My brother was at school with her. He threw her asthma inhaler out of the window.'

Rapes, murders . . . crime was in the air today. Natalie sat there, twisting the ring around her finger. It was the E-string from Damon's guitar, his Martin; before she had left that night she had sliced it off with his coke-cutting knife. Later she had plaited it into a ring, her small, erotic memento.

Natalie rallied. She thought: I've got nothing to lose. After all, I only have to look at the guys and see if any of them takes my fancy. Where's the harm in that? And if one of them delivered her from this, from the boredom and debt, the helplessness of it all, then who would care later what means had been used?

Natalie went outside. It was freezing. Hailstones bounced off the roofs of the cars. She thought: This time next year I'll be lying on a beach. This time next year I'll be free.

And how sweet that revenge would be.

CHAPTER TWO

Natalie, who could be kind to strangers, once helped an old man across the road. Afterwards she said: 'Shame you can't see me, because I'm really pretty.'

She was stoned at the time; that excused her. But it was true. She was slim and freckled, with delicate shoulder blades that melted the heart. Her body was firm; she worked out, she took care of it. In those days, before she changed her appearance, her hair was tinted red—curly, wayward hair pinned up with butterfly clips. People could imagine her at school—bright and restless, up to mischief—for there was a vibrancy to her, she radiated energy; next to her voltage other people dimmed. This came from the simplest of sources: she was basically happy. She had sloughed off her past; she travelled through life singing loudly in her car, living for the moment. Kieran had thrown her off-balance, but what the hell. She would show him.

The next morning she woke in high spirits. Her plan energized her, as if she were starting a new job. No, it was better than that. She felt like an actress who, with beating heart, prepares to step on to the stage. That her co-stars were ignorant of the roles prepared for them made her already feel tenderly towards them. She had felt this in the past, when she had stepped into a club and pinpointed the man she was going to fuck that night. While he was still unaware of her intentions there would be a vulnerable look to him that she always found arousing.

She had wedged the bathroom window with newspaper but still a draught whistled through. She didn't care; soon she would be moving out. Down in the street, in front of the barricaded shop, two boys were draped over their bike handlebars. They looked like fellow conspirators.

She applied her war paint, gazing at her parted lips in the mirror. Like many attractive people, she took her beauty for granted. If she put her mind to it, she could get almost any man. This face, this body was her means of escape; this and her quick

26

wits. This and her desire to screw everything she could out of NuLine. All her life she had lived in Leeds but she was destined for better things. This cramped, heavy, Victorian city was too small for her grand ambitions. Its recent attempts at sophistication in the city centre—pavement cafés, atria—were simply like an old lady dressing herself up in youthful clothes. Life throbbed more powerfully somewhere else—anywhere but here. All she needed was nerve.

*   *   *

Roz Lacock, a hefty girl with a good heart, was going on a sponsored bike ride across Cuba.

'Want to pledge some money?' she asked, on the way to lunch.

'I'm broke,' said Natalie.

'Everybody says that.'

'Yeah, but I'm *really* broke. I'm overdrawn two thousand quid, I owe Farida seventy pounds, I'm behind with the payments on my car—'

'OK, OK . . .'

Roz moved away. Natalie stopped her. 'Wait a sec.'

*   *   *

After lunch Natalie took the lift up to the eighth floor. Her heart beat faster. This building was no longer a dull and anonymous office block; with sharpened senses she noticed every detail—the fire exits, the sudden glimpse, through a window, of mist-dimmed moorland. She hadn't been up this high before. Overnight the building had become

27

transformed, as a house does during a game of hide and seek. A woman with a plaster over her nose opened a door, looked out, and closed it again. Natalie walked along the corridor to room 812.

'Come in,' said P. Tring (Product Development).

The strip light shone on his bald head. His desk was bare, his fingers poised over a calculating machine. Natalie had the strangest feeling that he had been sitting there all day waiting for her tap on the door.

'Would you be interested in sponsoring a girl in our department?' She told him about the bike ride. 'It's for Mencap. That's mental health.'

'I know it's mental health,' he snapped. He got up and fetched his jacket. She thought he was going to bring out his wallet but he rubbed his arms and said, 'It's freezing in here. What's happened to the bloody heating?'

By no stretch of the imagination could he be called an attractive man. Still, she perservered. 'Any amount would do.'

It was then that she noticed the AIDS ribbon—a red AIDS ribbon pinned to his jacket. No Yorkshireman would wear an AIDS ribbon unless he were gay. In fact, it took some courage to wear one at all.

'It never ends, does it?' he sighed. 'Once one's home was one's castle. There they come, knocking at the door with their tea-towels and their dishcloths, *Excuse me, I'm just out of prison, excuse me, I've got a disability.* It's take take take . . .'

'But this is give give give.'

He put on his jacket. 'Donald does the washing-up anyway. He says I leave the glasses smeary.'

He gave her two pounds fifty. She felt strangely

invigorated by this encounter. She had plucked up courage and done it; nobody had sensed anything wrong. Besides, she was helping Mencap because she gave Roz the money, of course. Natalie wasn't wholly dishonest. People didn't understand that, later. She had never shoplifted, for instance, though some years earlier, on one of her dad's brief visits, she had pinched forty quid from his wallet. After all, he deserved it.

Back at her desk she crossed *P. Tring* off her list. One down, five to go.

*   *   *

'I'm sorry about our little altercation, Natalie,' said Mrs Roe.

'That's OK.'

'We like to consider NT a friendly environment.'

'Yeah, but it's so big,' said Natalie. They were queueing in the canteen. 'I've been here two years and I hardly know anybody. Like, I've got a message for Mr Talbot.' She gestured around, at the people eating lunch. 'Who on earth is he?'

'Len Talbot?' Mrs Roe looked around. 'Can't see him. He's usually to be found in Dispatch.'

*   *   *

It was the following afternoon. Dressed for the kill in a leather microskirt, Natalie tottered down to Dispatch. Two men were heaving boxes on to a trolley. They straightened up; one of them whistled.

'Hi, guys,' she said. 'Will you sponsor some money for a bike ride?'

29

'I'm a bit short,' said one of them.

'Yeah, he's only five foot five,' laughed the other.

'What about you?' She turned to him. 'Just a few pence a mile.'

He was the better-looking of the two—lean and wolfish. As he wrote down his name she imagined caressing his hair. She looked at the piece of paper: *John Cousins.*

Just her luck. The other one was shorter, with a rash of pimples over his forehead. She suddenly realized who he was; Stacey said he had problem skin. 'You must be Derek Windsor,' she said.

'How do you know?' he asked.

'Oh, I just read your name somewhere,' she said casually. 'Is Mr Talbot around?'

Derek shook his head. 'You want him?'

Natalie nodded.

'He's along there, in the stock room.'

The other one turned to Derek. 'Maybe I should go with her.'

'Why?' asked Natalie.

'He's a dangerous bloke.'

'That true?'

'He gives off this animal magnetism.'

'Really?' Natalie's spirits rose.

'Animal.'

'You just be careful, OK?'

Natalie walked along the corridor. She passed the toilets, her high heels clacking on the concrete floor. She passed the room set aside for the Muslims to pray in; it had a notice saying DANGER: 240 VOLTS on the door. Finally she arrived at the stock room.

She opened the door on to a cupboard filled with shelves of stationery. An elderly man sat

30

there, eating a doughnut.

'You'll be wanting the rubber bands,' he said, heaving himself to his feet.

He looked bloated, somehow pumped up from within. She recognized him; he delivered supplies to their department. They called him the Walrus, on account of his moustache.

'You're Mr Talbot?' she asked.

He nodded, and gave her a cardboard box. 'For Mrs Roe, with my compliments.' Beads of jam hung from his moustache.

Natalie stifled a giggle and made her escape. Unable to face the boys in Dispatch, she hurried out through a yard filled with dustbins. A cook, muttering into a mobile phone, shot her a glance.

Back in the office she gave the box of rubber bands to Mrs Roe, her supervisor. If only she could confide in somebody; maybe, then, they could laugh about it. Except they would think she was insane. Sitting at her desk she told herself: Natalie, keep your head. Nothing ventured, nothing gained. You're only sizing up these blokes, after all, to see if one of them takes your fancy. And if, by any chance, one of them does, then you can take it from there.

'Got a hot date?' asked Sioban.

Natalie smiled enigmatically, but already she felt distanced from her colleagues. This would get worse, much worse, but even the beginnings of a secret sets us apart. It's not what we're doing—for she had done nothing yet—it's what lies in our heads. Natalie's surprise at her own audacity made her a stranger even to herself, and there is nothing lonelier than that.

The phone rang. 'Miss Natalie Bingham? I have

Mr Blasham on the line—'

Natalie slammed down the receiver. Mr Blasham was her bank manager. She pressed the Engaged button and reached for the pile of envelopes.

*   *   *

Storms blew across the hills, dusting the peaks with snow. Outside Natalie's office the wind, whistling past the window, carried not just snow but also messages, voices blown through the ether on phones and e-mails, eddying around the twelve-storey NT building, conversations caught and alchemized into money, into profit—tears and jokes and mobile-phone conversations (*I'm on the train, I'm on the train*), talks that changed lives (*I'm pregnant, I'm leaving you*), talks that sold flats and bought holidays, that told lies or the terrible truth; conversations between strangers became, under the staff's quick fingers, pounds and pence, transferred, with the press of a key, into NT's account and swallowed up for ever.

As Natalie sat at her desk, gossip drifted past her, unheard. She was in a strange state during those weeks; later she could admit it. She felt like a racehorse, pawing the ground as she waited for the starting pistol. She felt restless, she couldn't sleep—she, who usually slept soundly. She felt she was embarking on a long voyage; one night she suddenly missed her friend Gloria, with whom she had worked at a health club in Halifax; she needed to connect up with a comprehensible past. But when she phoned the number the line was dead. She was alone in the world, nursing her secret like a growth, a lump that gained weight each day but

32

whose existence she didn't dare reveal to a doctor in case he took action. Don't panic, she told herself. Keep your head. Remember, nothing's happened yet; remember, you've nothing to lose.

She had drawn a blank with the homosexual and the Walrus. The next on her list was I. Toole, in Sales and Marketing. The following week she plucked up courage and took the elevator up to the third floor.

The door was ajar. In the room, a young bloke was hitting a ball of paper into a bin. He jumped.

'Don't stop,' she said.

'Thought you were Mr Slaughter.'

'I won't tell.'

He grinned at her. He looked carefree and boyish, as if he had just dropped into the office on a whim. 'Like the boots,' he said. 'Have I seen you before?'

'In the canteen?'

'I think I would've remembered. How long have you been here?'

'Two years.'

'Two whole years! What a waste!'

She smiled. 'Can you cope?'

He shook his head. 'I'll need some help.'

'I know a good therapist.'

'Great,' he said. 'Is she free tonight?'

This was going better than she had expected. She had no need of Roz's Cuba trip. 'Well, there was this Pilates class . . .'

'Who needs Pilates?'

'Then I was going for a drink with my friend Rhona, who does it with me . . .'

'Who needs Rhona?'

'I could always video them both and watch them

later.'

He laughed, and gave her a coin. 'Here's twenty pee. Phone your mum and tell her you won't be home tonight.'

Just then a side door opened. A woman put her head into the room.

'Ian,' she said. 'Your wife's on the phone. Do you want to take it?'

There was a silence.

'Ah,' said Ian Toole. He smiled ruefully at Natalie. 'Sorry, my little boy's teething.'

*   *   *

In the toilets, Roz asked: 'Got any pledges?'

'One or two,' said Natalie. 'But people are funny, aren't they? Just when you think they're going to deliver, something happens . . .' She shrugged. 'Still—win some, lose some.'

Roz brushed her hair. 'It's really kind of you, Natalie. Sometimes I think everybody's just out for themselves, know what I mean?'

*   *   *

The last three were swiftly eliminated; she realized this the moment she saw them. Terriaki, K. (Credit Control) was Japanese, and Japanese men had small dicks. The filing cabinet behind Tichmarsh, C. (Trainee Management) was covered with *Congratulations! It's a Girl!* cards so that counted him out. Tanner, J. (Security) was simply repulsive.

It was early December by now. Natalie gave up. In fact she had lost heart some days earlier, after the visit to Ian Toole. The last three Ts were simply idle curiosity.

The whole idea was ludicrous. It was lucky that she had come to her senses before she made a complete idiot of herself. How on earth could she have hit on a man for his surname? And, even if she had seduced him, why should that lead to marriage? Even then, suppose that all happened— that she was actually attracted to somebody, fell in love with them, got married—would she really have had the nerve to carry out her plan?

The possibility, however, had put a certain fizz into her life. It was Tuesday afternoon, and time had come to a standstill. For those in mindless jobs, Tuesdays are the slowest day. By Wednesday one is halfway to the weekend; it's downhill from then onwards; by Thursday there is a quickening in the air and the countdown can begin.

'You noticed how the clock doesn't move?' she said to Farida. 'It stops at three and just stays there?'

'Never mind. This time next year I'll be in Winnipeg.'

'Huh. All right for some.'

'Don't worry,' said Farida. 'Somebody'll come along. Somebody better than Kieran.'

'A bloke's not the answer. I've realized that.' She gazed at Damon's photo. *To Natlie*. One corner had come unstuck; the photo leaned towards her as if Damon were trying to tell her something. Soon, when the rest of the Blu Tack lost its grip, he would fall behind her desk. 'If you want to change your life, you've got to do it yourself. Forget blokes . . .'

Her voice died away. The far door opened and a man came in. He was accompanied by a group of Japanese businessmen. He gestured around; he looked as if he was giving them a tour of the building. His gaze stopped at Natalie.

She felt a jolt. She had felt it in the past, of course—the throb of it, the melting sensation in her guts—but not for some years. He was tall and rangy; dark hair. As a rule, she wasn't attracted to men in suits.

'Who's that?' she asked.

'Search me.'

Stacey leaned out from behind her partition. 'It's Phillip Tomlinson, the new Personnel Director.'

Natalie paused. 'Tomlinson?'

*   *   *

'Come in,' said a woman's voice.

Natalie opened the door. It was a large room—beige sofa, pictures—up on the twelfth floor. There were two desks, one of them empty. A middle-aged woman sat at the other one. She looked up irritably from her computer screen.

'Yes, can I help you?'

'Is Mr Tomlinson around?'

'He's in a meeting. Can I ask what it's about?'

'I'm collecting some sponsorship pledges.'

Her phone rang. The woman picked it up. 'He's still under sedation,' she said. 'They've given him a new knee.'

As she spoke, Natalie looked at the other desk. On it was a pack of Marlboros and a lighter.

The woman looked up. 'You'll have to make an appointment,' she said.

*   *   *

36

Stacey, putting on her coat, gazed at Natalie in the mirror.

'It's not fair,' she sighed. 'I've seen you in the canteen, tucking into all those chips.'

'Yeah, but you should see my tits. Two E's on an ironing board.' Natalie wound her scarf around her neck. 'How's it going with Derek? Got into his trousers yet?'

Stacey nodded. 'Last night.'

'He took long enough, didn't he?'

'I tried everything, but then we had this row.'

'What about?'

'Leeds' chances in the Cup.' Stacey picked up her bag. 'I mean, I don't give a toss but I read this article in *Marie Claire* which said that anger's a turn-on.'

*   *   *

The NT building was L-shaped. Smokers in Phillip Tomlinson's wing used another doorway. Natalie found him there at tea-time, the next day.

'Was it your decision, to clobber the smokers?' she demanded.

'I beg your pardon?'

'It was way out of order.' She pointed to his cigarette. 'Bet they don't deduct *that* from your wages.'

'It was nothing to do with me—er—'

'Natalie.'

'Natalie. I only arrived last month.'

'You've even got your own doorway. I suppose I need a place on the board to smoke here.'

'It's not specially for directors,' he said. 'It just happens to be near my office.'

37

'The whole thing's pathetic.'

Phillip held out the packet. 'Would you like one?'

Close-up, he had smooth, regular features; he looked like a golfing pro. Not her type. He even wore a polo-neck jumper under his sports jacket. Natalie felt another surprising jolt of desire.

'I don't want your poxy cigarettes,' she said. 'See, it's the little things people notice, the people in my position, it's the little petty things.' Her voice rose. 'We're the ones who keep this place going and if you treat us like shit we leave. It's so stupid, so bloody un-cost-effective, because then you've got to get somebody else, haven't you? Advertise for them and interview them and train them up—and all for a fucking seven minutes!' She paused for breath. 'See, *we* notice seven minutes. So go and tell them to stuff themselves.'

He stared down at her. 'Wow.'

Natalie turned on her heel and left.

Back in the office she sat at her desk, shaking with silent laughter.

*   *   *

The afternoon raced by. Stacey pressed her fingers into her stomach. 'I think I'm getting fibroids,' she said.

Sioban put down the phone, her eyes brimming with tears. The deal on the Scarborough flat had fallen through. 'It had asbestos in its extension,' she said. 'It's a sign I shouldn't go. I wasn't cut out to be the other woman.'

'Try these,' said Farida, passing out St John's Wort tablets. 'My auntie swears by them.'

Natalie blithely swallowed one, her mind elsewhere. Skittish and insouciant, she sped through her work. At five thirty, when everyone was packing up, she hurried outside to the car park. His Audi was parked in its designated space: P. TOMLINSON. There was room next to it, so she backed her car into the gap and returned inside.

Management always worked late. Natalie lingered in the toilets. Through the window she could see the twelfth floor, up on the other wing of the building. His window was still lit. She misted herself with Arpège.

You press this, here, it immobilizes the engine.

How helpless a woman is when her car won't start! How hard Natalie tried, the engine turning over, grindingly, and soon dwindling to the feeblest of groans. Only a few moments and she believed in her own lie, she was good at that, she came from a family of self-deluders.

In the rear-view mirror she saw Phillip emerge from the building and, bent against the wind, make his way towards her. He knocked on her window. Reluctantly, she wound it down.

'What seems to be the trouble?' he asked.

'Nothing. I'm fine.'

'You sure?'

She burst into tears. She could do this, by thinking of her goldfish that had died.

'Don't cry,' he said.

'I'm fine,' she sobbed. 'Go away!'

'Budge up.'

She shifted into the passenger seat. 'Bloody car,' she muttered and blew her nose.

'A damsel in distress . . . such a rare sight nowadays.' He tried to rev the engine. 'Battery's

39

flat. Allow me to come to your rescue with my trusty jump leads.'

His eyes flickered down to her legs. Her skirt had ridden up, exposing her thighs.

'Haven't you got to get home?' she asked.

'I'm in no hurry,' he said.

'That true?'

'I'm utterly at your disposal.' He smiled at her.

The car park was almost empty now; there was room for him to reverse his car and manoeuvre it into the mating position next to hers, bonnet to bonnet. He fiddled inside the engine, fixing the leads. She could tell, by the hunch of his back, that he knew she was watching him.

Straightening up, he rubbed his fingers with a handkerchief. 'Ready to be charged up?' he asked, eyebrows raised.

'I feel awful, after what I said to you,' she snuffled.

'Don't think of it.' His eyes moved up and down her body. She smiled, weakly.

They sat in their respective cars, revving the engines. Natalie's didn't fire. Through the leads, she could feel his lust vibrating. Catching his eye, she shrugged at him. He shrugged back and switched off his engine. Through their windscreens they gazed at each other. She felt a rush of gratitude, that he was helping her even as she tricked him, that they were both in this together. He opened her door and held out his hand.

'Do you forgive me for earlier, Natalie?' he asked.

She nodded.

He took her hand. 'Come on,' he said. 'I'm driving you home.'

He accelerated fast, up the slip road. Flung back in her seat, Natalie thought: How manly he is! She could forgive him the laborious, damsel-in-distress gallantry. As he sped along the motorway, veering around lorries, flashing dawdling cars, she surrendered herself to voluptuous anticipation. She knew she had ensnared him: first through anger, then through tears. They were already plunged into intimacy.

She turned to him. 'Sorry I snapped at you,' she said. 'I was in a bit of a state. My boyfriend and I, we split up last month.'

'Ah.' He paused. 'So how do you feel?'

'Great.' She smiled at him. 'Really great.'

He turned to look at her. 'Footloose and fancy-free?'

He was nervous, she could tell. The bravado of his driving was only to impress her. One hand casually gripped the wheel while the other clenched and unclenched in his lap. She gazed at his profile. Like many faces, when seen from the side he was another person: weak chin, beakier nose than she had realized. This, however, didn't dampen her lust—the sharp and thrilling lust one feels for a stranger with whom one plans soon to be intimate, their skin as yet unfelt under their clothes.

'Aren't I the lucky one,' he said. 'Taking home the prettiest girl in the office.'

He parked outside her flat. He gazed out of the window. A torn police tape dangled from a lamp-post; another incident must have taken place.

'Crap area, right?' she said. 'I don't plan to stay

41

here long.'

Phillip switched off the engine and turned to her. The streetlamp illuminated the fur around his ears. She thought: We're just animals, the two of us. Mammals on heat.

'Want to come up for a drink?' she asked.

*   *   *

She closed the door. Phillip pulled her against him and kissed her clumsily, their noses bumping. Even Natalie was taken by surprise. Dropping her bag, she clasped him in his bulky sheepskin jacket. His head knocked against the wall; the mirror skewed sideways.

'I've been wanting to do this all day,' he muttered.

They fumbled off each other's coats and stumbled into the bedroom. It was chilly, its curtains still closed from the morning. In the darkness Natalie groped for the bed, pulling him with her; she helped him yank off her tights and knickers. He slewed her round on the bed, manhandling her as if she were a rag doll. He pushed her legs apart and plunged his head between them.

She had to admit that he was a skilled lover in a virtuoso, look-at-me sort of way. She could tell he was going through his paces to show her what he was capable of—first the moist nuzzlings, his lizard tongue flicking in and out, then the swift undressing, the nipple-licking, the cunty kisses on her mouth and the efficient rolling-on of a condom. He slid in, startling her. 'Am I hurting you?' he whispered smugly.

42

She pulled his head close and silenced him with her lips. Wrapping her strong, thin arms around him she was flooded with such pleasure that she forgot there had been a plan to this.

*　　　*　　　*

The next two weeks were a surprise to her. Heated by Phillip's passion, her heart melted. He wasn't her type—too clean-cut, too male-model—but there was a thrill to it, having an affair with her superior: snatched kisses in the toilets, a frisson when he stood in the office talking to Mrs Roe ('No can do, Stella') and their eyes met. Passing him in the corridor when he was talking to a colleague ('It's your turn to give Fraser a bollocking'). Sitting at her desk, thighs aching from lovemaking, Natalie found messages to *hotlips* on her screen. *Can't wait for tonite.* When he wandered into Accounts—which he did nowadays on the smallest pretext—when he paused at her desk the sounds around them drained away, as they did when she thought of her plan; they left herself and Phillip, alone in the world.

And he was besotted, no doubt about that. Lying in her arms, listening to the shouts echoing down in the street, he whispered: 'I'm going to take you away from all this.'

'Where to?'

He ran his finger down her freckled arm. 'Anywhere but here. You deserve better.'

'I know.'

He enfolded her, he made her yielding and female, she astonished herself. But then he went home. He never stayed the night, he said he had to take his dog around the block before bed.

'What's his name?'

'Arnold. He has a prostate problem.' He stroked her cheek. 'You can laugh, you're not a bloke. Thank God.'

He never asked her over to his place, which was out beyond Dewsbury. His ex-girlfriend, with whom he had recently split up, still had a key.

'Thing is, people think we're still together. She hasn't told anyone.'

'They've got to know, sooner or later.'

'She's taken it very badly. She's still got some stuff in the flat and she just pops in, without warning.'

'Sounds loopy to me.'

'If she saw you, she'd go berserk.'

'Why don't you change the locks?'

'I'll get it sorted out, I promise. You don't mind, do you?'

With the generosity of the victor, Natalie shook her head. She was still drugged with love. She smiled at the security guard in Reception; she sent Phillip an e-mail when he was in the middle of a meeting with some people from Stuttgart. She pictured his face as he read it. *Excuse me, ladies and gentlemen*, he'd be saying, rising to his feet. *I have to check some data in the other office.* She waited for him in the ladies' cloakroom, her knickers draped over the cubicle door. How thrilling, the danger!

'What if someone comes in?' he whispered.

'Shut up.'

She unzipped his trousers, sat him on the toilet and, straddling him, fucked him with a furious passion. Afterwards they slumped against each other, limp and laughing.

He gazed at her, wiping her damp hair from her forehead. 'Oh Natalie Natalie, where have you been all my life?' He zipped up his trousers. 'Listen, sweetheart—don't tell anybody about us, OK? Don't want any gossip, you know what offices are like.' He kissed her. 'I want to keep you all to myself.' And then he went back to his meeting.

The new, compliant Natalie went along with this. She lived for the night. The flat was no longer desolate for her, with its relics of Kieran's occupation—his scrawled writing on her video cassettes, his *Teach Yourself Spanish* from his short-lived evening class. So potent once, they were now defused and could no longer upset her; Kieran had gone, and simply left objects behind. Her flat was transformed by erotic anticipation; for two weeks it became a palace of love as if it had never known a normal, hair-drying, telly-watching evening. She was a terrible cook but she bought prawns and mangoes and put wine in the fridge to chill. She bought scented candles and stuck them around the bathroom, as one does in the early days of love; she and Phillip sat in the bath together, their jack-knifed knees draped with foam, her toes caressing his balls.

As they sat there, the mirror steaming up, she told him about her childhood. She had worked it up into a series of anecdotes by now; they gained in drama with each telling. By now her past felt as if it had happened to somebody else.

'Shredded Wheat?' he asked. 'For three days?'

'I was only little. I didn't know how to work the tin opener.'

'What about the baby?'

45

'I gave it to him too. He liked it, actually.'

'Didn't the milk go sour?'

'I nicked some from outside the flat next door. And then my mum came home so that was all right.'

'Doesn't sound all right to me. The woman was an alcoholic.'

'Is. She's still around, somewhere.' Applying the word 'alcoholic' to her mother was as startling as applying 'arranged marriage' to Farida; it made her into a case, something no doubt her mother would cheerfully admit. Janey, when she wasn't boozily weeping, was a cheerful woman. You could say that for her.

'Weren't the social services involved?' he asked.

'They took away two of the younger ones but we kept moving around, see. They couldn't catch up. Halifax, York . . . I knew it was going to happen when she told me to keep my clothes on when I went to bed.'

'You're a survivor, aren't you?'

She scooped up water and spilt it over his knees. 'You've got to look after yourself in this world. Nobody else is going to do it for you.' She could always get a man's sympathy by talking about her parents. This was the one thing they had done for her. 'My parents never grew up, see. They were sixties kids.' She told him how her father had bailed out when she was little, going to Ibiza and smoking dope, working on the boats, going off to Thailand to live with what's-her-name.

Phillip gazed at her tenderly. 'Do you miss him?'

'Oh, there's been plenty since him. No shortage of blokes when my mum was around.' She thought of Raymond, creeping in at night when her mother was asleep. She would save the Raymond stories till later. 'She's been shacked up with five of them since then.'

'That the truth?'

She nodded. 'I wouldn't lie about something like that.'

'What *would* you lie about?'

'What would *you*?'

'I asked first,' he said.

She gazed at the sliver of soap. 'Sometimes I start with a lie, then I find out it wasn't needed at all.'

'Why not?'

'Because it's become the truth.'

For once, she had spoken from the heart.

Phillip left, to go home. She gazed at him over the landing as he descended the stairs. He was nearly forty; from here, she could see his thinning hair.

Back in the bathroom she stood in front of the steamed-up mirror. In the condensation she wrote, with her finger, *N. TOMLINSON* . . . She watched the letters weep.

*   *   *

She longed for Phillip to spend the night. She wanted to wake up with him in the morning and lend him her toothbrush. Maybe he liked listening to the *Today* programme. She didn't mind; she ought to know what was happening in the world. He could even bring his dog around; she liked all animals except the slithery kind. She lusted after him, she wanted to see more of him; it was as simple as that.

47

She didn't see him on Thursday; he was at a conference in London. By Friday she was missing him keenly. During her morning break she went to his smokers' doorway but he wasn't there. Taking the elevator to the twelfth floor, she sauntered past his office but his desk was empty. She didn't dare enter; he had advised her not to, it might arouse suspicions. 'Mrs Johns has eyes like a hawk,' he said. Back at her desk Natalie rang his mobile but it had been switched off.

At lunchtime, in the canteen, she saw Mrs Johns. Lips pursed, she was picking her way through a biryani. Natalie stopped at her table. 'I've been looking for Mr Tomlinson.'

'He's in meetings all day.' Mrs Johns removed a piece of cinnamon bark and placed it on the side of her plate. 'If you want an appointment, phone on Monday.'

Outside there was a rumble of thunder. Natalie comforted herself with the knowledge, gleaned from Phillip, that Mrs Johns's husband had left her for a twenty-eight-year-old IT consultant.

She sat down with Sioban, who closed the book she was reading, *Do It Yourself Conveyancing*. 'Did you know that the best way to get rid of wrinkles is to rub them with haemorrhoid cream?'

I'm getting old, thought Natalie. I'm nearly thirty-three, there are lines between my eyes, soon I'll be too old for anybody to love. Sioban's bookmark was a boarding pass. Her security guard had taken her to Paris for an illicit weekend. *They* had spent the night together; they had woken in a strange hotel room and brushed their teeth in unison.

All afternoon the storm raged. Over the blips of

the computers and the hum of conversation—its volume always rose on Friday afternoons—over this Natalie could hear the rain lashing at the windows. Why didn't Phillip phone? As yet they had made no date for the weekend. In fact, both weekends she had known him he had been busy, the first at a badminton tournament and the second visiting his parents in Keighley.

At the time she just felt mild vexation. He was busy, after all; his work was a lot more demanding than hers. This wouldn't be difficult. 'You're wasted in that job,' he said, 'bright girl like you.' She suspected nothing, for love had made her stupid.

At five thirty the others started packing up. She waited until six, then she wrote him a note, *Home all evening, phone me.* She slipped it into a plastic folder extracted from Mrs Roe's cupboard. She and Phillip often stuck things under the windscreens of each other's cars—jokes, assignations. Like the e-mails it gave them a frisson, thrumming beneath the surface of their days.

Natalie left the building. The wind sent her reeling; the moors had their own climate, ten degrees colder than anywhere else. Up on the twelfth floor, Phillip's window was still lit. Bent against the rain, she hurried across to his car.

Another vehicle, however, was parked in its place: a hatchback. Natalie pressed her face against its window. A child's seat was strapped into the rear.

Puzzled, she straightened up. Around her doors slammed, engines revved. A man was getting into the next car; she recognized him, he had been smoking with Phillip that first day.

'Whose car's in Mr Tomlinson's space?' she shouted at him, through the rain.

'Must be Melanie's.'

'Whose?' She raised her voice.

'MELANIE'S!' he yelled. 'His wife's.'

*　　　*　　　*

A good liar knows about detail—not too much, which might arouse suspicions, for which innocent person can accurately itemize their actions? Just enough to casually suggest a life, a fictitious scenario of which only the iceberg tip is visible. It's an art, of doubtful moral value but more useful than most, and Natalie herself was a deft practitioner. Indeed, over the coming months she would exploit her skill to breaking point. Part of the pain, in discovering Phillip's deception, part of the pain and loss was the discovery that in the lying stakes she had met her match. He was a man after her own heart.

Phillip had a wife, Melanie, and two children: Kelly, eighteen months, and Tom, four. He didn't have a dog. Arnold, whose urinary problems had roused Natalie's sympathy, was simply a figment of Phillip's surprisingly fertile imagination. No wonder he had had to get home each night. What was Natalie called? Late meetings, business dinners?

All this Natalie discovered as they sat in her car, the rain drumming on the roof. She had ambushed Phillip as he left the building.

'I'm crazy about you,' he said.

'Oh yeah?'

'Crazy.'

'You creep!'

'I was going to tell you—at the beginning I thought you must know—but then it was too late—'

'You lying prick, you—you—' She tried to hit him but there was no room. Uselessly she pummelled him with her fists; the sheepskin jacket was too thick.

'Melanie and I—'

'Fuck Melanie—'

'Melanie and me, we're not happy, the marriage has been dead for years—'

'Oh shut up.'

'It's you I love—'

'So you're going to leave her then?'

There was a silence. The rain had stopped. By now the car park had emptied.

'Get out,' she said. 'Get out and fuck off.'

*   *   *

Tears pricked Natalie's eyes but she was not going to cry, not her. She drove along the motorway, back towards Leeds. The oncoming headlamps blurred. Traffic was heavy; it was Friday night, people were on the move. How senselessly busy they all seemed! It felt like a week—a month—since that morning, when she had driven in the opposite direction. Time had been dislocated, its joints swinging loose. She couldn't believe her own stupidity: why hadn't she seen the signs? Was she really such an idiot? And there she was, almost falling in love. Almost dreaming up a *future*.

Natalie left the motorway and drove towards the city. Lights dazzled her, blurred by her angry tears.

Revving up, she swung out to overtake the car ahead. An oncoming car hooted, blinding her with its headlights. She braked and slipped back.

As she drove into Leeds she thought: So that's the end of my plan then. It was almost a relief, to feel it finally dissolve away. Strangely enough the affair with Phillip, which might have turned it into reality, had made it irrelevant.

She stopped at some traffic lights. It was a crazy idea, truly crazy. Maybe Phillip had sensed something odd about her, from the start. Oh, the *bastard*.

The lights changed to green. Natalie pressed the accelerator pedal. Nothing happened. The engine had cut out.

Behind her, cars hooted. Flustered, Natalie tried again. The engine turned over, grindingly, but didn't catch. She tried again: nothing. This time it was for real; her car truly wouldn't start. Behind her, cars reversed. A huge McDonald's lorry rumbled past. It was then that she noticed the warning light on the petrol gauge. The tank was empty.

You think you have fallen as low as you can get, that you've hit rock-bottom. Then the floor collapses and you fall still further. As Natalie trudged the two miles home—after a lengthy wait, she had persuaded a passer-by to help push her car on to the pavement, where it would no doubt collect a ticket—as she trudged past lit pubs, laughter issuing from them, other people's Friday nights, she thought: Fuck it all. It had started to rain again; her shoes were sodden, she was freezing cold. She passed an NT Phone Shop, empty and brightly lit. NT, IT'S YOUR CALL. She had tried to phone a cab but her mobile battery was flat and when she tried to use a phone box it swallowed up her twenty-pence piece. Cars hissed past her as she walked along the main road.

Betrayed and sodden, Natalie trudged along the pavement. One of the cars slowed down and parked, a few yards ahead of her.

Natalie stopped. There was nobody around; just a sliding stream of cars passing. She pretended to inspect the wall. Somebody called Kevin had sprayed SUCK MY KNOB on it. Out of the corner of her eye she could see the car, waiting.

Thursday last, a girl was stabbed along there. Natalie started running. She darted up a side street. *That girl who was raped? My brother was at school with her . . .* She ran past a row of houses due for demolition, their windows boarded up. Calm down, she told herself. She hummed a Sheryl Crow song: *A change, change, change will do you good . . .*

Then she was out on a main road, somewhere she didn't recognize, and Kieran waited at the traffic lights. Her heart leapt. There he was, on his motorbike, clouds of exhaust billowing into the night air.

A damsel in distress . . . such a rare sight nowadays.

'Kieran!' she yelled. She had never been so pleased to see anybody, in all her life. They would sit in a pub together, like old times. All that rancour would be forgotten.

'Kieran!' she shouted again, but he didn't hear.

She rushed up to him and tapped his leather jacket. He lifted his visor.

She stepped back. 'Oh. Sorry.'

*   *   *

By the time Natalie reached home she had made a decision. This time she would really do it—cut her losses and jack it in. Monday morning she would give in her notice; she had had enough of the whole bloody business. As she climbed the stairs, hurrying before the light switched off, as she fumbled, with frozen fingers, for her keys, she thought: I'm getting out of here. I'll go to London, it's high time I bailed out. After all, my mum did it enough times. I'm bright, I'll get by. Something will turn up.

*   *   *

Next morning she was woken by the ring of the bell. She wrapped herself in a towel and opened the door.

A young man stood there: square, sturdy. He wore some sort of official work-clothes.

'Sorry to disturb you, miss,' he said. 'I'm from the gas company.' He shifted from one foot to the other. 'I hate this bit.' He had a broad Yorkshire accent.

She moved aside. 'The meter's through there.'

'No.' He cleared his throat. 'I—er—regret to inform you that I've come here to disconnect your supply. For non-payment of your bill.'

Natalie stared at him.

'Here's my ID.' He held out a card. Sheathed in yellowing plastic, it showed his photo, *Registered Gas Fitter* and his name: C. TAYLOR. 'My authorization,' he said.

She bent closer to read. 'Taylor.'

He nodded. 'That's the name. Colin Taylor.'

54

A moment passed. Then Natalie, clutching her towel around her, put out her hand. 'Pleased to meet you,' she said.

Surprised, he put down his metal case and shook her hand.

'Come in,' she said, and smiled at him.

CHAPTER THREE

Colin, fondly known as Stumpy to his friends, was one of life's innocents. Unworldly, generally of a cheerful disposition, he was bemused by the litany of violence he heard on the radio when he was driving hither and thither in his gas-board van. How could folk do that to each other? It was beyond his comprehension, for he still believed, against all the odds, in the innate goodness of human nature. Thinking the best of people gave him, at this point in the world's history, a quaintness, as if he should have been born in another era. As if he should have remained a boy.

Which, in a sense, he had. 'Stumpy' suited him, for he had the rolling gait and eager, open face of a chubby little boy in dungarees, running open-armed to embrace what life had to offer. If it were a slap he would pick himself up and start all over again for he was a born optimist, a simple soul, and everybody loved him.

Nobody loved him more fiercely than his mother. He had lived with her all his life and she protected him with a passion. Her name was Peggy and she came from a long line of grim, determined Yorkshire farmers, who worked the unforgiving land and who had no truck with displays of feeling.

Ah, but she had feelings, powerful ones, and they centred around her son. Colin was her only child, born to her in her middle years when all hope of motherhood had faded. His father was long since dead. Her son was a miracle to her, though she would have gruffly pooh-poohed such a word. They lived together on the edge of Leeds, on a bleak estate where rain lashed the grey stucco houses. Colin was her sunshine, he was the love of her life.

Colin was twenty-five. Whether he was still a virgin was a source of some speculation to his mates. They were not aware of any girlfriend, past or present, and he expressed no interest in women. In the pub, when they told dirty jokes, he simply looked blank. Sometimes he tried to join in, to show willing, but he hadn't a clue. And he was not a bad-looking chap—shortish and squat, rugger player's thighs, and a charming, twinkling smile that lit up his broad face. They just wished he would stop wearing that woolly hat, but Colin was a loyal sort of bloke, he refused to be parted from it. Once he attached himself to something, it was for keeps.

All in all he was a kind young man; that was why he hated his job. He had trained as a gas fitter but recently he had been transferred to disconnections. The pain of it, ringing a doorbell and seeing the smile wiped off a face . . . His heart bled for them. What was their crime? Murder? Child molestation? They simply didn't have the funds to pay their bill.

That Saturday, the morning that would change his life, Colin had already made two calls: a black woman who had broken down in tears and an elderly woman who had slammed the door in his face. He wished he had been a postman. In general, they were regarded with affection; this seemed to persist even if they were the purveyors of bad news. Everyone, except dogs, liked postmen.

So it was with a heavy heart that Colin trudged up the stairs of Meadowview—a misnomer if ever there was one. It was an ex-council block, smartened up and sold off some years before, but the neighbourhood was a poverty-stricken one; he had visited it on many occasions to perform his melancholy task. He pressed the doorbell of Flat 28.

The young woman who opened the door looked neither startled nor suspicious. This was unusual. Judging by her attire, or lack of it, she had probably been in the bath.

Colin, shuffling and looking at his feet, explained himself. She turned away to lead him to her boiler. He tried to avert his eyes—she wore only a towel—but he couldn't help glimpsing her shoulders. They were frail and bony, and her skin was as freckled as a wall lizard. Stumpy was one of the few people in Britain who had successfully bred these in captivity. This warmed him to her. He was proud of his hatching record: six eggs in the past year.

'To be honest with you, I don't want to do this,' he said, following her into the kitchen.

'Don't then.' She flashed him a smile. He felt a shifting sensation inside. 'Let's have a cup of tea and forget all about it.'

She adjusted her towel—it was in danger of slipping. Colin felt a blush rising up his neck. The

57

poor girl must be frozen. He took out his tools. 'I'm ever so sorry,' he said.

'There's nothing I can do to persuade you?'

His face reddened as he switched off the boiler (Potterton Suprema, 40,000 BTUs). 'They'd only send somebody else and you'd pay another disconnection charge.'

'They charge me for this? Great.' The tap hissed as she filled the kettle. 'Oh well, if that's the case, I'd rather have you.'

As he turned off the main gas cock, he explained the procedure to her: how once the bill was paid she would have to make an appointment for a reconnection and there would be another charge for that. 'It's daylight robbery,' he said, 'downright senseless.' He heard the rattle of china. Was she doing it all with one hand?

'It's just that I'm broke,' she said.

He got out his spanner. 'They don't give a monkey's, these big outfits . . .'

'They don't care if I freeze to death . . .'

'Not a monkey's about ordinary folk . . .'

'People like you and me. Sugar?'

'Two, please.' He leant his weight against the spanner, pressing hard. The blooming union was stiff.

'NT, where I work—you know it?' she asked. 'They don't even send out a reminder. They send out a final demand and if the customer doesn't pay within seven days they cut them off, just like that, the tossers.'

He flinched at her language. 'Don't I know it,' he replied. 'They did it to me and a whole crate of tortoises died.'

'Tortoises?'

Finally, he disconnected the pipe and capped it. ' 'Cos the bloke at the airport tried to ring me, see, and he couldn't get through.' He sat down heavily at the table. She passed him a mug of tea. 'They know me there, the customs fellas at Manchester, they know I've got a way with them.' He pushed some crumbs into a pile. 'Not wanting to blow my own trumpet, but I'm a bit of an expert. It's all down to, I suppose, that I like them and they like me.'

'Who do?'

'Tortoises.'

He looked up at her, his face ablaze with pity. 'They're banned from being imported, it's illegal, but sometimes these crates arrive from these places, Turkey, places like that, and my pals in customs, they smell a rat—'

'Or a tortoise—'

His eyes pricked with tears. 'They're in a terrible state, half of them dead—dehydration, starvation. There was this crate last summer, fifty-four Hermann's tortoises, beautiful creatures . . .' His voice broke. 'Only eleven responded to resuscitation.'

She gazed at him. 'That's horrible.'

'Cold-blooded murder. No other word for it. How could folk be so cruel?' He wiped his nose.

'I love tortoises,' she said.

'You do?'

She nodded. 'Love them. Funny little shells and funny little faces. And so sort of . . . slow. In fact, I love all those kinds of animals.'

'Reptiles, you mean?'

She nodded. 'I adore them.'

'Like, lizards?'

She nodded.

'Snakes?'

She nodded again. The sun had come out; it flooded the kitchen with light.

He gazed at her wonderingly. 'What about amphibians?'

'What?'

'Frogs and toads?'

She nodded. 'Them too.'

The sun shone on her shiny, curly hair. It was the colour of his mother's treacle pudding. He realized, with surprise, that she was really pretty. 'Never met a lass who liked frogs and toads.' He paused, overcome with emotion. 'I breed them too.'

'Where do you keep them?'

'At home.'

She lit a cigarette, drew in the smoke and exhaled. He coughed. There was a silence as he shifted the crumbs into another pile. He thought: I'm alone with a nearly naked young woman. A wave of panic hit him. He climbed to his feet.

'Better be p-p-pushing off.' He always stuttered at moments like these. Not that they came very often. 'Now remember, you can't use your gas cooker either—'

'Can I see them?'

He stared at her. 'See what?'

'Your frogs and toads and everything?'

Colin's jaw dropped. He gazed at her as she sat at the table. The towel was knotted expertly around her chest, leaving both of her hands free. She tapped ash into a saucer and smiled up at him.

'You want to see them?' he asked, stupidly.

She nodded. Quite a lot of her chest was

revealed. This, too, was scattered with freckles. Were all females this freckly? His experience was minimal; mostly limited, in fact, to the swimsuited girls he saw at the leisure centre. She was gazing up at him, her eyes bright, waiting for an answer.

He gathered his wits. 'How about, you could c-come for tea,' he suggested. 'Give her warning and me Mam'll bake us a cake.'

*   *   *

'Who is she? What does she want?'

'She wants to see me reptiles, Mam. She's that keen.'

His mother gave him one of her looks. He knew her face so well: grimly set, for the most part, but sometimes weather passed over it, like clouds or—more rarely—sunshine, darkening or lightening an outcrop of rock.

'I said you'd bake her one of your sponges,' he added.

Colin was devoted to his mother. The thought of her dying, as she one day must, filled him with fathomless panic. They were everything to each other; they knew each other through and through. He would walk through fire to earn her approval. Oh, he had her love, he knew that, but sometimes it was an uphill struggle to please her. Life had been hard for Peggy, her husband and sisters dropping off one after another. There were just the two of them left, clinging to the raft.

He watched his mother as she opened the larder door. She moved slowly, her joints stiff, but he knew better than to help her. She put a bowl on the table and crumbled flour and butter together. Her

61

knuckles were hugely swollen; she worked more slowly than usual. From the way she sat, rigid, he knew that she knew that this was something special. Already he could feel a loosening between them.

'Don't stand there like a lump,' she said. 'Go down the shop and buy me a couple of lemons.' She lifted the flour and let it fall through her fingers. It was graceful, the way she did it. 'There's a good boy.'

*   *   *

It was the next day, Sunday. Natalie was due to arrive at four. Outside a gale blew. Next door's motor scooter had fallen over; its plastic cover snatched and billowed in the wind. Colin, propping it back on its stand, worried about Natalie, her thin frame freezing in her unheated flat. He couldn't get the image of her, all but naked, out of his head. What did she look like, dressed? He had kept his eyes lowered; he could hardly remember her face.

Colin wore his tartan shirt, freshly ironed by his mother, and a clean pair of jeans. Waiting for Natalie, he saw his street through her eyes: the boarded-up windows, the single tree with a bin liner caught in its branches. The houses were dwarfed by the pylons that marched behind them, across the high ground. Nothing stirred except pieces of plastic; Rowton Crescent was sunk into the torpor of Sunday afternoon. Where were the kids? Colin had grown up here, he had played in the street with his gang. Nowadays children had disappeared like the lapwings on the upland meadows. Their cries were silenced.

Suddenly, powerfully, he wanted kids of his own.

He longed for them, he longed to be a father, tying their little laces. The idea made his legs weak.

'Come in, you'll catch your death!' his mother called.

He pretended not to hear—his own small rebellion. It was ten past four. He looked up and down the road. How would Natalie travel? By car? By the unreliable bus service from the centre of Leeds that stopped at the main road, six streets away? He should have offered to collect her, that was what people did.

But she wasn't coming anyway. The whole idea was too far-fetched. Natalie was a chimera, dreamed up in yesterday's sunlight. She didn't exist, she wouldn't come. Why should a young woman like her want to have tea with him anyway?

And then he heard it: the *thud-thud* of a sound system. It grew louder, pounding down the street as a silver Honda hove into view. It juddered to a halt beside him.

Natalie stepped out. Colin's heart turned over. How pretty she was! And quite different, fully dressed. In her flat she had looked maybe thirty years old. Alarmingly experienced, anyway. Now she seemed like a young girl arriving at a birthday party—buttoned-up coat, velvet band in her hair.

Indoors he helped her remove her coat. A powder-blue cardigan was revealed beneath. He glanced at the bumps of her breasts and closed his eyes. His mother came out of the lounge.

'Hello, Mrs Taylor, I'm so delighted to meet you.' Natalie shook his mother's hand. 'What a lovely home!'

There was a pause. Standing there, Colin felt clumsy and male. Even his mother seemed to be wearing some sort of perfume, or maybe she had just squirted the hall. Guests made her conscious of the smell that lingered in the house; he himself never noticed it.

Natalie cocked her head, listening. 'Is that a phone ringing?' she asked, frowning.

'Oh,' said Colin. 'That's crickets.'

'Crickets?'

'I feed them to the lizards.'

'Ah.' She laughed. 'They sound just like trill-phones, don't they?' She turned to his mother. 'I work for a telecommunications company.'

Demure, that was the word. She looked demure, and neat, and polite. Colin hadn't expected this, not from their first encounter, but then women were changeable creatures. You never knew where you were with them.

She was looking at a plate which hung on the wall. 'That's so pretty, Mrs Taylor,' she said. 'Did you buy it on your holidays somewhere?'

'We don't go on holiday,' said his mother. 'You'll see why soon enough.'

'Tour first, or tea?' asked Colin.

'Tea.' Natalie smiled at his mother. 'I've heard you're a wonderful cook. I could eat a horse.'

*   *   *

If his mother was thawing, there was only the slightest of signs. Her wintry face gazed at Natalie, who took a third slice of cake.

'Mmm,' she said, munching. 'Wish I could bake things.' She glanced at Colin. 'Not that I could at the moment anyway.'

'He doesn't like cutting folk off,' said Peggy. 'It's

not in his nature.'

'Oh, I'm not staying there long anyway.'

Alarmed, Colin asked: 'Where are you going?'

'I hate the city.' Natalie turned to his mother. 'I'd like to move to the country, I adore the country—you know, animals and flowers—that's where I really want to live. Besides, the city's no place for children.'

'Children?' asked Peggy.

'Well—you know—one day . . .' Natalie sipped her tea.

This moment of pensiveness over, she brightened. Sitting there, arms clasped around her knees, she asked Mrs Taylor about Colin's childhood.

'What was he like?'

'Such a soft-hearted boy, always looking after the smallest ones in the street.'

She asked Mrs Taylor about her husband. He was an embittered man who had lost his farm and who had worked, for an unhappy period, as part of the British Rail catering team. Peggy didn't tell her any of this.

'He was a good man,' she said shortly.

Natalie offered to wash up; Peggy refused. As they left the lounge Colin whispered 'Something tells me you've made a hit.'

He felt staggeringly intimate with her. Yesterday morning he hadn't known that Natalie had existed. She had popped up from nowhere and stepped into the centre of his life, wolfing down his mother's lemon sponge and interesting herself in things he had hardly noticed in fifteen years of living there. She was so vibrant; the house blazed with her presence. All his life he had been dozing and now

65

he was jolted awake.

He led her upstairs, into his bedroom. The chirrup of crickets filled the air, louder here.

'It's like being abroad!' she exclaimed. 'Club Med or something.'

'Club Med?'

'Somewhere nice and sunny. Anywhere but Leeds.'

Cardboard egg-boxes were stacked on the shelf. These housed the crickets, until it was time to drop them into the terrariums. He pointed to a tank.

'There's a mink frog in there. It's developed red-leg, that's a serious bacterial infection.'

The floor was crowded with pens filled with straw. He hadn't realized they covered such a large area of the room.

'I call this the intensive-care unit,' he said. 'There's two spur-thighed tortoises there, *testudo graeca*, they've got broken shells.'

'You like rescuing things, don't you?'

'In that one there's a monitor lizard that's poorly.'

She peered at the heap of straw. 'Where?'

'Better not disturb it.' He saw the bedroom through Natalie's eyes. For years he had been used to negotiating his way between the pens, from bed to washbasin, but now he saw how it might strike a stranger. He also noticed the powerful smell. 'Mam kicks up a fuss but it's just temporary, till I build another shed.'

'You've got more?'

'Oh yes,' he said proudly. 'These are just the invalids.' He led her downstairs. 'What I really want is a python.'

'A python?'

66

'They make lovely companions but I don't have the funds, not as yet.' He chuckled. 'Have to take out a mortgage for one of those.'

Opening the back door he had a strong desire, which he resisted, to take her hand. Instead he paused, with Natalie at his side, and surveyed his domain. It was impressive, no doubt about that. Sheds of various sizes lined one side of the garden; on the other side a large pond reflected the darkening sky. He led her to it. The perimeter was muddy; her shoes made a shy, sucking noise.

He pointed into the water. 'This one's got your friends in it.'

'What friends?'

'Frogs and toads. Plus newts, all three species— common, palmate and greater crested. *Triturus cristatus.*'

She stood her distance and vaguely looked in. 'Where are they?'

'Hibernating.'

Suddenly he felt deflated. The afternoon had defeated him; he wasn't up to it. She stood beside him, shivering. He led her into his largest shed.

'It's nice and warm in here,' she said.

'Each shed's got its climate—tropical, desert, temperate.' He pointed to the electric heater. 'It's thermostatically controlled, at thirty degrees C.'

'Huh,' she snorted. 'Lucky for some.'

'I'm sorry—'

'It's OK. So what's in here?'

This shed was his pride and joy. He had wired it up with ultraviolet lights, on timers. They hung from the ceiling, illuminating his rows of terrariums. Each tank contained a midget sandy desert, a micro-world in which he had placed twigs

67

and stones in artistic arrangements. He pointed to a tail protruding from behind a rock. 'That's a Sudanese plated lizard.' He pointed to another tank. 'There's a couple of Berber skinks in there, just under those leaves—'

'Christ! What's that?' She pointed to a saucer. Its contents were moving.

'Mealworms. That's their tea.'

'They eat *maggots*?'

'No—maggots are softer and whiter—'

'All right, all right,' she said.

He moved her to the next tank. A leather whip was lying languidly on the sand. Its tail trailed in the water bowl like a starlet's fingertip in a swimming pool. Natalie's presence made him think of things like that. He opened the lid and lifted it out. Natalie yelped.

'What is it?'

'My garter snake,' he replied. 'It's all right, she's a pussycat. Do you want to hold her?'

Natalie, backing against the wall, made a small noise in her throat.

'Just stroke her head,' he urged.

Tentatively she put out a finger, hesitated, and withdrew it.

'Sorry,' she said. 'I love all snakes except small ones. I forgot to tell you that.'

'That's all right then. Wait till I get my python.'

There was a silence. It was suffocatingly hot. Colin felt a failure. His collection of reptiles was a disappointment to her. To him, in fact, now that she was here. Today they all seemed hidden or hibernating or torpid with antibiotics. He felt like a father who wants to show off his children and all they do is sulk. Come out from under your pebbles!

he urged them. Show her your paces! She would clap her hands in delight and be at one with him in his passion. Here she was, a confessed reptile-nut, and his had failed to rise to the occasion.

He decided against taking her into the other sheds. They stepped outside, into the biting wind. It was dark in the garden, but the light from the kitchen illuminated her face.

'Oh Colin, that was great!'

The way she said his name, *Colin*, made his heart lurch. There, in full sight of the kitchen window, she pulled him to her and kissed him on the cheek.

Colin's legs buckled. Suddenly, everything was all right.

*   *   *

That evening was a momentous one in Colin's life. He did something which, until that weekend, would have been unthinkable. In doing so, he stepped into another universe, that of the law-breaker, and was changed for ever. It might not have been a big deal, to the world, but it was for him, because he had lived a blameless life.

He drove his van to Natalie's flat. It was nine o'clock, he had left his mother dozing in front of the TV. He drove down into Leeds, down Hall Road and through the centre, across the river and south to where the tower blocks rose up into the starry sky. It was a beautiful evening, crisp and thrilling to him.

The intercom at Meadowview was broken and the door hung ajar. He walked up the stairs. When Natalie opened her front door—she looked surprised, as well she might—he heard the closing music of his mam's TV show in her lounge. It seemed scarcely believable that the same quiz was playing when he himself had travelled so far, across the canyon that separated his former life from this.

Natalie must have been washing her hair. This time a towel was wrapped around her head; she wore a black top thing and black leggings, she looked as sheeny as a seal. Exuding an exotic scent, she was utterly new to him, all over again.

'I've come to reconnect your gas,' he said, boldly stepping into her hallway. 'Bugger the lot of them.' He didn't swear as a rule but *bugger them*.

She stood behind him as he opened the boiler cupboard. 'A knight in shining armour,' she said. 'Such a rare sight nowadays.'

'Stuff the lot of them.' He placed his tube on the meter's u-gauge, for the soundness test. 'Shouldn't be doing this,' he said gruffly. This was something of an understatement. With his spanner, he wrenched off the cap and reconnected the pipes, a surprisingly easy operation if people knew how. Yesterday's procedure was undone, as it might be when a man who has fallen suddenly in love has his vasectomy reversed. His heart swelled as he tightened the nut.

Behind him he heard the pop of a cork. He squatted down, struck a match and lit the pilot light. It, too, popped, though more discreetly. 'There you are,' he said, straightening up. 'Back to normal.' Which was the last thing he felt.

'Colin, you're a star.'

He turned round. She was pouring wine into two glasses.

'I never drink when I'm on duty,' he said.

70

'But you're not on duty now.' She looked at him. A tendril of wet hair had escaped and was stuck to her forehead like a question mark. 'Isn't that the point of what you've been doing?'

They stood there, listening to the murmur of the boiler as it sprang into life. 'Want me to t-turn up the thermostat?' he asked.

'Come here.' She moved out from behind the table. 'Know something, Colin?' She laughed softly. 'You've turned *me* on too.'

Colin snapped shut his toolbox. 'Got to be going,' he muttered and scraped past her, heading for the hallway. 'I'll let myself out.'

He clattered downstairs. Outside, in a doorway, a group of youths huddled together in a cloud of strange-smelling smoke. Colin beamed at them; they, too, were up to no good. He had stepped into a world of criminality, a world fraught with danger, and all because he had fallen in love.

*   *   *

'Hi, I'm not here but leave a message, OK?'

For three days Colin flunked it, putting down the phone. Her voice was so breezy; somehow it seemed addressed to anyone but himself. Natalie must have hundreds of friends; a whole teeming life. She was way out of his league; she was an angel, how could he presume to touch even the hem of her garment?

And then he remembered her smile. *You've turned me on too.* The invitation had been unmistakable. Was it just gratitude for reconnecting her gas supply?

Colin was in turmoil. There was nobody to

71

whom he could turn for advice. Not his mother, that was for sure. A glint came into her eyes when Natalie's name was mentioned. Nor could he talk to his mates, whose crude jokes would trample over the rarefied sensations he was experiencing. Colin stood for long periods in his shed looking at the rows of terrariums. Bathed in the glow of his lamps they offered up microcosms of domestic contentment: his pair of blue-tongued skinks, lounging side by side as they sunbathed; his garter snakes coiled so tightly around each other that you couldn't work out where one ended and the other began. Their embraces rebuffed him. They remained motionless, their black tongues flicking in and out. Ever since Sunday he had felt let down by them. They no longer gave him that old sense of fullness, of a solid centre in his life.

On Thursday evening Colin plucked up courage again. After all, he had phoned girls before. Hannah something, whom he had met on a rock-climbing weekend, he had taken her out on several occasions. He had held hands with girls from his class at school and sometimes kissed them in bus shelters—a cautious, experimental activity which, though stirring, had somehow left them even more unknowable than before. On two occasions, in fact, he had actually gone all the way, but both times proved to be ultimately dispiriting, as neither girl, being drunk at the time, had remembered a thing about it. No, he wasn't entirely a novice; just shy. Besides, there were so many other things to do. How did people find *time* for all that? And then there was his mam.

This time Natalie answered. 'I thought I'd scared you off.'

'Want to come for a walk with me, up in the Dales?' He said it like that, bold as bold. His stutter had gone.

'I'd love to,' she replied. 'I love walking.'

They fixed it up for Sunday.

*   *   *

All his life Colin remembered that day. When he was an old man he looked back on it as one of unclouded happiness. Nothing that happened later, none of the terrible things, could spoil his memories, for it remained inviolate.

It was a fresh, sunny day in mid-December; the rocks cast razor-sharp shadows. He loved the rocks, rusty-red, stained with black, breaking from their thin scalp of turf; he loved knowing that even when hidden they were just beneath his feet. He took her up from Pateley Bridge, up towards Brown Bank Head. Great patches of heather spread around them, dark like cloud-shadows. Wearing a furry coat and slip-on shoes, Natalie scampered beside him. The spongy grass put a spring into their step as he led her up the hill; she slipped her gloved hand into his quite naturally.

'Let's get lost!' she said.

'You won't get lost with me,' he replied proudly. 'I know these moors like the back of my hand.'

'I mean, let's get lost and never go home.' The wind whipped away her words.

'I'll keep you safe.'

'You're so *nice*. You don't know what shits most men are. Lying shits with the morals of polecats.'

'I can't bear you being hurt,' he blurted out. The snow had recently melted; he steadied her as she

73

skidded on the slippery grass.

'You wouldn't believe the things they tell you . . .' She jumped over a puddle; it was thinly filmed with ice. 'The things they tell you, just so they can . . .' Her words blew away.

'You can trust me.'

She was out of puff now. Leaning against a dry-stone wall, she paused for breath. Her dear nose was reddened by the cold. Manly and experienced, Colin waited beside her. They were up on the plateau now, bleak as tundra, its bleached grass pale in the wintry sun.

'I love it here,' he said. 'The Pennine Way, Haworth, that's where folk go, hiking and picnicking and whatnot, but here—it's like you're alone in the world.'

'Except *I'm* here.'

It was then that she kissed him, full on the lips. Her nose was icy, but how warm were her lips against his, how moist her tongue as it slid into his mouth! Trembling, Colin held her in his arms. His tongue probed hers, diffidently at first and then more keenly.

Then they were hugging wordlessly, her head buried in his shoulder. Stroking her beret, he feared he would burst into tears. He looked up at the sky. Far above them, a bird circled lazily.

'Look!' He pointed.

Still in his arms, Natalie followed his gaze. 'You mean the plane?'

'No, the hen harrier.' He pointed. 'And there's a kestrel, look! It's hovering, ready to drop.'

She was gazing at the plane, however, high up in the sky. 'Just imagine . . . Florida, New York . . .' A shadow passed over them as it crossed the sun.

'Wonder where they're going, lucky sods.' Urgently she gripped his arm. 'Don't you long to get away from here?'

'But it's beautiful—'

'Not here—Leeds, boring job, no money, working for dickheads . . .' She sighed. 'Oh, I just can't wait for life to begin.'

Boldly, he touched her cheek with his gloved finger. 'It has.'

*　　*　　*

That evening she took him into her bedroom. It was stiflingly hot, the radiator exhaling illegal heat. Three candles sat in saucers; Natalie lit them, one by one. Colin stood there as she unzipped his anorak and tenderly, expertly removed his clothes. He was strangely unembarrassed; this day existed in a bubble of its own, separated from the timid confusions and inadequacies of his normal life.

'I've got something to tell you,' he said.

'You're gay.' She smiled at him. 'You're married.'

He shook his head. 'It's just . . .' What could he say? That his experience was pitiful?

She nuzzled his chest. At the same time she deftly shed her own clothes, yanking down a trouser leg with her other foot.

'Come to bed,' she whispered, pulling her T-shirt over her head. Underneath she was naked.

He stood there, transfixed by her skin in the candlelight. Wonderingly, he put out his hands and cupped her breasts. They were small and firm; their hard nipples pressed against his palms. Though he was aroused, Colin didn't want to move.

75

He wanted to hold this moment for ever.

'Come on,' she whispered. Moving away, she slipped under the duvet and held out her hand. 'Come in here.'

*   *   *

Salamanders occasionally have difficulty shedding their skins. Place them in a container thickly planted with tradescantia and carry out frequent water changes. There they perhaps will succeed in casting the skin among the tangle of plants and roots.

If snakes have problems in shedding their skin, administer a lukewarm bath for several hours. You must ensure that they receive sufficient air through the nostrils. Weak or chilled animals should not be subjected to such a procedure. By oiling with cod liver oil or any other oil, the skin can sometimes be softened and removed. This must be done very carefully, particularly in the head region and on the eyes.

That night Colin sloughed off his past. It lay there, an empty skin. He stepped out of it, into a new life.

*   *   *

The wedding was fixed for January. The speed of events left Colin breathless. Natalie took everything in hand, fixing the register office and a party afterwards at somebody's uncle's restaurant, arranging the mortgage (a hundred per cent) on a starter home (appliances included) in a new development out on the Selby Road.

Colin sleepwalked through it all. Dazzled with

love, sluggish with satisfied desire, he surrendered himself to the current. He lived for the nights, when the world closed down and he held Natalie in his arms under her striped duvet. So this was what he had been missing! He felt cocky and proud, he felt he had joined the human race. And yet he pitied other people, for nothing they experienced could approach the intensity of his passion for Natalie—and hers, it seemed, for him.

For she seemed to love him; that was the miracle. His mother was suspicious. 'She's after something, that young woman.'

'Her name's Natalie, Mam.'

'What's she want from you?'

'She loves me!'

'It's not your money because you haven't got any. And it's not your blooming reptile collection, she's not that daft.' Her eyes narrowed. 'She's an ambitious hussy, what's she doing with you?'

'Please try to like her, Mam. For my sake.'

To tell the truth, he could hardly be bothered about his mother—he, who had been her devoted son. Love blinded him to her feelings. He became, for a short while, uncharacteristically ruthless.

'Think of it,' he said cheerfully. 'No cages cluttering up your house—'

'Our house.'

'No terrapins in the sink. Remember the fuss you kicked up about the toad spawn?'

'It was in the ruddy bath—'

'I'll visit you every week, that's a promise. You'll be fine.'

He kissed her lightly on the forehead—he, who never kissed her!

'She a local lass? What's her family?'

Where did Natalie come from? Colin hadn't asked. She had mentioned moving from place to place, mostly in the Leeds–Halifax area. What little he knew about her parents seemed unsuitable for his mother's ears. He could picture Peggy's face. *Her mum, she's had kids with four different men. She's run away to Dundee with a fella half her age and her dad sells drugs on a Thai beach.*

'Her mum's called Janey, she lives in Scotland at present. Her dad's a businessman, he works in the Far East.'

His mam paused, taking this in. 'What's the hurry?' she asked. 'She pregnant?'

Colin assured her to the contrary. He already felt foreign—new clothes, bought by Natalie; a new, secret existence his mother couldn't penetrate. Had she ever felt like this about his dad? The thought made him queasy.

Whatever her misgivings, Peggy was built to soldier on. She put a brave face on it and even had her hair permed for the big day.

*   *   *

The wedding was on a Saturday. Natalie drove round to Colin's house, to collect him. His mother, dressed in her best coat and hat, was sitting on the edge of the settee; she had been sitting there, motionless, for some time.

With Natalie's entrance the room lit up; her presence switched it on. Colin marvelled at her beauty. She wore a silky trouser suit thing with a flower in its buttonhole. His drab past was shunted into a siding; it was redundant. His real journey started here, at this moment. Somehow he still hadn't believed that she would turn up, that she would go through with it. She sat down on the arm of a chair and smiled at them both. 'Ready?'

'You're wearing a ring already,' said Peggy. 'I noticed it the first day.'

Natalie looked at her hand. 'I forgot.' The ring was made of plaited wire. She tried to pull it off. 'It's nothing. I just wear it for fun.'

'On your wedding finger?'

She was still tugging. 'Got some scissors?'

'I can do better than that.' Colin hurried out and returned with his toolbox. Opening it, he produced a pair of pliers. 'Sure you want me to cut it?'

She nodded. 'It doesn't mean anything, it's just a bit of wire.'

So he cut it off, snip snip snip. He did it with great delicacy, for his huge hands were surprisingly sensitive. He could fix wiring; he could swab, with a moistened cotton bud, the gummed-up nostrils of an ailing iguana.

And an hour later, in Leeds Register Office, Colin slipped on her wedding ring.

A book was produced and she wrote, with a fountain pen, *Mrs Natalie Taylor* in her best schoolgirl writing.

*   *   *

The party was held in a Greek restaurant. Natalie's mother Janey, who had been tracked down to Dundee, had arrived late. She had a tan—how had she got that, living on benefits?—and had dyed her hair a startling shade of purple.

Draining her glass, she stared at Colin. 'That one?' she spluttered, her throaty laugh startlingly loud. She and her boyfriend Greg were already merry, having stopped to celebrate on the journey south. 'Blimey. No wonder he looks like all his Christmases have come at once.'

'He's really nice, Mum. He wants to look after me.'

'But you're not that sort of girl.'

'I always have been,' said Natalie. 'You just didn't notice.'

She looked at the line of grey along her mother's parting, where the purple was growing out. Where were you, she thought, when I needed you? She felt a rush of warmth for Colin, who had restored order into her life; it was like starting out again, but properly this time. Colin would never betray her and she loved him for this. She realized: I want to make him happy. It was such an unfamiliar sensation, it startled her.

'Oh well.' Janey raised her glass. 'Here's to you, babe.' She was overcome with her smoker's cough.

In a sudden spasm of family feeling Janey had brought along one of Natalie's half-brothers: Lawrence. He had been removed from Care for the day as this was a special occasion. Lawrence was a cheerful, coffee-coloured boy whom Natalie hadn't seen for years, and now his voice was breaking and he would soon be a man.

Colin clutched Natalie's hand. The appearance of this motley little family made his love for her all the stronger. She was vulnerable, a frail vessel adrift and he was the harbour. Where was her parents' sense of responsibility? *He* wouldn't be like that. He would stay married to Natalie for ever, they would grow old side by side.

They made their way from one table to the next,

greeting friends. The man she had lived with, Mr Motorbike, hadn't been invited. Colin would have thumped him. No—he would have pitied him, for losing her. *No*—he would have hugged him in gratitude. Colin's head swam; he wasn't used to drink. Nor had he ever been the host of a party; it was as novel a sensation as being a bridegroom. Both, for a moment, felt equally momentous. Strangers shook his hand; someone refilled his glass. Men envied him, he could feel it. Who could not envy him this woman of experience and spirit, so radiant, so vibrantly alive, whose every movement was entrancing—the way she turned her slender neck to blow smoke past someone's face, the way she leaned over the table to pluck an olive? But he could feel, too, a generosity of spirit, for it was the big day of his life and they were happy for him.

As time passed, the room grew blurred and voices boomed, as if underwater. He saw his mother gazing at a shish kebab as if it was about to explode. He stood up, to go over to her, and sat down again. He smiled at everyone, oblivious to the undercurrent in the room.

He's ever so sweet, but . . .
Maybe he's a great fuck . . .
You must be joking . . .
Why so quickly? She pregnant or something?
She's older than him, maybe her biological clock's ticking . . .

There were fifty guests at Andy's Taverna: Colin's mates and schoolfriends, with whom he had loyally kept in touch; Natalie's friends from college, friends from other offices where she had worked in the past, the girls from NT. The same thought

81

passed through all their minds: what on earth did she see in him? But then this often happened in marriage: the office stud choosing the dumpy home-maker, mismatches of this kind. Maybe people thought this looking at their own partners, love being far too mysterious for logic.

Natalie sat beside him, backed by a trellis plaited with plastic vine leaves. With her fork she tenderly fed her bridegroom chunks of kebab. Pointing to her hair, he whispered to her; she laughed and shook her head like a dog come in from the rain. Confetti spilled on to the table. She looked exhilarated; she wore the look of those in love, the unmistakable look of somebody guarding a secret: *I know something the rest of you don't.*

*   *   *

A honeymoon was out of the question. 'We'll have one later,' said Natalie. 'When we can afford it.'

'I don't mind,' he said.

She smiled. 'Oh, we'll manage it somehow.'

Sunday they spent in bed, only emerging to fry some chicken nuggets and drink Red Bull for their hangovers. The heating was on high. Natalie liked it that way but Colin felt suffocated, not to mention the expense. While she slept he opened the window. Wind whistled in and blew their wedding cards off the chest of drawers.

So this is marriage, he thought. I am a married man. When I walk into a room she'll be there. Or she'll be in another room, doing whatever she does. He thought of the tune from *Friends*, a show she loved: *I'll be there for you.* I'll hear her moving about, the miracle of her, the miracle that she's alive, on this earth. And that it's me she wants.

He picked the cards off the floor and closed the window again. He climbed back into bed. Cupped around his wife, he listened to the banshee wails that echoed from the multistorey car park. As he fell asleep they became the curlews, calling each other across in the place where she had first kissed him. Their cries echoed across the moors that were so near yet so far; they echoed down the years of his future.

*   *   *

The rains had ceased, long ago; the floods receded. Village high streets had re-emerged and life had returned to normal. That dark, miserable autumn was just a memory now.

On Monday Natalie was back at work. She sat there, a married woman, twisting her slightly loose wedding ring round her finger. Somebody had stuck a yellow Post-it on her screen: HERE'S LOOKING AT YOU, MRS TAYLOR. It must be from Phillip; *Casablanca* was his favourite film, in fact he had promised to lend her the video. But she had forgotten about Phillip. That was all behind her now, in another life.

Safe behind her frosted glass she slit open envelopes one by one. The cheques were all made out to *NuLine Telecommunications plc.* Finally, after thirty or so, she pulled out a cheque for £269.23. It was written to *N.T.*

Natalie held it in her hand. She held it gingerly, as if it might give her an electric shock. Its *chequeness* was intense; it was as if she had never held a cheque in her hand until this moment. This was the buzz of crime, the kick of it. She felt fizzingly alive to her fingertips.

The customers (Mr and Mrs L. Dimshaw) had used black biro. Natalie looked around—an instinctive, criminal gesture—but why should anyone be watching? Nobody could see her anyway, with partitions either side. She reached into her bag and rummaged around for her collection of pens at the bottom. She lifted them out and selected a black ballpoint.

Carefully, copying the writing on the cheque, she altered the *N.T.* to *N. Taylor*.

Then she slipped the cheque into her handbag.

PART TWO

CHAPTER ONE

Morning light glimmered through the curtains. The bedroom floor was strewn with clothes: tights, knickers, tracksuit bottoms. Beside the bed a digital clock glowed: 10.45. The walls were covered with posters: girl bands, boy bands, two posters of O-Zone and one featuring Damon alone—skin-tight leather and a sneer that said *Everything I want, I get.*

It was March. Outside it was cold, the clammy grey sky clamped down on the city. The bedroom, however, was stifling; its occupant liked it that way. Traffic thundered past, down in the street; it was used as a short cut between the motorway and Manchester city centre, it was always busy. A police car screeched past, its siren wailing.

In the bedroom, however, all was quiet. The sleeper, a humped shape under the duvet, exhaled a snore. The duvet stirred as she shifted her position. Young women, dreaming of love, can sleep their lives away.

A tap at the door. No response. Another tap, a little louder, and a woman stepped into the room.

'Pet? It's time to get up.'

The duvet moved. There was a groan, and a face emerged.

'Your dad wants you downstairs; Lennox is going to be late.'

Chloe groaned and turned over.

'I'm sorry,' said her mother, and closed the door.

Chloe climbed slowly out of bed. She was not an unhelpful girl; in fact, she was generally good-

87

natured. An amiable lass, was how she was regarded by the regulars. She just found it an effort to get out of bed. The air was thick; it was like soup, to be moved through sluggishly. And sooner or later, as part of the dressing process, she would have to come face to face with herself in the mirror. While she was still dozy, Damon whispered, *I want you I want you*. Once she was awake, however, and gazing hopelessly at her wardrobe full of clothes, the girl bands (Lurex, Mob Effect) would be looking at her contemptuously from their posters. *In your dreams*, said their glossy lips. *Lose some weight, darling.*

Chloe wasn't fat; just big-boned. Besides, men liked girls with some flesh on them. Waifs were yesterday's news. That was what Chloe told herself as she made her way to the bathroom, locked the door and lowered herself on to the toilet. The seat creaked.

On the wall hung a framed collage of photographs: herself as a baby; herself aged eight, dressed as an angel in the St Cuthbert's Nativity play; herself aged eleven, holding up a rope of seaweed on the beach at Morecambe. Her dad had taken the photos; there were more of them, a drawerful somewhere. None of them were recent.

Chloe's eyes filled with tears. She tore off some toilet paper and bunched it in her hand.

*   *   *

Downstairs, David was opening up. As he unlocked the door he heard the clunk as Sheila put ashtrays on the tables. As usual it was she, his wife, who had cleaned up and mopped the floor. David thought irritably: Where's my lump of a daughter? Does she expect her mother to do all the work? Chloe was twenty-one; was the girl going to snooze her life away?

The bar smelt of stale cigarette smoke, the odour of his working life. He stood outside, on the pavement, breathing in the air. A Texas Homecare lorry thundered past. Every morning David stood here for a few moments before his first customer arrived (Archie Bacon, inevitably).

Opposite, Mr Hassan stood outside his shop, Europa Food and Wine. Next to it was an electrical repair shop belonging to Mr Hassan's cousin, and next to that a computer shop belonging to the cousin's brother; the family had taken over the street. David thought: If only Pakistanis drank, if only there were a verse in the Koran extolling the virtues of alcoholic beverages, then he would be a rich man. There was a rush of office workers at lunchtime and, briefly, at six, but his customers were mainly of pensionable age, men who had lived in these few streets of Manchester all their lives. He was fond of them. As Sheila said: 'They might be old lags, but they're our old lags.'

David stood in the cavernous street; it was part of a one-way system and the traffic funnelled through as if blown by a giant bellows. Dwarfed by commercial premises, the Queen's Head was the standard Victorian public house: etched glass, fancy plasterwork, a building whose charm was thrown into relief by the sixties office blocks that loomed up on either side of it. Sheila had planted daffodils in the window-boxes. She was a born home-maker; wherever they lived, she would settle in and make do. She was a placid woman, easily contented. 'Well, one of us has to be,' she said.

For David was a turbulent man, a prey to his emotions. Today he was seized with irritation. He looked up; his daughter's curtains were still closed. What was the matter with the girl? At her age he was working at two jobs, moonlighting from one to play in a band, drinking all night, getting stoned, getting laid, composing songs to girls whose faces he had long ago forgotten and burning up the motorways in his old MG. Was Chloe going to do nothing with her life?

Right on cue (eleven o'clock) Archie Bacon appeared, hobbling down the street accompanied by his bull terrier. David folded up his paper and went inside. Sheila was on the phone. She stood behind the bar, polishing glasses as she spoke, the receiver wedged between her shoulder and her ear. There was something girlish about the way she did this; suddenly the years fell away and he saw her as she had been then, the first time they met. She was dancing with her baby sister, holding both her hands and pumping them up and down as her sister jumped about. The floor was filled with families—parents, teenagers. It was the last night of the holiday, Saturday, and the atmosphere had briefly revved up a notch, as it did on the final evening. Just for a couple of numbers, everyone took to the dance floor, but it was Sheila's gaze that David held as he belted 'Wild Thing' into the mike. *You make my heart sing.* She wore a green dress and a necklace made of white plastic shells that bounced up and down as she danced.

David didn't tell her he remembered this. They spent their lives together, working side by side, they were in each other's company day and night. They had all the time in the world to speak of such things, yet somehow the moment never came up, did it? Not when you had been married for twenty-eight years.

As he pulled Archie's pint Sheila's gaze met his, but without registering; she was talking to her mother. 'Give it a good jiggle around in cold water,' she said. Every day they talked on the phone; how could they find so much to say? Sometimes David was amused, sometimes awestruck. Today he was irritated. How female they sounded! Everyone they knew seemed to be suffering from some life-threatening ailment. Then there was the saga of her mother's neighbours and the ongoing debate about the definitive fish pie—cheese on top or not? David knew that this was one of Sheila's few pleasures. The pub was their workplace, their home, their tyrant. Unless they came in for a drink, phone conversations were the only way Sheila could stay in touch with her family. Still, it irritated him.

'Crying shame, eh?' said Archie.

'What?'

Archie pointed to the newspaper. A woman's body had been found dumped in a wood next to the M6 motorway, near Congleton. She had been raped and strangled. Archie looked obscurely gratified. 'Now who would do a thing like that, eh?'

Sheila, who had finished her conversation, came over.

'Oh no,' she said. She sat down next to Archie and looked at the paper. 'The poor girl.'

Sheila was good with the customers—friendly, confiding, always ready to commiserate. Whatever happened to them she could pluck, from her large family, something of a similar nature. *I know just what you mean. My Uncle Patrick, he had it too and it moved to his kidneys . . .* and they were off. There was an ease about her which David admired, for he was incapable of it himself. He was a good publican—honest, fair, firm with drunks—but he was not a chatty man and people gravitated naturally towards his wife. He had few intimate friends. In fact, none. All he had in this world was his small family—his wife and daughter.

Chloe ambled in. David gazed at her. She was wearing a shapeless print dress. Her big, pallid arms were bare except for a wayward bra strap that had slipped down her shoulder. His daughter always wore slightly unsuitable clothes, never quite right for the occasion. Today, too flimsy and middle-aged. *Frumpy.*

'Shouldn't you be starting on the lunches?' he demanded.

Chloe looked like a startled rabbit; Sheila, too, jumped up. 'Come on, pet,' she said. 'I've made a start on the veg.'

'Seen the news?' said Archie, with grim satisfaction.

'Don't show her,' said Sheila, 'it's upsetting.'

Chloe moved closer and picked up the paper. David was standing behind her. He gazed at her vast hips. Her upper arms, from the back, were ruddily mottled; her elbows dimpled, and sunk in flesh. A spasm of pain passed through him.

Chloe let out her breath. 'How awful . . .'

'Listen, Chloe—'

She swung round, jumping to attention. Why did he have that effect on her?

'Wherever you are,' he said, 'whatever the time,

it doesn't matter how late . . .' David wanted to put his arm around her but he hadn't done that for years. 'Day or night, if you need picking up, just phone. Understood? Just stay there and I'll come and fetch you in the car. Is that a promise?'

Surprised by the passion in his voice, she looked at him. 'OK.'

'Phone me. That's what your mobile's for,' he said. 'And make sure it's charged. You know how forgetful you are.'

Sheila gave him a sharp look. He shouldn't have added that; it made the whole thing accusatory. His irritation rose.

'And run across and get some tomatoes for your mother.' He thrust a note into her hand. 'They weren't in the delivery.'

Chloe made for the door.

'Put on your coat!' called Sheila.

But their daughter had gone. Traffic rumbled, as the door opened. David felt a familiar sense of failure.

'You'll catch your death!' Sheila called.

*   *   *

The pub filled up, first with the regulars, then with the lunchtime crowds from the nearby offices—gaggles of girls (Chardonnay by the glass) and young blokes (Stella Artois, Czech imported Pilsner in the bottle) who shouted and blew smoke into David's face as he served them behind the bar. They took the place over, pulling chairs away from the tables (*You using this, mate?*) and leaving the old boys marooned with their pints, looking like a nearly extinct species, which indeed they were.

These kids spent money—where did it all come from? If the brewery had its way, which it was threatening to do, this last genuine local would be revamped into some themed Slug and Lettuce bollocks, transforming it from a pub that served food into an eatery that served drinks, because that was there the profits lay. And the few old lags who stuck it out would find themselves shunted into the corner, gazing glumly at a bottle of balsamic vinegar. Finally they would feel so out of place that they would just melt away. It was happening all over. Where did they go? Into some corner where they quietly died of natural causes?

David felt equivocal about this. He couldn't make a livelihood out of his pensioners, eking out their pints, but on the other hand he had run this pub for nine years; he knew their wives and their grandchildren, he had presided over their family celebrations in the function room upstairs. Besides, he too was feeling his age.

Only fifty, he told himself, and then he would catch sight of his face in the mirror on the way to the gents'. A large expanse of his forehead was visible now; this left his eyebrows looking thicker and somehow comic. A person's first reaction wouldn't necessarily be: Look, a bald man. But he had to admit that a certain amount of his hair had disappeared, leaving alien, shiny skin that burnt in the sun. It seemed only yesterday that David had had a full head of it—thick brown stuff that just existed, taken for granted. He had even pulled it back in a rubber band when he went on stage. His moment of glory now seemed pitiful. What had he been? A Green Jacket at Warner's Holiday Camp who had fancied himself as a singer. That young

94

man had long since disappeared, to be replaced by this familiar stranger, his inappropriately clownish face lined with disappointment.

Lennox, his barman, had arrived. Lennox was a virile young Australian who sported a full head of hair. He treated the customers with relaxed, almost insolent familiarity. 'No worries,' he said, with irritating regularity. He *had* no worries. Soon he would be off elsewhere—Montreal, Cape Town. The world was his for the asking; no doors had been closed to him, one by one. Lennox's tanned arms flexed as he pulled the pumps; their blond hairs shone in the light.

It was one thirty, and the decibel level was rising. David could set his watch by the volume of noise— it peaked at one thirty, and at ten thirty in the evening, just before closing time. Having consumed his usual pint and packet of pork scratchings, Archie rose to leave. The dot com whizzkids shouted over his head, moving aside to let him pass. David gazed at Archie's dog. Its back legs were bowed, to accommodate its enormous balls. Their size was unseemly. *Look at me and all I'm capable of.* They rubbed against each other as it walked, stiffly, to the door. David lifted the mixers nozzle. Squirting some tonic into a glass he tried to remember the last time that he and Sheila had made love. Two weeks ago? Three?

He gazed at his wife as she rubbed *Lasagne* off the blackboard. From the back she had spread, but in a shapely, feminine way. She was still an attractive woman. The knot of her apron had come undone; one tape hung down. This touched David. When had he last caught her in his arms and kissed her properly—a deep, passionate kiss, just like that—on the landing or in the bathroom?

He was resolving to do it later when he heard a shout. 'Chloe!'

*   *   *

A girl was worming her way through the drinkers. She wore an air stewardess's uniform and dragged a small black suitcase on wheels. Chloe was standing behind the cold food display, slowly assembling a tuna baguette.

The girl pirouetted round in front of the sliced meats. 'Guess where I was this morning?'

Chloe gaped at her old schoolfriend, Rowena. 'Where?'

'Lisbon,' replied Rowena. 'Lisbon, Portugal.' She had just completed her training, she said. 'The crew was divine! There's this guy called Tim—last night, my dear, we were staying at the Marriott, and guess what—'

'Pull a finger out with that sandwich, pet,' said a customer.

Rowena moved away to the bar. When the rush had eased, Chloe went over and sat down with her. Lennox had treated Rowena to a vodka and tonic and was chatting her up, a situation with which Chloe, who fruitlessly loved him, was only too familiar.

'I'm fast-track, they say,' breathed Rowena, shooting a glance at Lennox. 'Next year I'll be on long-hauls—just think, Chloe, Miami! LA! Four-star hotels, you can work on your tan. Go on, I'll give you the number, you'd be great at it—like, knowing about serving and everything.'

'I couldn't,' replied Chloe. 'I'm scared of flying.'

96

Rowena caught Lennox's eye. 'Don't be a wuss.'
Chloe shook her head. 'Anyway, I get airsick.'
Behind the bar, David gazed at his daughter.

*   *   *

That night, when he had closed up, David paused outside the bathroom door. Chloe was in there, singing. She sang when she thought nobody was around.

'Once I had a sweetheart and now I have none . . .'

When she was fourteen he had bought her a guitar, and for a few months she had learnt folk songs.

'Last night in sweet slumber I dreamed I did see, my own precious true love sat smiling by me . . .'

She had a beautiful voice, pure and true.

'But when I awakened I found it not so . . . my eyes like some fountains with tears overflowed . . .'

The lavatory flushed and Chloe came out.

'Oh,' she said, her face reddening.

'You should take it up professionally,' he said. 'Why did you stop the guitar?'

'Were you outside all the time?' Her blush deepened. He had been listening to her on the toilet!

'No—I just heard . . .'

But she hurried away into her bedroom and closed the door.

David tapped and let himself in. Chloe was sitting on her bed.

'I was only trying to say—'

'Please, Dad—'

'I was only trying to say you should do something with yourself.'

'What do you mean?' Her hands flew to her face.

'You've got a nice voice. You've got—well, a lot of things going for you . . .'

'Like what?'

'Chloe! Stop being so bloody negative. You'll never get anywhere that way.'

'I want to go to sleep.'

'Isn't it time you got off your behind and did something with your life?'

Sheila appeared in her dressing gown.

'Mum, tell him to stop!'

'David—'

His voice rose. 'Look at Rowena—don't you want to see the world, go places?' A terrible pity seized him; the way her thighs rubbed together now when she walked. When she *waddled*. 'You can't just sit here, rotting away—'

'David!' said his wife.

'Do you really want to end up like me and your mother—'

'What do you mean?' demanded Sheila.

'Stuck in a pub seven days a week? You really want that?'

'Dad, stop it!'

His wife put her hand on his arm. 'That's enough,' she said.

*   *   *

Later, Sheila came into their bedroom.

'You shouldn't have talked to her like that,' she whispered.

'I was only trying to help. She takes everything the wrong way.'

'It's how you put it.'

David lit a cigarette. He knew that Sheila disliked him smoking, up here in the bedroom, but he just did. He was standing at the window, gazing down into the back yard.

'Don't you see?' whispered Sheila. 'She's happy, in her own way. You just upset her, talking like that.'

'It's for her own good.' Down in the yard, the barrels glinted in the lights from the office block. The windows were lit all night; it was a crying waste of electricity.

'She's not ambitious, not in the way you want her to be. You can't mould her into the sort of person she's not.' Sheila sat on the bed. 'You're such a tyrant, Dave. Don't you see you're taking away her confidence, what little she has of it? Maybe she feels she's too overweight to be an air hostess.'

'Why doesn't she go on a diet then?'

'Ssh!' Sheila lowered her voice.

'Make herself a bit more attractive. She might even get a boyfriend—'

'She's perfectly pretty—just a bit plump—'

'Plump? If she got on a plane it wouldn't be able to take off.'

'David!' She stared at him. 'That's a horrible thing to say.'

David turned and looked at his wife. He thought: If you hadn't got pregnant I could have been a professional, I could have gone on that tour.

'She'll do what she wants,' said Sheila 'in her own good time.'

'You want to keep her here.' He thought: You want to stop her growing up, you want to tie her to your apron strings. 'You want to keep her here just so you've got some company.'

Sheila glared at him. 'Well, can you blame me?'

*   *   *

David thought: And this was the night I was going to kiss her.

In her bedroom, Chloe pulled the duvet over her head and slid under it like a tortoise into its shell.

CHAPTER TWO

'I'll do it my . . . way!'

Natalie belted it out at the top of her lungs. She had a terrible voice but she didn't care. She adored karaoke. They had to practically drag her off the stage.

Some of her friends from work were there. She went to the bar, waved a twenty-pound note, and ordered drinks. Sioban and Farida gazed at her as she handed out the glasses. There was something about Natalie nowadays; she gave off such heat, such exhilaration that she almost throbbed. She swore she wasn't expecting a baby. It must be marriage—it was two months now—but who would have thought it? They gazed at Colin with new respect as he sat at the nearby table, guarding their seats. Maybe he was, in fact, a terrific fuck. He looked more confident these days, more mature. He wore a new sweater in a bold zigzag pattern; Natalie had smartened him up. There was a sharper definition to his face; men looked like that at work, when they had just been promoted. Ah,

100

and the way he gazed at Natalie as she brought over his lemonade! It was a look of such naked adoration, such rapture, that they felt intruders, even to be in the same room.

A big bloke was singing 'Love Me Tender' way off-key. Natalie sat down next to Colin and ruffled his hair. He took her hand.

'You've got a lovely voice,' he said.

'It's crap,' she said, 'but you're sweet.' She laid her head on his shoulder and hummed, '*I did it my way . . .*'

Farida, also recently married, sat down next to her.

'How are you two getting on?' Natalie asked.

The recent months had also changed Farida. Her girlishness had disappeared; she had become dignified and distant. She answered politely that she and Bashir were getting on very well.

'Remember us talking about it?' asked Natalie. 'How it's all a lottery?'

'What is?'

'How love comes later, you've got to work at it?'

Farida looked blank. Wincing at Natalie's cigarette smoke—she had given that up now—Farida sat there, composed, her hands in her lap.

These sort of conversations embarrassed Colin. He turned to Natalie and said: 'When you're ready, love, we better make a move. Big day tomorrow.'

Driving home, Colin ventured to mention something that had been on his mind. 'We got to pull in our belts, Nat,' he said. 'What with all the expense coming up. It's different in a house, see, there's the bills and putting down a deposit on the settee.' He added, with pride: 'There's a lot of hidden expenditure when you own your own home.'

'Don't worry about that.' Natalie sat beside him, her hands clasped around her knees.

'But we've been spending money like nobody's business. Drinks all round, the stuff you've been buying me . . . it's ever so generous of you but I don't reckon we should—'

'We'll be fine.'

He indicated the seat belt. 'Buckle up, love.' He drove out of the city centre, across the river and down the Dewsbury Road. 'I mean to say, where does it all come from?'

'I told you, they paid me another bonus.'

'But they paid you one already, last month.'

'NT's doing really well. Retail outlets and shit, it's expanding all over the place. They're really aggressive with marketing.' She spoke with breezy authority. 'We're seeing off the competition, Stumps, we're even putting the wind up BT, and know why?' She polished an imaginary lapel. 'Because of us, me and my mates. We're the ones that keep it going, not that they'd notice, the bastards. You should see their profit margins.'

Colin was impressed. He had no head for business, it was all beyond him.

She ruffled his hair. 'We're happy, aren't we? Isn't that all that matters?'

Colin's heart was full. He nodded.

*   *   *

The next day they moved into their new home. Colin stood in the back bedroom. It was a small white room; it smelt of fresh paint. It smelt of the future, of infinite possibilities. Outside, the sun

102

blazed; it was only March but it felt like the first day of spring. Beyond his back garden lay the small muddy squares of other gardens. Some had been turfed and planted; some of the houses backing on to theirs were already occupied, while others had SOLD signs stuck to their windows. The houses, though detached, were packed close together; you could barely slip a knife between them. Colin liked this. He felt companioned in his happiness.

The new development was out on the Selby Road, near the Temple Newsam golf course. Two models of homes were available: the Commodore (Tudor style) and the Burlington (more Georgian). Theirs was a Burlington. One day, Colin thought, he was going to wake up. He would find himself back in Rowton Crescent, back in the lounge with his mam, the clock ticking and his only future the false dawn of the convector fire's radiant glow. He still couldn't believe that this house belonged to him and Natalie, that she was downstairs, putting their new pots and pans into the kitchen (he could hear the clatter). That she loved him, and was living with him. What had he done to deserve this? He had always been slow, teachers jiggling impatiently; the speed of what had happened took his breath away. He still hadn't caught up with himself.

Colin stood at the window. Maybe none of this existed. After all, a year ago it hadn't. A year ago, none of these houses had been built. This place was the grounds of an old mansion, now a conference centre. It was overgrown shrubberies, then, and secret places. When Colin was a boy he used to explore here, slashing at nettles with his stick and collecting frogspawn from the pond

103

which, if he remembered correctly, now lay somewhere beneath the turning area for numbers 15–21. The whole place had been concreted over.

The same process seemed to have happened to his life. The dazzling appearance of Natalie (oh, that towel!) had obliterated his past. He still went to work, of course, and returned to Rowton Crescent to visit his mother and feed his livestock, which would soon be removed to his new home when he had prepared their living quarters. But all that seemed strangely irrelevant. Even his reptiles (which Natalie called his pets, though they weren't pets, they were wild creatures which he was privileged to tend), even they felt distanced from him. They were like pupils whose teacher has lost interest in them once he has a family of his own.

He heard the bare boards creak as Natalie came up the stairs. She put her put her arms around him. 'Our first day,' she said.

He crushed her thin body against his. 'Happy?'

She nodded, her hair rubbing against his face.

'I was thinking, this could be baby's room,' he said. 'When we have one.' Disentangling himself, he gestured around. 'I could make a cot and a little cupboard, I'm handy with my hands.'

'Hang on, Colin,' she said. 'It's a bit early for that.'

'Don't you want a family?'

'Aren't we happy just as we are?'

'You said you wanted children,' he said. 'I can look after you, now we're settled. You could give up your job.'

'Give it up?' She looked at him.

'You're always complaining—'

'I'm liking it more now.'

104

'Why?'

She paused. 'I just am.'

She blushed. He had seldom seen her blush; the pink bloomed beneath her freckles. Maybe he had introduced the subject too abruptly; he hadn't had any practice in this, in any of it.

'Anyway, I've *got* you a baby.' She took his hand and led him out of the room.

Baffled, he followed her downstairs. They went into the lounge. Amongst the piles of belongings—suitcases and bulging bin liners—stood a cardboard box.

'Open it,' she said.

He pulled open the flaps. Inside, curled in straw, lay a python.

'That's our baby,' she said.

It lay there, its great flanks wedged against the side of the box. Its blond skin was patterned with the palest zigzags—olive green, yellow. It was curled tight; when it started to move, its skin slid in two directions like traffic on the motorway.

Colin, his mouth hanging open, stared at it. Slowly it raised its small, shapely head and looked at him, its tongue flicking.

A reticulated python. An *albino* reticulated python. So rare were they, so precious, that they seldom came on the market. It was a perfect specimen—two years old, he would guess, still a juvenile.

'Natty . . .' His voice croaked; he cleared his throat. 'I don't believe it . . .'

'Like it? She's a female, they said, two years old.'

He couldn't speak. The beauty of the snake moved him profoundly. What touched his heart, however, was Natalie. He had had a suspicion that

105

she wasn't as keen on reptiles as he had believed; after that first day she had expressed little interest in talking about them. What a dolt he had been.

'I told you I liked snakes.' Smiling, she unzipped his fly.

'Natalie—'

'Got a nice big one in here?' Her fingers slid in; they caressed him through his underpants.

Colin was a modest young man. Living with Natalie had loosened some of his inhibitions but he suddenly thought: What if my mam came in now? This was stupid, of course; she didn't even live here.

'Come on,' said Natalie. 'Let's christen our bed.'

'But the bloke will be delivering the settee. Saturday p.m., he said.'

'Fuck that.'

She led him upstairs to the master bedroom where their new brass bed waited. She had driven to Sweet Dreams, just like that, and bought it. No instalments, nothing. She pushed him on to the mattress.

'And we got to fetch another vanload—' he began.

Straddling him, she stopped his words with her mouth.

*　　　*　　　*

'. . . *presenting the latest government initiatives to tackle crime . . .*' said the radio. Natalie sped along the motorway. It was April, and she was on her way to work. '*The most recent figures show that throughout Britain the crime rate is rising . . .*'

Natalie was in high spirits. It was a beautiful day.

The cassettes, warmed by the sun, lay in a heap on the passenger seat. She picked up O-Zone—she had bought their latest—and slotted it in.

'Giveittome giveittome giveittome...'

Natalie shouted along with Damon; the music thumped. Unlike her husband, she was not a country lover. During their walk back in December, she had practically frozen to death. This was how the moors should be seen: at speed, from a car, with the sunroof open and O-Zone belting out at volume 23. In the valleys stood empty mill buildings, their rows of windows glittering in the sun. People had left this area in droves and who could blame them? Here and there, amongst the trees, vast chimneys rose up. She thought: They look like penises sprouting through pubic hair.

This turned her thoughts to Colin. She was filled with affection for him. Oh, she had been fond of him from the start—who wouldn't be? He was so sweet. But her warmth towards him had grown. He was such a devoted husband. He brought her little gifts, like a dog dropping a bone at her feet, and gazed at her with his spaniel eyes. He carried her tea up in the morning and cooked dinner at night—he was a much better cook than she was, he had learnt it at his mother's knee. He emptied her ashtray; he picked up her clothes from the floor, folding them reverentially and laying them on the chair, giving them a little stroke. He fussed around her—'Won't you catch cold?'

This could become stifling but as yet she didn't mind, because most of the time Colin was busy outside, hammering away in the workshop he had erected in the garden. He was an enthusiastic home-maker. Each weekend he was occupied knocking up shelves, whistling happily, or tending his repulsive pets. He kept them away from the house, thank goodness, though she sometimes found evidence of his hobby: fly-traps, painstakingly assembled from wire mesh; a bag of frozen mice in the freezer. She was too contented to mind, however; she could even joke about it. Only that morning she had pretended that the trilling of the crickets was the phone ringing. 'Hello, Natalie speaking,' she had said, lifting up the receiver, 'how may I help you?' They larked around a lot, in those early months.

Having money helped, of course. If their house closed in on her she could simply jump into her car, drive three miles into the city centre and go shopping. Natalie adored buying clothes, she had an insatiable hunger for it. Briefly satisfied, it would well up again and she would surrender. Their bedroom floor was scattered with tiny plastic T-shapes, dropped when she wrenched off price tags.

They could go to the movies; they could buy a microwave. Every morning, as a matter of routine, they drank Sainsbury's freshly squeezed orange juice, with bits in it. It surprised her, how quickly one got used to it. Natalie was extravagant by nature, spending recklessly and hoping that when the credit-card bills arrived it would sort itself out, but to tell the truth she had been rather desperate before she got married—panic-stricken, in fact. Now the pressure had eased and she felt an airy sense of liberation. Who said money didn't buy happiness?

Colin was a worrier but she soothed his fears. All she had to do was put her arms around him and silence him with kisses. That did the trick. He was in thrall to her body; he was hers, utterly. At first he had been shy in bed but she had coaxed him, releasing in him a clumsy passion which had alarmed him—was he hurting her? But she was teaching him how to please her. She would take his hand and move his fingers over her body, murmuring to him, and his eagerness to learn touched her. He really was a nice boy, and though they had little in common their shared life drew them together. They were young, healthy, and well-disposed towards each other. They had never quarrelled, not yet, and they loved their new home; to her surprise, she had even enjoyed a trip to IKEA. It seemed as good a start as any to a marriage, though 'husband' seemed an odd word to apply to Colin. Maybe everybody felt like that at the beginning.

So that Tuesday Natalie settled down to work with a sense of benign goodwill towards the world. It seemed ridiculous, that the job had once bored her. Every day now she felt a quickening of the pulse; it gave a zip to things. Each time she picked up an envelope she was a fox, sniffing for a scent. When she slit it open, would she find her quarry? Her senses were heightened; everything seemed in sharper focus. The very desks seemed more desk-like, as if she had never noticed them before. Her separation from her colleagues was palpable; she was amazed they didn't feel it. They worked and chatted, blithely unaware that she lived in a different world. She thought: spies must feel like this. She didn't use the word *criminals*, even to herself. After all, she was just milking the system. And why bloody not?

Some days there were four cheques she could use; some days none. Her secret word for them was *hits* (*two hits today*). She only chose those for modest amounts—up to two hundred pounds. Little and often was her motto. That way they were less likely to be detected.

But they wouldn't be detected. Even if these small shortfalls were noticed, they couldn't be traced back to her. That was the beauty of it. Her scheme was so clever that even in the years to come, when she would look back on her activities with mixed feelings, even then she would feel a glow of pride at this particular aspect of it.

For if she simply paid the cheques into her own account, sooner or later people would realize that something was wrong. Customers who had presumed they had paid their bill would receive a final demand, or even find their phone cut off. They would kick up a fuss, NT would search its records and discover that the cheques had never been paid in. Presumably this would result in some sort of internal investigation. Only an employee, and an employee in the accounts section, would have access to cheques. It would simply be a matter of time before Natalie was traced.

Her method was foolproof. For security reasons, registering and processing payments were two separate departments. They were served by two separate programs on the computer, but it was easy to access the processing program. All she needed was the password and the name of somebody in that department and she could log in.

It only took a matter of minutes. Natalie tapped in the password, which she had obtained from her friend Belinda, logged in Belinda's name, and downloaded various customer accounts. She ignored the small, domestic accounts; what she used were the accounts of large companies—multinationals, big industries from all over Britain—whose phone bills were so great that an additional two hundred pounds or so would go unquestioned. After all, what was two hundred quid here or there when a bill was in the thousands? It would either go unnoticed or be written off as staff making personal calls—un-itemized local ones. She moved the sum to these accounts, processed the original bills as PAID and pocketed the cheques.

The beauty of this was that the bills were indeed paid, but by large firms. None of Her People—for that was how she fondly thought of them, as her unwitting collaborators—none of Her People who had so helpfully written *N.T.* on their cheques would know that anything had happened. For their bills would go through and nobody was the wiser.

And nobody came to any harm, did they?

And nobody knew. The only person she had told was Kieran, but he would have long since forgotten. Chemical abuse had wrecked his short-term memory; besides, he and Angie, who was Australian, had moved to Melbourne; he had another life now. Like the white dog, he had disappeared for ever.

All in all, it was going even better than she had expected. That day, however, there was a hitch. Natalie returned from lunch to find the computers down; the server had crashed. People sat around. Sioban played cards with Amir, who had only started work that week; Stacey disappeared to Dispatch to visit Derek. None of them minded, of course. This had happened before; with any luck they could go home early.

An hour passed. In her office the new supervisor, Mrs Coles, was talking to the Financial Director. Through the glass, Natalie saw him shaking his head and looking at his watch. When he had gone she went in.

'What's the problem?' Natalie asked.

'It hasn't been traced yet. They're working on it.'

'Do you know how long it'll take?'

Mrs Coles raised her eyebrows. She looked gratified, that a member of staff displayed such impatience to get back to work. 'There's a possibility they'll still be down tomorrow. Such a curse.'

Natalie thought: What the hell. Three cheques had arrived that morning, all final demands. They sat on her desk; she hadn't had time to process them. Oh well, she thought. Just this once.

So, at the end of the day, she slipped them into her bag. And on the way home, as usual, she stopped at a post box and sent them to three of the various building society accounts she had opened in her new name.

By the time Natalie got home, to the smell of chicken cooking, she had forgotten all about them.

CHAPTER THREE

A middle-aged woman called Margaret was walking along Brighton beach. *April is the cruellest month . . .* The poem rose to the surface, sentence by sentence. So many words lurked there, in the sediment of her mind. Stray phrases popped up at unexpected moments, like bubbles of escaping gas.

Margaret had been a schoolteacher; she had taught T. S. Eliot, when he had been on the syllabus, to girls who had listened with varying degrees of incomprehension. They would be grown women by now. She thought about them a great deal, more frequently as time went by. They accompanied her like ghosts, her past pupils. They would have husbands now, and children. Their lives, stopped for her at eighteen, continued in unseen homes, scattered over Britain in unvisited towns. Maybe one of them—Annette, Diana, one of the brighter ones—was pausing as she brushed her hair, to remember the words from her A-level Chaucer: *Whan that Aprill with his shoures soote . . .*

Margaret doubted it. She had lost them long ago. For her, however, the words had resurfaced with horrible potency. April was indeed the cruellest month when she looked in the mirror, the sun's pitiless rays illuminating the whiskers on her chin. Recently, in Venice, she had picked up a mirror to inspect the Tintorettos on the ceiling of the Scuola Grande di San Rocco. Instead she had caught sight of the underside of her own throat, the turkey-wattle collapse of it. *Talk about ancient monuments*, she had joked to her companion.

All her life she had made the best of things, working diligently, heating up her Serves One meals in the evenings, keeping herself well groomed, but now she couldn't be bothered to make the effort. This was, in some ways, a relief. Her life had run out of steam while her phantom girls heedlessly matured. And so they should, for hadn't she wished the best for them? It was they who were striding into the future, it was their world now, tough and brutal, exhilaratingly free compared to the life she had known. However, she had to admit that their relationship with her seemed somewhat one-sided. Were they all too busy to write? Just a Christmas card would be welcome.

Margaret was scrunching along the pebbles, lost in thought, when she realized she was not alone. A dog was trotting beside her. It accompanied her as if they had just been separated for a few minutes and it had rejoined her for the rest of their walk. A dishevelled creature with curly hair, it stayed close beside her, raising its face from time to time to check that she was still there. When she stopped in her usual place, to look at the sea, it sat down next to her leg, panting.

By the time she reached the underbelly of the Palace Pier, its great iron struts sunk into the beach, she felt as if she and the dog had known each other for years. She knelt down, rummaged in its damp corkscrew curls and found a disc. On it was inscribed an address and a phone number, in Kemp Town.

The dog accompanied her home, pausing with her at the traffic lights. Its eyes, barely visible under its hair, were moist with love. She hadn't been the object of such devotion since an Indian newsagent, many years before, had made her the unlikely recipient of his sexual attentions. When he had pressed a Toblerone into her hand she had taken her patronage elsewhere.

Back in her flat she gave the dog a bowl of water. 'You're very appealing, but you belong to somebody else,' she said. The dog stopped lapping and looked at her, as if it needed permission to continue. Some of her more diffident girls had looked at her like this. 'To be perfectly honest, I'd love to keep you, but it would only be a temporary thing and I'd hate to have our hopes dashed.'

She checked the number on its disc and went to the phone. The dog's tail thumped.

She lifted the receiver. The line was dead.

Suddenly, she felt weak. It was moments like these that did it. Bottle tops she couldn't unscrew; a leak sprung in the bathroom pipe. Only the week before, when struggling to open the sealed plastic container of a prawn and avocado sandwich, she had suddenly and inexplicably burst into tears.

She couldn't use her neighbours' phones. 'Know something?' she told the dog. 'I don't think I would even recognize them in the street. Funny, isn't it, but I'm a busy person and once you start to talk to people, who knows where it might lead . . . They'd be ringing on my doorbell asking me in for coffee, my life wouldn't be my own . . .' Her voice trailed off. It was odd, talking aloud in her flat. Under its shaggy eyebrows the dog gazed at her, waiting for more. 'Besides, I'm perfectly happy with my own company, thank you very much. And somehow there's never enough time even to open a book, one's so busy.' There was a silence. The dog waited. 'We'll have to go to a call box. Now, do you want to stay here or come with me?'

She got up. The dog went to the door and waited for her. They went out together, to the phone box on the corner. The dog sat outside, its eyes fixed on her face as she punched NuLine's number.

A girl's voice said: 'Good afternoon, Ashley speaking, how may I help you?'

Margaret explained that there seemed to be a fault on her line, could she be put through to the engineers? Ashley told her to hang on. She was replaced by Pachelbel's *Canon*, a piece of music Margaret particularly disliked. Through the glass, the dog gazed at her confidently.

A man came on the line. 'Clive speaking, how may I help you?'

She explained again, patiently, as if to a slow learner. Clive was replaced by Pachelbel again. Her money was running out. She slotted in her last twenty-pence piece and cursed NuLine. She had only switched to them because BT had kept pestering her with calls in the middle of supper asking if she was satisfied with their service.

Finally somebody with a foreign name asked her to verify her number and then said: 'I regret to tell you, Miss Stoner, that your line has been disconnected due to non-settlement of the bill.'

'But I paid it!'

Hadn't she sent a cheque? She could remember writing it. Maybe she had forgotten to post it; her hormones had been playing merry hell during the past few months. She had always prided herself on her memory but it seemed to be letting her down. Only the day before she had discovered her gloves in the fridge. Then there were the mood swings. Suddenly, for no reason at all, she would burst into tears. Dr Scott was recommending HRT.

She was interrupted by a paroxysm of barking. A Jack Russell terrier was attacking her dog. Margaret put down the receiver and hurried out.

'Freddy!' yelled a voice. 'Freddy, get down!' A handsome woman in a leather jacket was struggling with the Jack Russell. She attempted to grab its collar. 'Freddy! You little bugger!' Finally she got a grip and pulled the dog away. Yapping and snarling, it skidded along the pavement. The woman snapped on its lead. 'I'm so sorry,' she said, looking up at Margaret. 'Is your dog all right?'

'It's not my dog.' Suddenly, inexplicably, Margaret's eyes filled with tears. 'I don't even know it.'

How terribly embarrassing. What was the matter with her?

The woman got to her feet. 'Are you all right?'

Margaret nodded.

A moment passed. Then she shook her head.

*   *   *

She was a tough old bird, Sally, a legendary figure in the business. For more years than anybody knew—for she lied about her age and nobody stayed long enough in their jobs to remember—for many years now she had been the fashion editor of a glossy magazine. Lifted, tucked and dressed in her signature black, she was ageless, a survivor in one of the world's most ruthless professions. She was feared and fawned upon by designers from New York to Tokyo but she was impervious to flattery—to every emotion, it seemed. Many years ago she had had a child; 'Was it a human?' asked Willy Landells, editor of *Harpers & Queen*. Nobody knew what happened to the child, it was never mentioned. Sally admitted to no personal life. She was a true professional, girt with steel.

Just sometimes, however, something touched her heart. She could be surprisingly maternal to young designers and wept at their boyfriends'

117

funerals. See, she was a softie, the old fag-hag. And sometimes her iron heart melted when she leafed through photographs of models.

She was doing this one day in April, sitting on a Brauer sofa with Berenice, the boss of a large and prestigious agency. Outside the sun shone over Carnaby Street, but Sally had never been interested in the weather. She was looking at the photographs of young girls, artfully lit and shot by Nick Knight and Mario Testino.

'A tabula rasa, that's what I'm looking for,' she said. 'Dewy, untouched by life. Something special—and very young.'

How short was their blossoming, these girls! Some were barely seventeen. Their hopeful faces gazed from the page. Some had beauty so fragile that in a few years it would vanish. Coarsened by drink or simply their own ordinary lives, they would lose their luminosity and be removed from the agency's books. Some would succumb to drugs and eating disorders. Some would simply disappear. Their moment was fleeting; caught by the camera, they were already history.

'And she must be available to fly out tomorrow,' said Sally. 'For the shoot.'

Eventually Sally found her. So many times she had felt this sensation in her bones, and she was invariably right. The girl—wide eyes, thin blonde hair falling like water, cheekbones to die for— gazed out of the photo. Moira Hunt.

'She's inexperienced,' said Berenice.

'I can see that. Why do you think I like her?'

'For such a big job. But I have to agree with you, darling. She's perfect.' The shoot was in Morocco, a five-page spread. Berenice turned to her assistant. 'Get her on the blower, sweetie, now.'

*   *   *

In a chemist's shop on Stanmore Broadway, Moira Hunt was stacking the shelves. Her hands were busy, moving plastic bottles of Pantene conditioner from the box to the display rack, HAIR PRODUCTS: SPECIAL OFFER. Her mind, however, was miles away. She was dreaming about Malta—what had happened there, and if he would ever phone. Three weeks, it had been, but she knew that he was busy, she had understood that much of the language. He was on duty breakfast, lunch and dinner.

Hindi words floated past her. The manager, Mr Ramesh, was arguing with his wife.

'The phone isn't working.'

'I know the phone isn't working.'

'What have you done to it?'

'Nothing. Go next door and phone the engineers.'

'I'm busy.'

'*I'm* busy . . .'

All that afternoon there were no phone calls; from the Maltese waiter, from anybody. Moira picked up the empty carton. She paused at the mirror above the Max Factor testers and looked at her face. He had told her how pretty she was. Exaggerating a little, she had replied that she was a model. After all, she had done small jobs. All she needed was a break.

But the agency couldn't get through on the phone, the line was dead, and Morocco never happened. Not to Moira, anyway. They chose another girl, whose life was changed instead.

*   *   *

Meanwhile, in Brighton, another life was transformed. For on that day of the dogs Margaret fell in love.

That it was a woman who caused this upheaval came as something of a surprise, but that soon passed. In fact, when she looked back over her past, it seemed inevitable. How blind she had been! Her emotions had never been stirred by a man, not deeply. Long ago she had had a couple of short affairs; these had petered out, however, through a mutual lack of interest. She had put this down to the demanding nature of her job. Besides, few men crossed her path—just married fathers on parents' evenings.

The dog had been returned to its owner; the sun had sunk over the sea. And now there she was, aged fifty-eight, eating pasta with a woman called Clare who that morning had been unknown to her but who now seemed her twin soul, her other half. She felt she had known her all her life.

'If I were an essay,' she said, 'I would write *cliché* all down my margin.'

Clare laughed. Margaret felt vastly funny; she amused even herself. And the woman had a Jack Russell, a breed of dog she found particularly unappealing—small and yappy, bouncing up like a tennis ball.

Later, they would tell people that they had been connected by a disconnected phone, that things sent to annoy us could have a glorious outcome. And in fact Margaret felt so warmly towards NT

120

that the next day, disordered by love, she paid her bill all over again.

*　　*　　*

In the following weeks such petty irritations would be forgotten. At the time, however, they came so thick and fast that David's nerves were stretched to breaking point.

First, Lennox the barman gave in his notice. He had decided to take six months off to travel around South America with his girlfriend.

Then Sheila lost the car keys and David had to go out and get some more cut. However, later, when he stopped at a garage to fill up with petrol, he discovered that he had forgotten to cut another key for the fuel-tank flap. This meant a bus ride back home to collect a crowbar with which, when he had taken another bus back to the petrol station, he had forced open the flap. This had resulted in damage to the bodywork and of course a broken hinge. All this undertaken under the impassive eyes of the Ethiopian cashier.

The final aggravation came the next morning when he checked on the delivery from the brewery and found it a barrel short. Back in the bar he paused, before lifting up the phone to ring them, and gazed at his daughter. Chloe sat leafing through a magazine. She lifted her feet as her mother hoovered under them.

'So, Chloe, what's the capital of Ecuador?' David asked.

'Pardon?' Chloe's mouth hung open. She had shapely lips, they were her best feature, but when loose like that she looked subnormal.

121

'All right then,' he said. 'The capital of Peru.' And why didn't she do something about her hair? Lank and brown, it was pulled back in a rubber band.

Sheila, who had stopped the hoover, said: '*I* don't know the capital of Peru.'

'Ask Lennox,' said David. 'He's going to see the world, he's going to do something with his life.'

'Yes, and where does that leave us?' replied Sheila. 'Without a bloody barman, that's where.'

How small were the horizons of his womenfolk! David despaired of them. Leaving them exchanging glances, he picked up the phone.

The line was dead.

'Shit!'

He borrowed Chloe's mobile and rang the phone company. By the time he had got through three voices who needlessly introduced themselves and then abandoned him to canned music, Sheila had opened up and was serving customers, with the help of Chloe, who had lumberingly risen to her feet. Finally David was answered by a female who told him that his phone had been cut off for non-payment of the bill.

Even Archie, not a curious man, swivelled round to listen to David's bellowed response. Finally David switched off the phone.

'Maybe there's some mistake,' said Sheila.

'But I paid it.'

'Are you sure?'

'Of course I'm sure.'

'There *must* be some mistake.'

'It's their mistake, not mine. I'm not going to pay a bloody bill I've paid already.'

'But David—'

122

'And they want me to pay a fucking reconnection charge.'

'Listen, love—'

'The fucking cheek.'

A man waited at the bar, waving a five-pound note between his fingers. Running a pub meant there was no privacy in one's life. David had to be there, ready to serve any stranger who, on a whim, happened to come through the door. The front room of his home, the heart of his family life, was constantly being invaded by people who sat on his chairs as if they had a right to be there. David didn't always feel this way, of course; only when he was in the middle of a conversation with his wife and suddenly he had to become a publican again and pull a pint. An argument had to be put on hold for hours until, having ejected the last drunk, David could continue it at the point where it had been interrupted. Over the years he had become accustomed to this; it was the rhythm of his working life, and sometimes, by chucking-out time, the quarrel had lost steam. Sometimes, however, it had gathered its own momentum and grown out of all proportion. It entirely depended on mood.

When they were closing up Sheila said: 'It's probably under a pile of papers somewhere.'

'What is?'

'The cheque. These people don't make mistakes, they've got computers.'

'Computers!' he snorted. 'Well, that's all right then.'

'Just pay it, David. We must have a phone. Mum'll be ringing tomorrow, about her test. And there's the Millers phoning about booking the room.'

'So I should just cave in?'

'Oh, don't be so stubborn.'

'Whose side are you on?'

She bolted the door. 'Why are you so touchy nowadays? What's the matter with you?'

He should have relented then. In the years to come, it was his most bitter regret. He should have said: *OK, you're right,* and paid the reconnection charge. He should have taken her in his arms and kissed her the way he had meant to do, all those weeks before, and told her: It's not about the phone, not really. It's everything else, and the phone is the final straw. The everything else is so vast that I cannot tell you, for fear you'll take it personally. Because it's not about you, it's about me. You are a wonderful wife and I still love you, and your chapped, reddened hands touch my heart. All these years you've put up with me and never complained, though you must have been feeling, in your darkest hours, the same as me. But I've never dared to ask, in case I find out it's true.

David said none of this. He swabbed down the bar and hung the damp tea-towel over the pumps. Sheila paused, on her way upstairs.

He switched off the lights. 'I'm not paying it.'

*   *   *

Throughout the next day, Friday, David tried to get through to the NuLine Customer Services Manager. Despite yelling down the phone he got nowhere. Fridays were the busiest day of the week, people knocking off early and putting away a few drinks before they legged it into the city centre. By five o'clock the pub was packed.

'Where's Chloe?' David shouted.

'She's upstairs, getting ready.' Sheila swiped the froth off a Guinness. 'She's going out, remember?'

*   *   *

Chloe gazed at her reflection in the mirror. The bed was heaped with clothes. She had tried them all on and they had all looked terrible—correction, they looked terrible with her inside them. The dresses made her look like a cleaning lady. The skirts (size 16 now) revealed her bulging stomach. This isn't my body, she thought. It has swollen around me, an alien growth, it belongs to someone else. Take it away, please! Deep in her heart she knew why her father had stopped taking photos of her: he was ashamed of what she had become. A great mutant creature, spawned by him. How could he possibly love her?

How could anybody? Two floors down she heard the hum of voices; people had spilled out on to the pavement. Somebody laughed. Down in the bar they stood there, chatting each other up. A stage on—how well she knew the courtship ritual, from her position on the sidelines—a stage further on they would be sitting together, touching all the way down and inspecting the cinema listings in the evening paper. The next stage on, the breeding period (oh she longed for children), they all but disappeared from sight, though the bloke might drop in to watch the big match on Sky. But he had a home to go to, a life. He was loved.

Chloe finally chose black leggings—repulsive when seen alone, straining over her bulges, but slightly less so when covered by a voluminous top.

The front was scooped, revealing her cleavage. She suddenly thought: One day, will my breasts drive some man crazy? For they were the only part of her body of which she felt remotely proud. My feet aren't bad either, she thought, but who's going to bother with them? Only I have ever noticed my slender toes, that seem to belong to another person entirely.

Chloe clumped down the stairs and made her way through the bar. Lennox had his back to her. He was collecting empties. She had never known any man who could hold so many empty glasses in one hand; it was just another wonderful thing about him.

It was a shame she was all done up and he didn't see her go. Her mother was nowhere in sight. Her dad, however, was in his usual position behind the bar.

He looked at her and paused. A spasm of what she took to be irritation crossed his face. His last words to her were: 'Got your keys?'

*   *   *

It was Rowena's birthday party—Rowena the air hostess—and she had booked a club in the city centre, somewhere behind Debenhams. Chloe wasn't an habitué of the Manchester club scene. This was a place called Pixies. She could hear the music out in the street; there was a roped-off bit around the entrance, and even a bouncer. She nearly told the minicab driver to turn round and take her home again. It was only the thought of her parents' faces, the humiliation, that stopped her.

Inside, the room was crammed. Chloe was seized

126

with panic. She knew she should be doing this; it was called having a good time. *You've got to live*, said her father. He had been a bit of a raver but why should she? You fought through bodies to get a drink you didn't particularly want. You shouted at other people, who couldn't hear what you were saying and who wouldn't be interested anyway; you roared with laughter at a joke whose punchline you had missed. It was the same in the pub every night, the shouting, the getting rat-arsed, the incomprehensible slide into oblivion.

Clutching a cocktail, Chloe longed for her bedroom. Its peace, its fringed lamp, the unread *Elle* magazine waiting for her. *You can't just sit here, rotting away.* How could her father have said that? *Rotting away.* She wasn't dead yet; she was just biding her time. She would join the Civil Service; she would show him. Once she had decided what it would be, she would do it. He was such a bully, and so insensitive. Couldn't he see that nobody would want her as an air hostess?

Chloe drained her glass. She never drank as a rule, she didn't like alcohol, but the cocktail was pleasantly syrupy. She recognized a few faces from school—Shelley, Anne-Marie. She shouted at them and they shouted back . . . *hairdressing . . . little boy aged three . . . anyone hear from Andy?* She knew what they were thinking—Christ, Chloe's put on the pounds.

After her second cocktail, however, this seemed to matter less. Nor did it matter that, in all probability, she was the only virgin in the room. She had been fondled upon occasion, but mostly by boys who were pissed, and she was a publican's daughter, she felt contempt for drunkenness. One

127

day she would find her true love. *Your breasts*, he would say wonderingly, *I worship them*. Not just her breasts—herself. They would gaze into each other's eyes and hold each other close and nothing else would matter.

As time passed, Chloe felt airier. *What will be, will be . . .* She loved the old standards, the ones her father had taught her . . . *Que sera, sera . . .* The words rocked from side to side in her brain, like brandy in a glass. The future would take care of itself. For, to her surprise, Chloe was starting to enjoy herself. By ten o'clock she had slipped into another gear, she was starting to see the point of it all. She even danced with a group of girls—their hands, separate things, clapping above their heads. *Thank you for the days*, sang Ray Davies. It was one of her dad's favourite songs and she felt a wave of warmth towards him. He wasn't that bad, he loved her really.

This warmth included them all. She even realized, with a smug, settling feeling in her stomach, that not all of them were that good-looking. Some of the girls were in fact quite plain, though they had made an effort, as she had. The world wasn't divided into beautiful people and herself, a great lump. They were all in it together, struggling along, they were all just part of the human race. This struck her as beautiful. Why hadn't she realized it before?

With surprise, she thought: I'm having fun. So she was tipsy, who cared? Then the music stopped and they all sang 'Happy Birthday', and Rowena staggered on to the stage and sang 'Happy Birthday To Me' and then other people were being urged to get up there and sing and then Mandy somebody, another gratifyingly beefy girl from school, was pulling at Chloe's sleeve.

'Come on, Chloe, you had a wicked voice.'

And now Chloe was standing up there and she was singing in her pure, high voice.

'If I had wings like Noah's dove, I'd fly up the river to the man I love . . .'

They gazed up at her, startled. Her self-consciousness melted away.

'When I wore my apron low, I couldn't keep you from my door . . .'

Her voice always surprised her. She possessed it, the sound came from her only-too-familiar body, but it was also something apart from herself, like a bird that flew from her open mouth. She adored singing.

'But now my apron, it's too much in, You pass by but you don't come in . . . Fare thee well, oh honey, fare thee well . . .'

The room was silent; nobody else knew folk songs, they couldn't shout along to the words. The song poured out of her, tapped from within like liquid gold. How sad it was, and how beautiful! Even those in the room who looked so happy, they must know that love is fleeting, life is fleeting, all that we can be sure of is this moment—here, now—just for this evening.

'One of these days and it won't be long, Call my name and, honey, I'll be gone . . . Fare thee well, oh honey, fare thee well.'

She stopped. They clapped.

'More, more!'

But the spell was broken. Blushing, she stepped down from the stage.

And then a man was clasping her hand in both of

his. 'I cry and I cry,' he said in a thick foreign accent. 'It is beautiful.'

His eyes were, indeed, moist. He was a huge man with a great slab of a face, pitted with acne scars.

She recognized him: it was the bouncer. They started talking.

'My name is Cheddar,' he said. They called him this because nobody could pronounce his real name. He said he had served in the Yugoslav army and that Manchester was a big and lonely city.

'For a moment I hear my village,' he said. 'I hear my mother singing as she washes the clothes.' He said his village was in the mountains and that you could hear a goat cough in the next valley. At least, that was what Chloe presumed he said; he coughed to demonstrate.

She moved with him back to his position by the door. He continued to gaze down at her, his eyes searching hers.

'So beautiful.' He wiped away a tear. 'The world, so evil, and this so beautiful.'

'My dad used to sing for a living, long ago, but he's stopped now.'

'Even this place . . .' Cheddar jabbed at the street. 'Even this city, there are men they kill each other.'

'He bought me a guitar but he kept nagging at me, I was never good enough at it.'

'I look into men's eyes. It is my job. They come to this place and in one moment'—he held up his great finger—'this quick moment I make up my mind. Do they come in anger, do they cause trouble?'

'You have really big hands,' she said.

130

He mimed a strangling motion. 'Six men,' he said. 'The first man, I cry and I cry.'

'You mean you killed them, back in Yugoslavia?' She shivered. But he wasn't alarming; there was something sorrowful about him, as if he had only done it with the greatest reluctance.

They stood there for a while. She felt easy with Cheddar; he demanded nothing of her. She thought: neither of us fit in.

'The English girls, they are so cold,' he said.

'I know.' She nodded. 'English people are very polite, they never say what they mean. That's why they like getting drunk, it's the only way they can loosen up.' She laughed, briefly. 'Tell me about it. My parents run a pub.'

'English girls—thin like this.' He made a small, contemptuous gap between his thumb and forefinger.

She nodded enthusiastically. 'All skin and bone.'

'Skin and bone?'

'Oh, shit—I don't mean dead.' Where he came from, he probably thought that.

With his hands he mimed an hourglass shape. 'I like this.'

'Good. A lot of men do, actually.'

People were leaving. Cheddar nodded goodbye to them; he had courtly, East European manners. A British bouncer, she was sure, wouldn't behave like this.

Standing beside his bulk, Chloe felt an unfamiliar sensation—so unfamiliar it took her a moment to identify it. She felt fragile. Cheddar made her feel like a young woman in need of protection. She thought: I really am drunk.

More people were leaving. They washed past

him but he remained, like a rock when the tide receded. Chloe was in a strange state that night: buoyed up by the euphoria of her performance— how special she had felt!—and now cherished by this gentle giant who liked his women big. In his village, no doubt, they were all her size. She pictured hunky women in headscarves, lifting hefty babies; she must have seen a photo somewhere. And how could she pity herself? Think of the tragedies he had seen.

'My aunt . . .' He slid his finger across his throat. 'Her three little babies . . .'

'That's terrible!'

He said that during the day he worked in a car-wash and sent money back to his family in the mountains.

'You OK?' asked Denise, a girl from school, who was leaving with her boyfriend. 'Want a lift?'

Chloe shook her head. Denise glanced at them both, gave them a conspiratorial smile and walked off.

'You are going home?' asked Cheddar. 'You have a car?'

She shook her head. 'I'll get a minicab.'

'No—I mean to say—you come to me one day and I give your car a washing?'

Her heart jumped. 'Ah, I see. No, I don't have a car. I can't drive.'

'You come to the Pixies again?'

She nodded. 'Tomorrow—' She stopped; that sounded too eager. 'I mean, sometime I shall.'

'I want to see you again.'

There was a silence. They stood in the hallway. Stars made from Bacofoil hung from the ceiling.

The last people seemed to be leaving.

132

'*Arrivederci*, babe,' said Rowena, the birthday girl, as she stumbled out. 'You were great . . .' Her words were swallowed up in the night.

'I have a car,' said Cheddar. 'Volkswagen Polo. You come for a drive one day?'

Chloe nodded. She was held in a spell but she knew she should be getting home.

'Excuse me a moment,' she said, and went to fetch her jacket. The girl in the cloakroom was putting on lipstick. She too had wonderful possibilities ahead of her; they were all in it together. Chloe fished out her mobile and dialled the minicab number.

'Nothing for a hour, duck,' said a voice. 'And that's optimistic.'

Chloe paused. She didn't want to wait for an hour. Much as she liked Cheddar, she didn't want to hang about any longer. She wanted to go home and think about him. She wanted to lie on her bed and replay this night over and over again. Besides, it was half past one and the place was emptying.

She punched in her home number. *Wherever you are, whatever the time . . . just phone me . . . I'll come and fetch you in the car.*

The phone line was dead.

Of course it was dead. They had been cut off; that was why her dad had been in such a filthy mood all day.

Chloe stood there, undecided. She could hardly ask Cheddar to drive her home in his Volkswagen Polo. For one thing, he was still on duty. For another . . . well, she couldn't, could she?

'Do you know another minicab number?' she asked.

The cloakroom girl gave her a card. Chloe tried

them but a man said: 'Fifty minutes at least. We're rushed off our feet.'

There was only one option: she would walk home. It was only a couple of miles, the exercise would do her good.

In the doorway she shook Cheddar's hand; she couldn't think what else to do.

'You walk alone?' he asked, his brow furrowed.

'I'll be fine.'

*   *   *

The moon was full. It slid out from behind a building, startling her. So huge it was, tonight! Veiled in cloud, it was blurred like a pill dissolving in water. Around it, the sky glowed with its radiance.

Chloe clumped along the street in her heavy, strappy shoes. She walked past the side of Debenhams, an Adidas display in the windows, and across Piccadilly. Stepping over the tram lines, she walked down Mosley Street, wide and grim, with closed banks on either side. It seemed strange that the minicabs were busy, yet the streets so empty. If she turned left and took a short cut through Chinatown, she would emerge on Oxford Road. Then it was straight home.

The restaurants were closed. Woo Sang Cantonese was dark, with a pile of rubbish bags outside. Even a place called the Long Legs Table Dancing Bar was shut up. Where had everybody gone? Empty doorways reeked of urine. She turned right; should she have turned left? She had a poor sense of direction. She passed a humming extractor vent. The buildings were taller here, looming up in the darkness. When she got to the end of the street she found a bar across it and a sign saying NCP CAR PARK.

She retraced her steps, paused at the junction and turned left. The street looked vaguely familiar; maybe she was walking back the way she had come. If she turned right, surely that would lead her to Oxford Road? She changed direction and took the right turn, walking down a street of shuttered shops. When she reached the corner she saw a discount store: EVERYTHING MUST GO. Its familiarity reassured her; she had bought her CD player there. If she kept straight on she should get to that road which led to Oxford Road and then she would be all right. She would walk under the bridge, past the BBC building and in another mile she would be home.

Chloe shivered. The wind blew a plastic bag along the pavement; it bowled along, rolling over and over towards her as if it had her in its sights. The sodium light cast a shadowless glow. In the city, she thought, you never saw moonlight bathing the streets. In Cheddar's village, however, she would stand on a hilltop and raise her face to a sky which was spangled with stars and where a full moon hung, its light bathing her face with an eerie beauty. None of the other stuff would matter any more—her father's strictures, her mother's anxious and protective love. *Do something, see the world*, said her dad. She would show him! Wait until she eloped to Yugoslavia, or whatever it was called now, see his face then! First she would have to find out about Serbs and Croats. And what about the Muslims, where did they fit in? She had never listened to that part of the news. Cheddar, however, wouldn't criticize her for her ignorance. Unlike her father, he was a kindly and patient man.

Goodness, it was cold! Chloe wrapped her jacket tightly around herself. *April is the cruellest month.* Where had she read that—in school? She was no longer tipsy; just happy. Never before had she felt such closeness with a man. How pitifully immature, by comparison, was her hopeless lust for Lennox! Heading for the main road, she thought of Cheddar's skin, ravaged with acne scars. His appearance, too, had caused him suffering. This was another thing they had in common. They were soul mates.

Chloe stopped at the kerb. This wasn't the main road. It was a one-way street, empty of traffic. At the far junction, traffic lights switched to red. She had never been here before.

She looked up. The moon had disappeared; all that remained was a milky bloom. It seemed to have shifted way to the left. Surely it should have been ahead of her?

She turned and hurried up a side street, keeping the milky glow ahead of her. She wasn't alarmed; she was cold and tired, and her shoes rubbed, but inside she was warm. She knew that Cheddar was drawn to her, that sooner or later he would come for her. With his great hands he would pluck her out of her present existence and they would be happy.

The street divided into two. She seemed to have lost the moon entirely. The sky was suffused with orange. What produced that glow? Maybe she had been walking in circles and she was now heading back to the city centre. Ahead, a church spire rose up, needle-sharp. Its illuminated clock said four twenty. Chloe felt confused: it couldn't be that late, surely? She seemed to have been walking for hours.

She checked her watch: ten past two. The clock must be broken. The night was dislocated, as if she couldn't catch up with herself. As she stood beside the church she heard the faintest hum. It sounded like traffic on a motorway. But which motorway? Maybe the hum was inside her head.

Chloe didn't panic. She turned and walked briskly back the way she had come. If she found the route back to the discount store she could start all over again. Suddenly she wished, with all her heart, that she were safely home, snuggled under her duvet. *Where have you been, pet?* her mother would say, standing in the doorway in her dressing gown. She would bend over Chloe and kiss her goodnight. *Thank God you're home. You should have phoned*.

But she couldn't phone, could she?

Chloe decided to retrace her steps back into the city centre. She had an urgent need to be amongst people, even a few drunken stragglers, and to see some lights in the windows. If she found her way to Piccadilly Station, perhaps she could pick up a cab from the rank. Unless the last train had gone.

Chloe walked faster. Of course it would be gone. The station would be empty. Bags of rubbish were heaped on the pavement; bulging with shredded paper, they glinted in the lamplight. They were so full that the tapes had come unstuck. Had she come this way before? She passed a Chinese takeaway but this wasn't Chinatown; the buildings were bigger and more spaced apart. And here she was, crossing the canal when she had never crossed it before. She hurried past office lobbies, dark and silent and waiting for Monday. She passed an underground car park, its illuminated sign saying SPACES. She didn't recognize any of it. Or did she? Her father always said she was dozy. *Pay attention, for goodness' sake!*

It was then that she heard the car. Faint at first, but growing louder. It was coming up behind her.

For a moment Chloe was frightened. Then she thought: It's him, of course. She had known Cheddar would rescue her, she had sensed it from the start. *You walk alone?* he had asked, frowning. He was anxious about her, she knew it. How? Because they were destined for each other. They had recognized it the first moment.

Cheddar had tracked her down, in his Polo, and he would drive her home and kiss her on the doorstep and soon she would be calling herself Mrs Chloe whatever-it-was, his beautiful, unpronounceable foreign name.

Chloe kept walking. Smiling to herself, she thought: Play hard to get. The car drew up beside her. She turned, her face lit with a smile.

But it wasn't him.

PART THREE

CHAPTER ONE

Saturday dawned pink and dewy; there was a balminess in the air, like summer. By mid-morning Colin, who was digging a pond, had stripped to his shirtsleeves. The clay was heavy; he heaved out a spadeful and dumped it on to the pile. Beside him the rubber lining was folded, ready. By the end of the weekend it would be finished, and then he could transfer the tadpoles (for the spawn had hatched) from his old pond to their new home. The deeper he dug, the wetter the clay. He heaved it up and flung it behind him.

'Look, Mum, he's going to put a dead person in it!'

'Dominic—ssh!'

A family had moved in next door. The child, who must have been standing on something, gazed at him over the fence. Colin straightened up.

'I'm not burying anything,' he said. 'It's for frogs.'

'Ugh,' said the child and disappeared.

The woman pushed back the hair from her face. She too was perspiring. 'He watches too much TV,' she said.

'Used to be a real pond near here.'

'At night he checks the doors are bolted. Funny, isn't it, a kid doing that.' She turned away. Over the fence he saw the top of her head moving back towards the house.

Natalie was still asleep. She was missing the best of the day but Colin was used to it by now. She should do just what she wanted. Knowing that she was there, dreaming under the duvet, was enough—more than enough; it filled him with amazement. He kept thinking that one day he would go upstairs and find her gone. Simply gone, as if she had never been.

He heard the doorbell ring and went through the house. Two men stood in the porch.

'Delivery for Mr Taylor. One flat-pack garden shed.'

Colin stared. Behind him he heard footsteps on the stairs; Natalie appeared, tousled from sleep, in her T-shirt and knickers. 'It's for you.'

'But love, I'm building them myself.'

'It's a present.' She kissed him on the cheek. He could see the men eyeing her up and down. 'They've been taking you ages. I took pity on you. And this one's much better.'

'But we don't have the money.'

She nuzzled him. 'We do.' She smelt of sleep, of their secret nights together. Her face, bare of make-up, looked scrubbed and vulnerable. He loved her like this—the private Natalie that was his alone. 'I know you want to move the rest of your pets here, your mum's getting fed up with them. This way you can bring them here quicker.'

She still called them pets but he didn't like to correct her. She wasn't interested in the scientific side of it, his breeding programme and rehabilitation unit. He said: 'The boy next door, he thought I was a murderer.'

She laughed. 'Just what I said when I saw you first—Christ, it's the psychopathic gas fitter!'

He suddenly thought: It's true. I could kill someone. If a bloke harmed my wife I would bludgeon him to death. Since meeting Natalie he

142

had had so many surprising thoughts, so many new sensations, that this one hardly gave him a shock. Given the circumstance, who could predict their reactions anyway? Most people never had to find out.

'I don't want you slogging your guts out to buy me things,' he said.

'I don't slog my guts out.' She tickled his chin. 'Trust me.'

By Sunday he had lined the pond and edged it with stones. He only had to install the pump, fill it up and pour in the anti-chlorine solution and it would be ready for its occupants. It was another blazing day—too hot for April, unnaturally so; the weather was weird nowadays.

Colin looked at the shed panels, stacked on the lawn. To be frank, he would have preferred to build his own. Those ready-to-assemble jobs were so flimsy that they fell to bits after a year or so. But he could hardly tell Natalie that.

At noon she appeared in a bikini and lay down on a blanket.

'You got suntan lotion on?' he asked. 'Don't get burnt.'

She lowered her sunglasses and grinned. 'Just carry on with your erection.'

He blushed and turned up the radio. The news came on. He pulled open a plastic bag of screws—totally inadequate, a quarter-inch—and gazed at Natalie as she lay there sunbathing. She looked white and defenceless, like a hatched grub.

'. ./ . *The young woman found murdered in Manchester this morning has been identified as—*'

'Ugh!' said Natalie. 'Turn it off.' She rolled on to her stomach.

After work on Monday, Natalie found a bunch of flowers stuck behind her windscreen wipers. No note, but she could guess. Stupid bastard, she thought. Anyone could have seen him doing it. It was a miracle he hadn't set off the alarm.

Phillip had been appearing in the office more often during the past few weeks. Ostensibly talking to Mrs Coles, his eyes had been fixed on Natalie. Her ex-lover looked gaunt—thinner and somehow diminished. Somebody—guess who?—had cut his hair too short. It didn't suit him. Natalie ignored him. From time to time, however, she had discovered gifts on her desk; the previous Thursday she had found a box of Terry's All Gold, wrapped in ribbon.

She dropped the flowers on to the floor of her car where they remained, withering in their wrapper. She had no time for Phillip; she was surprised she had even fancied him. Her life was far too engrossing.

The evenings were lighter now. Colin had erected his final shed, the one she had bought him, and was going to fetch his last load of tortoises. They had recently emerged from hibernation. 'Like me,' he had said. 'I was hibernating too.'

He spoke like this nowadays. The tongue-tied Colin was developing into a talkative young man; love had loosened the words from him.

'Come with me,' he said. 'You haven't seen me mam for weeks.'

Natalie shook her head. His mother made her uneasy. Those narrowed eyes seemed to bore into

144

her soul. Mrs Taylor—she couldn't bring herself to call her Peggy—was the only person whom Natalie feared.

'She'd rather see you on her own,' Natalie said. 'She sees precious little enough of you as it is.'

Afterwards she thought: Don't be stupid. I've got nothing to worry about.

*   *   *

Still, the next day her heart jumped when Sioban whispered: 'There's a thief in our midst.'

'What do you mean?' asked Natalie.

'Someone's been nicking things. The Walrus found out.'

'Ah.' Natalie paused. 'You mean, stationery and stuff.'

'He's beadier than he looks, the old sod.'

Sioban ground out her cigarette. Since Farida had gone matronly and given up the fags, Sioban had become Natalie's smoking companion.

'NuLine's such shit,' said Sioban. 'Who do they think they are, Big Brother? If I could think of a way of fucking them up, big-time, I would. What's a few paperclips, for Christ's sake?' Her cheeks reddened with irritation. 'We all do it. It's not stealing.'

'No,' said Natalie. 'It's a redistribution of wealth.'

*   *   *

At five thirty, however, she had another unwelcome shock. When she went down to the lobby, two policemen stood there. They were stationed in the doorway, stopping staff and searching their bags.

Natalie registered this at a glance. She turned round and ran back up the stairs. At the first-floor landing she paused, thinking fast. She had two cheques in her wallet, the day's hits. If her bag was searched, they might be found.

She hurried into the toilets. Nobody was there. She went into a cubicle and shot the bolt. Rummaging in her wallet, she took out the cheques. Where could she hide them? It was a warm day; she wore just a skimpy top and skirt. She thought for a moment, then she stuffed the cheques into her knickers.

She stood there, breathing heavily, and gazed at the toilet-paper dispenser. Calm down, she told herself. They won't be looking for cheques anyway. The paper felt awkward between her legs. She imagined hobbling downstairs, her legs bowed like a Greek granny, and burst into giggles. She made a swift calculation: £226.40 plus £212.25 equals . . . £438.65. All that money, nestling against her pubic hair. She thought: Nobody can call me a cheap date.

The main door opened; she heard its sigh and click. No footsteps, however, no cubicle door opening. Whoever it was must be standing at the mirror, silently applying their lipstick.

Natalie waited for them to leave. She remembered past moments in toilets—snorting cocaine when she was temping at a firm of accountants; trying to insert her diaphragm, in her pre-pill days, in a Greek karsey with flies buzzing around and a German called Hans waiting to take her down to the beach. Several shags, including the one with Phillip. Toilets held fond, illicit memories

146

for her. And now, wedged in her knickers, she had funds for a weekend for two in Paris, all-inclusive, plus that pair of fake snakeskin shoes she had seen in Pied à Terre. Real snakeskin would be better, she thought, thinking of Colin's python. What a creepy animal it was, wrapping itself around his body. *It kills by squeezing its prey*, he said. *Suffocates it to death*. All his reptiles were creepy, either sitting there motionless, eyes bulging, throats throbbing; or else suddenly, horribly quick.

Whoever it was, the person must have gone. Natalie pushed back the bolt and stepped out.

Phillip stood there.

'Go away,' she said.

'I've got to see you—'

'This is the ladies'.'

Lunging towards her, he gripped her shoulders. 'You're driving me mad.'

'Piss off, Phillip.' She tried to disentangle herself.

'I love you, I can't bear it any more—'

'You're bloody married.'

'I told you, me and Melanie—'

'I'm married too. Fuck off!'

He held her tight. She smelt the familiar scent of his skin.

'It's been hell, I can't bear it—'

'And stop leaving me bloody flowers.'

'I've got to see you again.'

He held her so tightly she couldn't move. She felt his erection pressing against her stomach.

'Somebody'll come in!' she hissed.

'I love you.' He pushed her against the washbasin. 'I love you, Natalie—I'm crazy for you.' His hand pulled up her skirt.

'Fuck off!' she shouted, panicking.

'You're driving me mad.' He started to pull down her knickers.

Natalie broke away. 'You want to bloody rape me?'

There was a silence. Phillip started sobbing. 'I'm sorry, darling . . . I'm sorry.' Tears ran down his cheeks.

She pulled down her skirt. Her heart was hammering. 'It's over, Phillip. Remember, you cheated on me? Remember that? Go home to your family, you snivelling little prick.' She picked up her bag and swung it over her shoulder. 'And if you try it on again I'll report you for sexual harassment.'

She walked out.

Blimey, she thought. That was a near thing.

A few moments later she was down in the lobby, smiling at the police officer as he opened her bag.

'Sorry about this,' he said.

'That's OK. You're only doing your job.'

He gave her back her bag and she skipped through the door, to freedom.

CHAPTER TWO

David slept heavily, those first weeks; he slept like the dead. It awed Sheila, that he could sink into oblivion, that the blackness could close him away from her as she lay beside him, waiting for dawn to lighten the curtains. Her pills were no use. They didn't send her to sleep; nor did they quell the panic.

For she was terrified. She lay there, very still, trying to control it. To hold her body together needed every ounce of energy she possessed; she had to concentrate on it. But the panic made her bowels churn and she would have to rise from bed, very slowly, and make her way to the bathroom. Like an elderly person, she gripped the doorknob for support. Once seated on the toilet, it seemed impossible to think of getting up again. If she moved, the chaos would open up. It would claim her, pulling her down into nothingness.

Besides, why move? What was the point of being in one place rather than another? This thought alarmed her; she needed to shake herself out of it. So she would heave herself to her feet in preparation for the long journey back to the bedroom. Outside Chloe's bedroom door she sometimes lost the will to move at all. When Chloe was small, Sheila would tiptoe in to check that she was still breathing. The miracle that she did.

Hours later Sheila would find herself sitting outside the bedroom door, chilled in her nightie. Dawn would arrive, eventually. Those early days in May, the dawns were beautiful. A detached part of her recognized this. There was one tree she could see, rising up behind the yard wall; it was misted with the tenderest green. Traffic was already building up, she heard the hum of it, but it seemed to be taking place a long way away, in another world entirely. It seemed extraordinary that they carried on driving, that people went on with their lives, getting in and out of cars, fuming in traffic jams, as if nothing had happened. People worried about things, about whether the plumber would turn up, wasn't that strange? And stranger still that the days passed, one remorselessly following another. Did nobody realize?

She would climb back into bed carefully, like an invalid. She lay apart from David, for fear of touching him; she felt his skin would bruise. Her body gave off a sour smell. It was too much of an effort to wash. This alarmed her, but in a sluggish way. Besides, it hurt to move. Her bones ached; her guts felt corroded with acid. The sheer physical pain sometimes made it hard to breathe. David smelt too, of all the cigarettes he had smoked since Chloe's death, thousands of them, and the whisky he was drinking at night.

So Sheila lay there, for what else could she do? She lay there, willing herself to stay sane. Ah, but the effort of it! Sometimes it didn't seem worth the bother. She would just surrender herself up and free-fall, into the pit. Meanwhile she willed David to stay asleep a little longer, in sweet oblivion. She dreaded the moment he woke, for when he opened his eyes, just for a moment, he was a normal, groggy person facing a normal day. Then, a moment later, he remembered.

And then the letters of condolence would thud through the door, still several each day, some from strangers. Mr Hassan opposite opened up his shop as if all that mattered was setting out his goods and putting them away again, that was the point of it all. He had slipped a note through their door. She supposed a lot of people knew; after all, it had been all over the papers. For several days reporters had pestered them, that had been hellish, but David had told them to fuck off.

Certainly their customers knew, the regular ones anyway. David had insisted on reopening the pub after three days. 'We'll lose business otherwise,' he said. 'You don't have to come down; Lennox and I will manage.' David was a man of routine. She knew he clung to it, now more than ever, that he too was fighting the chaos in his own private way. He showered in the morning, he ate two slices of toast, as he always did, and stood outside for a few minutes until eleven sharp when he opened up. Archie, however, had stopped coming.

Amongst the customers there had been a certain amount of shuffling, some muttered words of sympathy and avoidance of her eye. There were fewer of them these days; a lot of familiar faces had melted away. The past week, the takings were down twenty per cent. It was hardly surprising, for who wants to have a drink in a house of death? *Hey, let's go out tonight and get bladdered! How about the Queen's Head—know the one? Daughter murdered and dumped in Whitworth Street.*

Sheila helped him behind the bar. David needed her because that week Lennox was due to leave. 'May God be with you in your time of trouble,' Lennox said, for it transpired that he was a born-again Christian, a fact that she and David, in their former life, would have found hilarious. 'Take one day at a time, and keep our saviour Jesus in your heart.'

Being busy, she thought, might help. The trouble was, it was all she could do to put one foot in front of the other. She felt ill all the time, on the verge of vomiting. Stupid with grief, she mixed up the orders. David was patient with her. So were the customers. How many of them knew? She hardly had the energy to wonder, but some of them addressed her kindly, repeating their orders as if

151

speaking to the retarded. She stopped the lunches; cooking them was out of the question. Besides, the sight of food made her nauseous.

And she would suddenly find herself standing still, incapable of movement. In Europa Food and Wine, where she had gone to buy some lemons, she came to a standstill in front of the cooking utensils. She looked at a cherry de-pipper. Somebody had bothered to invent that, wasn't it odd? Chloe was dead and somebody had thought about taking stones out of cherries. Then she thought: Chloe's birthday is on June the twenty-seventh. She would be twenty-two.

It was hard, being exposed to the world like this, flinching when somebody shouted, feeling as if she had been flayed. Crossing the road frightened her—how huge and unkind were the lorries, thundering past! When a driver shouted at a car, 'Stupid cunt!' she jumped as if she had been shot. And every day she had to face the customers, their mouths opening and closing and noise coming out.

The funeral was long over. It had felt like the most terrible day of their lives, her and David's, but she hadn't known what lay ahead. For in those early days her family rallied around, her mother and her sisters, her uncle and nephews, the whole clan of Sampsons. They were a demonstrative lot; they wept with her and held her in their arms. Her mother, whose tests had turned out to be negative—at seventy-five, she was given a further lease of life—her mother went into Chloe's bedroom and tidied it up. She emerged with scraped-out yoghurt pots, their teaspoons smeary. When Sheila came into the kitchen her mother was throwing a half-finished packet of Jaffa cakes into the bin. She jumped, as if caught in a criminal act. And then, seeing Sheila's face, she made her a mug of hot chocolate, as she had when her daughter was small. Later Sheila heard the washing-machine rumbling with Chloe's clothes.

But her family was no longer around, they couldn't be there for ever. They too had lives. At some point Sheila had to face the long haul alone.

And she was alone. David sometimes put his arm around her shoulder. 'Are you taking your pills?' he asked. At the funeral he had cried briefly—loud, racking sobs that had alarmed her. But since then he had closed himself off. His fierce, stony grief was terrible to her.

Sometimes, late at night, he went out in the car. She heard the engine coughing into life, out beyond the yard, and then the whine as he reversed. An hour, two hours, he was gone.

'Where have you been?' she asked when he was undressing.

'Out.'

And then he climbed into bed and slept like the dead. Sometimes she resented this, and sometimes she was glad for him. Sometimes, during the long watches of the night, she slipped her hand into his. He would squeeze it briefly—was he really awake, and faking it? And then his hand lay there, inert, and finally she gave up and slipped hers out.

The next day, if she went out in the car, it stank of cigarettes.

*   *   *

'We'll get him, Mr Milner,' said the detective. 'It's only a matter of time.'

'A matter of time?' snapped David.

'We have thirty officers working on the case. *Crimewatch* created a huge response, we're following up a number of leads. You'd be amazed what crops up . . . memories jogged, things people have seen but thought nothing of at the time . . .' He laid two biros side by side. 'I know nothing I can say will help you, believe me, I do understand that—'

'Do you?'

'David . . .' Sheila laid a hand on his arm. She felt stagey, doing this. They weren't themselves. She would wake up and find it had all been a dream.

'We shall track this animal down and bring him to justice.' The man seemed to have learned some sort of script too. He was a new one; maybe he was an inspector, she didn't know. He had introduced himself but she hadn't caught the name. The whole scene had the glazed unreality of a TV series. But then everything seemed like that.

'What exactly are you doing?' David demanded. 'Six weeks this monster has been free.' Monster? He, too, sounded stilted.

'How about coming along to the Incident Room?' asked the man. 'Meet some of the people involved?'

'No!' said Sheila. They would all look up; *the victim's parents*. They might—God forbid—have photos pinned to the wall. She had seen those on TV, photos of the victim. At the time she had felt a pleasurable frisson. Wasn't that almost the strangest thing of all? She felt sick. She wanted to be taken home and tenderly laid in bed.

David was firing questions at the man. Who had

they interviewed? What about the forensic report? He sounded impressively knowledgeable, another person entirely, but he was badgering the man. All his anger seemed to be channelled in the police's direction. In fact, he had always been suspicious of them—drug busts in the past, that sort of thing. Sheila was a more trusting soul and used to tell him what a difficult job they had; it had been one of their regular arguments.

Suddenly, painfully, she missed their squabbles. How normally married such things now seemed! Chloe's death had bulldozed through the landscape of their relationship, scoring it open like a raw wound and squashing the plants—whatever they were, she could hardly remember now what the terrain had looked like.

David's aggression embarrassed her. She had wanted to come with him, however. The police were their allies. The world was so hostile; it pursued so heedlessly its own ends. Here in the police station Sheila felt briefly at home. Chloe might be simply a case to the police, but she was at the forefront of their minds. The same questions preoccupied them. Where exactly had she been killed? (Sheila couldn't even put a word to the other thing that had happened to Chloe before she was killed, not yet.) Somewhere on her route home, for the police had found out, by questioning people at the nightclub, that she had failed to get a minicab and decided to walk. But she had been discovered near the railway station, way off her route, left on a patch of waste ground (nor could Sheila say *body* or *dumped*). They suspected she had been killed somewhere else. They were agonizing, these speculations, but at least she was companioned in the horror of them.

'Of course it makes our task more challenging, that this was a motiveless attack—no links, as far as we know, to any other murders or serious sexual assaults . . .'

Nobody had watered the detective's spider plant. It sat alone on the windowsill, its roots bulging out of the plastic pot. But still it had struggled to produce offspring, the survival instinct was that strong. It had put out runners, with babies attached to them. They dangled down from the ledge.

'. . . but we'll get a break. Sooner or later he'll make a mistake, let something slip. Somebody, prompted by something else entirely, will make a connection. It's happened more times than I care to mention . . .'

The question she couldn't ask—nor could David. The question they kept secret in their separate hearts: *How much did she suffer?*

She put up quite a fight, someone said. Or maybe it had been in one of the newspaper reports she had tried not to look at. David had snatched them away, to protect her.

In the other offices, phones were ringing. They must be about Chloe; it was unthinkable that anyone could think of anything else. David and the detective had come to the end of their conversation; in fact they were standing up and shaking hands. Sheila didn't have the energy to get up.

Was nobody going to answer that phone? In the next room it rang and rang. It could be the vital call, the one they had all been waiting for. *I know the man, he's my next-door neighbour.* It could be a boy's voice. *I saw this car by the station, mister, and I*

156

got its number.

Whoever he was, the man, he was alive on this earth; that was the incomprehensible thing. He must be driving around in his car (that car). He probably looked like anybody else. He walked into shops and bought things, perhaps he had a wife and children. In this hot weather they would be getting the paddling pool out. He went out at night and his wife asked him, when he returned: *Where have you been?* And he replied: *Out.*

'Ready, darling?' David looked down at her, his eyebrows raised. They looked thicker, now he had lost so much hair. The bald part was cleanly bald, no stray wisps, but had the hair around his ears always been so grey?

They went out into the street. The sunlight assaulted her; it burnt her eyes. Crying had made them feel skinned; it seemed impossible that there were any tears left.

She died alone.

As they crossed the road, David held her hand. This comforted Sheila. She thought: We're in this together. If we help each other we might, just might, survive.

Encouraged by this, she said: 'Do you keep seeing her?'

'Seeing her?'

'On buses, in crowds. I keep just glimpsing her, and wondering why she doesn't turn round.'

David released her hand. They walked down the hill towards their car.

'Last night I heard a car stopping outside,' she said. 'I thought—it's a minicab, she *did* find one after all. I saw her getting out and she said, *I know I've been ages*—you know what she's like when she

157

apologizes, sort of abrupt—*I've been on a long journey but I'm home now.'*

There was a silence. Then David said: 'Thank you, pigeon.'

For a moment, Sheila thought he was addressing her. Then she saw the white smear on the windscreen.

David rummaged in his pocket for a tissue.

*   *   *

'He won't talk to me,' she said. 'He's closed off, more and more. I try to reach him but he won't let me.'

'It's his way of dealing with it,' said her sister.

'I want us to talk about her. If we don't, it makes her even more . . .' She couldn't say the word. 'Even more not here.'

Fiona, her sister, nodded. They were sitting in her kitchen in Hebden Bridge.

'He's always been bloody difficult,' said Fiona. She and David had never got on. They were too similar, that was why—touchy, prickly. Sheila had tried to defend her husband, smoothing things between them. In her family she had always been the peacekeeper. 'So bloody autocratic,' said Fiona, 'bossing you around. You should stand up to him more.'

'Now hardly seems the time.'

Fiona refilled their glasses. 'And he did the same with Chloe. That's why he feels so awful now.'

'He loves her. When she was younger he was a wonderful father.'

'Oh, underneath he did, I'm sure. But he didn't show it, did he? Always criticizing her and making

158

her feel hopeless.'

Sheila found this bracing. It was refreshing just to talk about her daughter, even in this irritable way. For a moment, she felt normal.

Fiona had a dim view of men in general. She had divorced her husband, a builder, some years earlier and was subjecting herself to a punishing regime of diets and line-dancing. She was on the warpath, searching for another lover whom she would soon find wanting. Her own children had found her alarming; so had Chloe.

'It's not just David,' Sheila said. 'Nearly everybody, they don't like to mention her name. I suppose they feel awkward or feel it'll upset me. Or they offer their condolences, people who've never taken the slightest interest in her, which sort of feels like intruding. It's as if the only thing she's done is to die. I want to talk about the normal things, even the annoying things, I don't mind.' *Know what my job is?* she'd once told Chloe. *I'm the Sponge Lady. I walk behind you, mopping things up.* Oh, their giggles in the kitchen. 'I want people from Clarence Street, and Morecambe, and all the places we've lived in to just chat about her, silly things; we'd just sit there chatting about that time she tried to wax her legs, or her disastrous driving test . . .' She stopped. '*Anything*. Don't they understand?'

She gazed at the walls. There were lines of rough plaster down them where Alan, Fiona's husband, had chased in the wiring but never got round to making it good. All the rooms were unfinished— the half-tiled bathroom, the unpainted lobby. Like her daughter, they had just stopped. Fiona didn't notice it any more; she had got used to it. And she wasn't the sort to do it herself. Visitors said: 'Just moved in, have you?'

Their mother lived in the bungalow next door. Maybe that was another reason for the departure of Fiona's husband; he felt outnumbered by this big, volatile family, that closed ranks at the first sign of trouble. If she were an outsider, she herself would feel unnerved. David had nobody to turn to; without her, he was alone in the world.

Sheila gazed at the day's letters, lying on the table. *Singles Nite at the Shangri La: First Cocktail on the House!* Suddenly the thought of David pierced her heart. How could she presume to feel alone?

'The awful thing is, he feels so guilty,' she said. 'He doesn't talk about it, the thing about the phone.'

'What thing?'

She told Fiona about it. Her sister had known about the phone being cut off, how Chloe couldn't get through and so she had to walk home. But now Sheila told her about the argument and how David had refused to pay for the phone to be reconnected. 'He blames himself, you see. He blames himself for her death.'

Fiona looked at her. Her eyes were piercingly blue; she wore tinted contact lenses. 'What about you?' she asked. 'Do you blame him?'

*   *   *

One night in June, two months after Chloe's death, Sheila went out. She could leave the pub because they had hired a supply barman. His name was Kit, that was all she knew. In the past she had been

160

motherly with the staff, commiserating with them about their love lives and asking them about their hopes for the future. Now she couldn't be bothered. She didn't even speculate about whether he knew what had happened. Grief does not ennoble us or deepen our generosity towards others. It doesn't make us a nicer person. It makes us self-centred and bitter and smelly. As Sheila sat in the bus she thought: Kit probably thinks it's because he's black. And I can't be bothered about that either.

Nor could she summon up much interest in the pub's continued loss of custom. Over the past weeks all the parties in the function room had been cancelled. 'In the circumstances, it seems inappropriate,' people said. 'We don't like to intrude. But if we can be of use . . . if there's anything we can do to help . . .'

'Hire the fucking room,' David muttered, behind Sheila's shoulder.

That night, Friday, was usually the busiest of the week but the place was half-empty. And no wonder. David stood behind the bar like a shop dummy—clean and smart as always, dressed in shirt, tie and jacket, but chillingly formal. He moved stiffly, as if he would spill. Nowadays he kept a glass of Scotch on the go but there was nothing convivial about this; he knocked it back alone. Sheila herself wasn't much better; greasy-haired, sleepwalking through the hours. Dust had settled on the table-legs; outside, the window-boxes were bare.

Nobody mentioned Chloe. It was as if she had never existed. Her name hadn't been spoken since Sheila had visited her sister, two weeks earlier. And people avoided her in the street; she could see them looking at their watches, as if they had just remembered something, and hurrying across the road.

Maybe it was due to the nature of Chloe's death. What possible words of comfort could they give? Illness or accident might, she supposed, be marginally easier to deal with. But this was so far beyond anyone's comprehension that there was no formula for dealing with it. She was set apart from the human race, sentenced to isolation as if she were infectious. But what, Sheila thought, can they catch from me?

Sheila got out of the bus in Piccadilly Gardens. It was nine o'clock. She made her way past Debenhams and down Tib Street. She knew the way. In the sixties she had bought clothes at a boutique on the corner; Chloe's age, she had been, and equally self-conscious. She didn't have the figure for mini-dresses—too big in the bust and hips—but she had caught the eye of Taboo's lead singer, hadn't she? David Milner, the sexiest bloke in the room. And within a month she had moved in with him.

The boutique had long since disappeared. The building had been renovated; there was an internet café and a sign saying *6 X Studio Apartments for Sale*. Once she had bought a lime-green miniskirt. Her little sister Monica had borrowed it without asking and spilt red wine down it. Would this have been more possible to bear if Sheila had had other children? Would they have been a comfort to her now? She couldn't imagine it; she couldn't imagine anything.

The sun was setting. PIXIES. The neon shone in

the fading light. Sheila heard music; kids were going in. It seemed perverse, to disappear into the gloom on such a golden evening, but they were young, weren't they?

A bouncer stood at the door. He was large and black. Was he the one? All she remembered, from the police report, was that the bouncer—the last man on earth, except one, to see her daughter alive—had an unpronounceable name.

She looked up at him. He had a kind face, she decided. She needed him to be kind.

'Excuse me. Were you on duty eight weeks ago, a Friday night like this one?'

He shook his head. 'I'm new—hey, not you, mate!' He turned and barred the way to a tattooed youth. 'I started this Tuesday, ma'am.'

'Do you know who it was? I want to talk to him.' She added weakly: 'I'm a parent.'

'Nope, no idea. Sorry.'

Sheila went into the building. She paused, for a moment, to adjust to the gloom. It was a narrow corridor, with stars suspended from the ceiling. Kids squeezed past her and went upstairs. She felt old, an obstruction. She tried to remember the surroundings for later—to remember them for Chloe's sake—but she couldn't connect this place to her daughter.

The police had also interviewed the cloakroom girl. She was the one who had told them about Chloe phoning for a cab. At the end of the passage was a booth. A girl sat there. Sheila went up to her and asked her the same question. Was she working in the club, that night?

The girl shook her head. 'I'm sitting in for my friend,' she said. There was something nude about

163

her face; she had plucked off her eyebrows, that was why. The skin moved, two ridges of it, as she raised them. 'Can I help you?'

'I'm looking for her.'

'Mel? She's gone back to New Zealand.'

'Ah.' Sheila paused. 'Or the bouncer who was around then. He had a foreign name.'

'Oh. You mean Cheddar. That the one? Big geezer, looked like a mass-murderer.'

'Does he?'

'He's left.' She stopped, and looked at Sheila. 'Hey, you OK?'

'I need to see him.'

'Want to sit down?'

'I'm fine.'

'Let me think. He had a day job, somebody said. Want me to find out?'

*   *   *

It needed a wash, the car. It had been neglected, of late. In fact, it had always been neglected. Sheila was naturally untidy and David, though a neat man in other respects, lost his will when it came to the Mondeo. Chloe had been the worst offender. Sheila remembered her husband's bellow when he had opened his *Manchester A–Z* and found it glued together with one of her sucked sweets.

Enboldened by her visit to Pixies, Sheila went into Chloe's bedroom. She needed to stir the air in it, to keep it alive. The clothes had long since been tidied away; she opened the wardrobe and sniffed the dresses like an animal. She had become an animal—aching, snuffling, farting, crying. She opened a drawer and handled Chloe's knickers.

They were familiar to her—some of them she had bought herself—and greyed by repeated washing. Large knickers, sprigged and striped cotton. Had they ever been touched by a man's fingers? Desperately she hoped so.

Sheila was beyond tears now, she had no more to shed. She pulled out a bra, 38C, frayed at the seams. For years now she hadn't seen Chloe naked. Once a carefree child, her daughter had become shy as she grew up. Beneath the underwear Sheila felt the crackle of wrappers. She drew out packets—Hob Nobs, Digestives—nearly empty packets with a few biscuits left.

This undid her all over again. She lay down on Chloe's bed and pressed her face into the pillow.

And now she was driving into the car-wash. A mannequin with a mechanical arm beckoned her under the railway arch: *Wash'N'Wax Valet Service.* She drove through a doorway into the great, vaulted darkness. Two men sprung out and lathered the windows. A sponge rubbed away the last smears of bird shit. The men were obscured by suds. Was one of them him? *Looked like a mass-murderer.* Suddenly the thought struck Sheila: Could it be him, the bouncer? He had followed her home?

How stupid she had been! Her brain was so slow nowadays, she could feel its cogs grinding and searching for a connection. Behind the foam the men-shapes shifted. A great hand, startlingly near, swabbed the window beside her. She heard words shouted in a foreign language.

Something struck the car roof. She jumped and sat there, rigid. A face loomed up at the window. It nodded.

She wound down the window. 'What do you want?'

The man smote the flank of the car. 'You go.' His finger pointed ahead. She tried to gather her wits: of course the bouncer hadn't killed her, the police had eliminated him long ago.

Engaging first gear, she slid the car on to tracks. They held it in a grip. Helplessly she sat while the car slid forward, through plastic curtains that slit open, and then great heavy fronds were slapping at her windscreen.

She put up quite a fight.

Jets of water squirted her from all sides. The car shuddered. Had the man locked the car doors? Why hadn't Chloe got out?

She's gone to join Jesus, said Sheila's Aunt Shirley, another Christian. *She's at peace now*. She had wanted them to have that inscribed on the headstone. Sheila thought: If only I believed in God. If I did, then I could believe that Chloe didn't die alone.

But how, if she didn't believe before, could she possibly believe now? The car slid forward. She heard a roaring noise; the droplets of water were blasted from the windscreen. They flew aside, shivering, and disappeared. And then the car slid forward again and emerged into the vaulted space. Men started rubbing it down.

Winding down the window, Sheila spoke to a man's belt. 'Is Cheddar here?'

There was a shout. The midriff moved away and a huge face filled the window.

'Yes please, I am Cheddar.' He squatted down on his haunches.

'I'm Chloe Milner's mother,' she said. 'The girl

166

who died.'

His mouth dropped open. He was a plain man, with terrible skin.

'I hear this noise, like an angel,' he said.

'An angel?'

'She is standing there, in the light, it is so bright, and she is singing.'

Sheila stared at him. 'You've seen her?'

Cheddar nodded.

Sheila's heart turned over. 'Is she all right?' The man might be mad but she needed to believe him. Never, in her life, had she needed to believe in something more strongly. 'Did you speak to her?'

He nodded. 'We have a little talk. After she sing the song and everyone is clapping her.'

It was then that Sheila realized what he was talking about. Chloe had sung a song at the party. Rowena, the hostess, had told her about it. *She looked so pretty, Mrs Milner, I always remember she had a lovely voice. I can't believe I'm never going to see her again.*

'Her singing is so beautiful . . . my heart, it feels like this.' His great hands spread open. 'I think— she is lonely too.'

Behind her, a car hooted.

'Did she look happy?' Sheila asked. 'Tell me she looked happy. I just want to know that.'

His eyes filled with tears. 'When I hear she is dead, I cry and I cry . . .' He wiped his streaming nose. 'And it is my fault.'

'Why?'

'I let her walk home. I am responsible.'

'Of course you're not—'

'It is all because of me.' He jabbed his chest. 'So I leave my job—I go away. How do I make my

167

promise to protect these people when I let this thing happen? When the beautiful fat girl is dead?' He blew his nose on a chamois leather.

Tenderness swept over Sheila. She suddenly felt intimate with him. He had been there; he cared. She put her hand through the window and stroked his pitted cheek.

'David, that's my husband, he blames himself.'

'We are men, this is our job, to protect our women.' He broke into renewed sobs. 'And we fail.'

Behind them the car hooted again. And another one, behind it. One of the men shouted at Cheddar in a foreign language, probably to move the car on.

'It's not your fault,' she said.

She took his great hand, pulled it into the car and kissed it. Then she wound up the window, started the engine and drove away.

*   *   *

Take it one day at a time, said her friends. *However long it takes, you will feel better.*

They were trying to be helpful, these people, but they hadn't a clue. How could they? For it didn't get better; if anything, it got worse.

And here Sheila was, a month later, back at Pixies. She had to do this thing; she realized it now. The sky was stained pink; somewhere behind the buildings, the sun was sinking. It was another glorious evening in midsummer, the ninetieth evening her daughter hadn't experienced. Another Friday, and the city was humming. A group of girls clattered past, making their way to the club. Sheila smelt their perfume. Why should they live? Sheila asked herself. What have they done to deserve it?

168

She walked past the corner where the boutique had been, where she too had dressed herself up. Two of the flats now had SOLD stickers on their windows. She knew the way home. Off and on, she had lived in Manchester all her life. What route would Chloe have taken when she had stepped out, alone, into the darkness? Her daughter had a poor sense of direction, it had been a source of irritation to both her parents. In the last place they had lived, Chloe had lost her way returning from the corner shop.

Sheila walked past Afflecks Palace, with its giant metal flower-lamps hung from the wall. This area had changed since she had been Chloe's age; it seemed a century ago that she herself had been young. She walked down the pedestrian precinct past Debenhams and into Piccadilly Gardens, the city centre. This much Chloe would have known. Sheila's feet made no sound. She realized, with vague surprise, that she was wearing her bedroom slippers. She crossed the road and walked down Mosley Street. This was the most direct route home. Above her the sky was a luminous blue, flushed with yellow. The moon hung there faintly, almost full. A blackbird was singing, surprisingly near; there must be a tree somewhere, here in the middle of the city. It was singing its heart out. *Her singing is so beautiful.*

I'm with you, she told Chloe. *I know I'm too late, but I'm here.*

Her noiseless feet padded past the Bank of Scotland. She reached Charlotte Street. A taxi stopped and two girls jumped out. *Did you turn left here and walk through Chinatown, or did you carry straight on?* She paused, waiting for a response. A

169

car passed, music pounding from its open windows. She left the main road and walked past a Chinese supermarket, loud with chatter, and a row of restaurants. *Unrescued by your father, were you starting to feel nervous?*

Chinatown was full of people. Even at that late hour, when Chloe had walked home, there would have been people around, certainly if she had stuck to the main roads. *Where did you lose your way, my darling? I'm treading in your footsteps, my foot fitting yours, I want to see what you saw . . . Oh tell me where you went.*

Darkness was falling. Sheila felt light on her feet, as if she didn't exist. *I'm never going home. I'm like you, I'm never going to get there.* Outside an office building, tubs were filled with bushes. Their flowers gave off the sweetest scent; it made her dizzy. *If only he had killed me, and let you live.*

A passer-by shot her a look. She must be talking out loud, a mad woman in fluffy slippers. She felt strangely light-headed. Nobody else mattered, it was just herself and Chloe, alone in the city. In fact, she herself was barely there; it was her daughter who seemed the real person, close to her now. She was her mother's guide; her presence walked beside Sheila as if she knew the way and it was her mother who needed looking after. *Don't worry*, she said, *I'm all right. It's worse for you than it is for me, honestly it is.*

In a cruel moment, David had said, *She waddles.* Chloe didn't now. She sprang along, as slim as she had been when she was ten. She escorted Sheila silently, under the moon. *It sees everything, the moon. It saw what happened that night. And does it get upset?*

170

Cheddar had seen her in heaven, singing. In her mind Sheila knew this wasn't the case, but her mind hardly mattered. Chloe looked radiant now, and quite calm. She led her mother down Faulkner Street, down the next street, past CLASSY FASHION: WE ALSO DO BIG SIZES. Sheila knew these streets but tonight they were as strange as if she were in a foreign city. *Sure you don't want to take a bus?* Chloe asked. *Come along then.*

Where are you taking me? Sheila spoke aloud. *You're not taking me home?*

They stopped at the traffic lights. The street was empty here. They were about to cross when a bus appeared, brightly lit. In it a woman, dressed in red, sat up straight. Then it was gone.

It wasn't blossom; Sheila could smell Chloe's hair—the musty, secret fragrance of her baby hair, when Sheila buried her nose in her daughter's scalp.

Of course I'm taking you home, Chloe said. *You can't come with me.*

Let me come! said Sheila, the panic rising.

Course you can't, said Chloe kindly.

Don't go!

But it was too late. The wind got up and she was gone. Far off, a car hooted.

Chloe had left her at Oxford Street. She had known the way, after all. From there, it was straight ahead, under the railway bridge, past the BBC building and under the motorway. A mile's walk due south and Sheila was home. It was eleven o'clock when she reached the pub. The door was open to the balmy air but the bar was empty. David, in a cloud of smoke, sat at a table.

He looked up. 'Where have you been?'

171

She decided to tell him. 'I went to that nightclub and walked home.'

She waited for him to flare up: *Why the hell did you do that, are you mad? Do you want to get killed too?*

But David didn't. He just drained his glass and asked: 'Which way did you go?'

Sheila looked at him. 'So you've done it too?'

He nodded. Outside, there was a rattle as Mr Hassan pulled down the shutters of Europa Food and Wine.

'So that's where you go,' she said.

He didn't reply.

'Why didn't we go together?' she asked.

CHAPTER THREE

Sitting in their paddling pool, the children heard the scream. It came from next door, where the murderer lived—an ear-splitting yell.

'I told you,' said Dominic to his sister. 'That's him killing one. He slits their throats, and he put them in his sheds and he does things to them there.'

'What things?' asked his sister, gazing at him.

Dominic flicked water in her face. 'Just things. I've heard him, in the night. Then, when he's done things to them he buries them in his garden. The bits of them that are left.'

Their mother hurried out from the kitchen. 'What was that noise?' she asked. 'It wasn't you, was it?'

Dominic shook his head. 'It was him next door.'

*   *   *

Natalie sat down heavily on the edge of the bath.

'I'm sorry, love,' said Colin. 'See, the phone rang and I forgot about him.' An iguana sat in the basin. 'He's got this fungal infection—'

'I don't give a shit what he's got—'

'And I was putting on his ointment.'

'For Christ's sake, Colin, I got such a shock. Just keep them out of the house.'

Colin hung his head. He looked like a puppy that had puddled the floor.

Natalie ruffled his hair. 'You're a funny bloke, Stumpy. Don't know why I put up with you.'

'I'll get rid of them all, if you want me to.'

'Christ, no.' If he didn't have his reptiles to keep him busy he would be hanging around her all the time. She was fond of Colin, but she had to admit that he was dull. In fact, that they had very little in common at all. His worship of her was starting to irritate, too. Though it was gratifying, to be gazed at as though she were a box of truffles, she was starting to feel stifled. Those sultry August days, the walls closed her in.

Colin lifted the iguana out of the basin. He supported it with both his hands, reverentially, like a priest carrying the sacraments on an altar cloth. He held it away from his body as he carried it downstairs. She stood at the window, watching him. By now all the houses were occupied—kids splashing in paddling pools, parents mowing their pathetic little lawns. How could people bear to lead such boring lives? The night before, Colin had yet again brought up the subject of starting a family.

She had realized: This is it. For Colin, this is what life is all about. It ends here, full stop. We live here, and we have kids, and this is it.

'Let's go on holiday,' she said at lunchtime. 'I'm owed three weeks and we didn't even have a honeymoon.'

'But Nat—'

'Let's go to Bali! I've always wanted to go to Bali. Or New York.' She fetched some brochures. 'I got these yesterday, there's this special offer—look—two weeks—'

'I can't leave them for two weeks. It's the breeding season.'

'Your mum can look after them. She's got bugger-all else to do. Come on, Stumpy, let's have some fun!'

She gazed at his round, sunburnt face. Back in January, marriage to him had spelt liberation. She hadn't really thought beyond that, it wasn't her way. Just for a moment, she could see the years stretching ahead.

It was the same at work. By now she would no doubt have left NuLine. During this past month her two closest friends had gone: Sioban had found a new boyfriend, unmarried this time, and gone to live with him in Harrogate; Farida, who was pregnant, had given up work altogether and would soon be leaving for Canada. Nobody in their right mind stayed long in such a monotonous job, and yet there Natalie was, the brightest of them all, still stuck at her desk. She could see the irony of it—she had spun her web and now she was caught in it. *O what a tangled web we weave, when first we practise to deceive!*

That afternoon, as she lay sunbathing, she heard

a voice: 'I thought you were dead.' The next-door boy gazed at her over the fence.

'I'm not dead. I'm getting a tan.'

'I heard you yelling,' he said. 'I thought you was being murdered.'

'Oh, nobody'll murder me.' She closed her eyes.

* * *

Sooner or later he'll make a mistake.

Or someone will.

On a hot morning in August, in a bungalow in Hastings, an elderly couple were eating breakfast. Ted and Muriel Cox had eaten breakfast together for forty-two years. On the veranda, the sun shone on a sleeping cat.

Ted and Muriel were that rare phenomenon, a contented couple. Not so rare amongst the elderly, for they had no vocabulary of dissatisfaction. They had not been brought up with those words. Their marriage had carried on, unanalysed, for nearly half a century. Besides, they were both of a cheerful disposition. The world's evil washed over them; petty irritations only briefly unsettled them.

There was one such irritation that morning; minor even by their standards. Muriel was opening the post. From one of the envelopes she pulled out a cheque. For a moment she thought: A windfall. Then she realized that it was signed by her own husband.

Through her glasses, she peered at the accompanying letter. 'It's from some building society in Leeds!' she shouted; Ted was deaf in one ear. 'They say they can't accept this cheque because you wrote last year's date, you silly billy.

175

They say you've got to change it and initial it.' She passed him the cheque. 'I mean, we all do it in January, but it is August now, dear.'

'What?' he asked, distracted.

She thought he hadn't heard. 'I said—' She stopped.

He was examining the cheque. 'It's written out to N. Taylor.' He looked across the table at her. 'Do we know an N. Taylor?'

Muriel thought for a moment. 'What's our window cleaner called?'

'Shawn. And we don't pay him ninety pounds.'

She took back the cheque. It took her a moment to realize.

'This is our phone bill,' she said.

*   *   *

It was the following Thursday. The weather had broken; rain lashed down. Natalie's car was buffeted by the wind as she drove to work.

She was in a good humour, however. Colin had agreed to a week in Penang at the beginning of September—cocktails, huts beside the pool. She pictured herself soaking in the sun like one of his lizards, but with better skin. Like all those who have won an argument, she felt warmly towards the loser. That morning she had decided to buy Colin a motorbike, a 1,000-cc Harley, the one she had pictured Kieran buying all those months ago, in her former life. It had been some time since she had bought Colin a present. Thank goodness he seemed to have stopped the *how can we afford it?* conversations. They had been starting to annoy her.

176

She had also made another decision. It was no fun at NT any more, with her friends gone. In the autumn she would give in her notice. By then she would have stashed away well over fifty thousand pounds in her various accounts. Maybe more. She was no miser; she didn't sit huddled over her building society statements, totting them up. In fact she simply stuffed them into the zipped pocket of her travelling bag, pushed to the back of her cupboard, where they radiated an energy sensed only by herself.

All good gamblers know they should quit while they're ahead. She was going to jack in her job and enjoy her freedom, certainly for a year or two. At some point she would think about what to do next. Her plans for the future were somewhat vague, but who cared? Sometimes they included Colin, sometimes she couldn't quite picture him in the same scenario. But nothing had happened yet, so why bother worrying about it?

It was still raining. Natalie parked the car and sprinted for the door. She wore new shoes. She didn't count her money but she did count her shoes—she adored shoes—thirteen pairs she had bought in the past months. Colin had made a special rack for them. By the time she reached the lobby this pair, pale suede, were soaking wet. She remembered this, later, for the shoes never recovered and she never wore them again.

She remembered thinking another thing. Leafing through the brochures, she had found several holidays in Thailand. Not once had the thought of her father crossed her mind. It was as if he had never existed.

She was considering this, with a mild sort of

surprise, when Mrs Coles, the new supervisor, walked over. She seemed to have been waiting for Natalie. There was an odd expression on her face. In fact, there was an odd atmosphere in the room. The new girl, Maxine, hadn't said hello; she had stayed still, a blur through the frosted glass. And nobody seemed to be doing any work.

Mrs Coles came close to Natalie and said, in a low voice: 'Natalie, could you come with me? You're wanted in the MD's office.'

CHAPTER FOUR

'I didn't do it,' said Natalie.

She was sitting in a police station, somewhere in Leeds. It was a small, windowless room and stank of the cigarettes smoked by all the people who had said the same thing. 'I don't know what you're talking about.'

On the other side of the table sat a detective, in plain clothes, and a female police officer built like a trucker. 'You know that's not true, Natalie,' said the detective. 'We have your statements here, from the account you opened at the Bradford and Bingley. That's the building society that sent back Mr and Mrs Cox's cheque. Since January this year you've paid in a hundred and seventy-six cheques, to the total value of fifteen thousand, seven hundred and twenty-five pounds . . .'

Was it that much? thought Natalie. She felt a throb of pride.

'We've traced them all back to NuLine customers. As you gathered from Mr Smythe, your

Managing Director, NuLine are taking this extremely seriously, as well they might. This is fraud on a very large scale.'

She hadn't called it *fraud*, even to herself. The word removed it from her—it did feel, in fact, as if somebody else had done it.

'What I'd like to know,' said the detective 'is how much more you've got hidden away.'

'I don't know what you mean.'

'I think you do, Natalie.' His eyes twinkled; he gazed at her legs as she recrossed them. The woman looked on, stonily.

There was a tape-recorder whirring, like on *The Bill*, and a downtrodden duty solicitor straight out of Central Casting. Natalie was the femme fatale, her black skirt riding up her thighs. She was that woman in *The Last Seduction*.

She had been given her rights. *If you are asked questions about a suspected offence, you do not have to say anything. But it may harm your defence if you do not mention, when questioned, something which you later rely on in court. Anything you say may be given in evidence.*

They had charged her with fraud, handling and deception. 'It would make everything a lot easier for yourself, and save everybody a lot of time, if you just told us about it now,' said the detective. He had one of those trim beards that looked quite attractive when seen from the front, but with an abrupt, shaved line around the jowls. It made his neck look fat. 'You're a bright young woman, I'm sure you can see that if this went to trial, in a Crown Court, the jury would without a doubt find you guilty. You haven't a hope in hell.' She had an urge to point it out: *Don't shave your neck, use*

179

clippers. Maybe his wife liked it that way, but Natalie doubted it. 'We can take a statement now,' he said.

Natalie crushed out her cigarette in the foil tart case. 'I didn't do it, and that's that.'

*   *   *

She remembered the name of a solicitor Farida had used and phoned him up. It was only three o'clock but the day seemed to have been going on for weeks. Could it really have been that same morning when she had stood in the MD's office facing Mr Smythe, a stunned Phillip Tomlinson and two policemen? As she was driven away, faces had appeared at the NuLine windows. She had waved at them, like royalty.

Natalie waited in the lobby of the police station. Out in the street a hearse slid past, slowly. It was heaped with flowers: GRANDPA. Other black cars followed it, then a van saying THORNTHWAITE AND SON: BUTCHERS. She thought: All that fuss when a human being dies, and there's a van full of dead meat. Nobody's mourning all those animals. Nobody's even kept the legs and shoulders together.

She was starting to feel weird, as if she had left the dentist's with a numb jaw and the sensation was returning. Where was Colin? She couldn't get through on his mobile but she had left a message at work. It made her uneasy, to think about him. She felt very alone, sitting on her plastic chair. Light-headed too, for nobody had given her anything to eat. Were they trying to starve the truth out of her? She felt sick, from the sweet tea.

180

And then the solicitor arrived and drove her to his office. He was a man, thank goodness, a large bluff Yorkshireman called Mr Wigton. She was better with men. And now she was sitting in his office, which was up an alleyway. Its window overlooked the rear view of Sainsbury's. A huge lorry was backed into its opening; unseen, its contents were being disgorged.

'Now, my dear, there's something you must understand. You needn't tell me anything you don't want to; what you choose to tell me, it's entirely up to you.' Mr Wigton had a large moustache, which he stroked. 'I'm here to act on your instructions, and we shall put up as good a case as we possibly can, you may be sure of that.'

A long way away she could hear the normal sounds: the lorry rumbling, a man shouting. Mr Wigton's office looked curiously temporary—flimsy partition walls, sparse furniture, as if when Natalie left it would be dismantled. There had been no secretary in the lobby either, just an abandoned desk.

She took a breath. 'Say—just say—they found me guilty. What would I—you know—get?'

'We're certainly looking at a custodial sentence. Eighteen months, two years maybe, depending on the judge. But let's not consider that. We shall fight it all the way.' He smiled at her, in an avuncular way. 'You're a bright girl, I can see you have plenty of fight in you.'

'What would be the defence?'

'That's what I'll discuss with counsel. Computer error—there's plenty of that about. Only last week I got a phone bill for six hundred pounds, turned out to be somebody tapping into an—ahem—an adult chat line in the Philippines.' He shuffled together the three pieces of paper that lay on his desk. 'We'll present you as a victim of a corporation cock-up, if you'll pardon the expression. NuLine trying to cover it up, trying to keep their shareholders' confidence; after all it doesn't look too good, does it? Especially with a big takeover in the pipeline. But these mistakes happen, don't they? We all know that. And there you are, the scapegoat, and all because your initials happen to be the same.'

'They weren't.'

'Come again?'

'I made them the same.' Natalie spoke in a rush; it was such a relief, to confide in somebody. 'I found a bloke whose surname began with T and I married him.'

The response was gratifying. Mr Wigton slumped in his chair, his chin resting in his hand, and stared at her. 'Can you just run that by me again?'

'I found this bloke—Colin—and I married him.'

'You married a man just to give yourself the initials N.T. ?'

She nodded. Mr Wigton looked enthralled. Natalie was starting to enjoy herself. So absorbed were they that neither of them heard the outer door open and somebody enter the reception room behind them.

'Did he know?' asked Mr Wigton.

'God no. He's sweet . . . he doesn't know anything. I mean, I liked him, of course . . .'

Mr Wigton's shoulders were shaking. He stroked his moustache, to hide his mirth. 'You're a clever girl, my dear,' he said, 'but not quite as clever as

182

you think.'

'Why?' she demanded.

'You didn't need to go to all that trouble. You could have just changed your name by stat dec.'

'What's that?'

'Statutory declaration—Bob's your uncle. Don't even have to do it by deed poll. Anybody can have any name they want.'

He was laughing at her! 'Oh, I thought of that,' she said, stung. 'But it would have looked a bit suspicious, don't you think? Suddenly just changing my name?'

Mr Wigton shook his head. His shoulders were still shaking. 'The poor bugger.'

'What?'

'Your husband. The poor bugger.'

She shouldn't have told him, of course. Just then she heard a noise in the other room. They swung round.

It was Colin. He had sat down, suddenly, in a chair.

*   *   *

They were sitting in Colin's van, outside the lawyer's office. It was rush hour. Traffic roared past; in the van, however, the silence was terrible.

'I can't believe it,' said Colin at last. 'I can't believe what I heard.'

'It wasn't like that,' Natalie blustered. 'Not really. I mean, I'm very fond of you and everything, you know that, Colin. It just popped into my mind, after I met you.' She reached out to touch his leg, and stopped. 'I mean, Farida had an arranged marriage and they've been getting along like a house on fire, she really likes him—'

'Fuck Farida.'

She jumped. Colin never swore.

'Haven't we been happy?' she said. 'Really happy? Nothing can change that, nothing can take that away, it's all quite genuine, honestly—'

'How can you say that? What sort of person are you?' He swung round to face her. 'I thought you loved me—'

'I do!' She put her arm around him but he shook it off.

'I thought—how could she love me?' He wiped his nose with the back of his hand. 'I was over the moon, I couldn't believe my luck . . .'

'Please believe me—'

'You cheated on me and you cheated on them. All this time, stealing all that money—'

'Who says I did it?' she asked weakly. Looking at him, she realized there was no point in protesting her innocence.

He was trying to take it all in. Rigid with shock, he was trying to catch up with it all. 'How could you do it, Natalie? I wondered where it was coming from . . . I can't believe it . . .'

'I'm sorry, Stumpy, I really am.' She tried to light a cigarette but the matches spilled. 'I didn't hurt anybody. Remember when we talked about the little people, people like us?' She scrabbled on the floor. 'I haven't hurt them, have I? You said how you hated the gas board, how they clobber old ladies, how they don't give a fuck . . .' She picked up a match and tried to strike it. 'Well, NT's the same . . . they didn't even notice it, they make such a stonking profit, so what's the harm?'

He stared at her. A tear hung on his lower lip.

184

'What's the harm? You ask, what's the harm?'

He turned away and started up the engine.

*   *   *

That night Colin slept on the settee. He didn't have the heart, it seemed, to pull it out into a bed. Natalie gazed into the lounge. He lay curled in his anorak, the lights blazing.

'Come to bed, Colin,' she said.

There was no reply.

*   *   *

Natalie overslept. Her first thought, when she woke, was: Christ, I'm late for work. And then she remembered. She wouldn't be going to NuLine, ever again.

She had woken to a changed world. No—a world that carried on regardless, but from which she had been removed. It was as if she had been diagnosed with cancer. A few words, and she was dispatched into a parallel universe which had been there all the time, but unvisited by all except the unlucky ones.

And now she was caught up in the momentum of this new life: another appointment with the solicitor, an appearance on Monday at the Magistrates' Court. This new existence brought with it a new vocabulary: *Custody Officer, Notice of Entitlements* . . . She had entered a foreign country with its own language and there was no going back.

On the floor lay her rain-stained shoes. Yesterday, in another lifetime, she had dressed for work. That young woman was unreachable now; for a panic-stricken moment Natalie felt a stranger even to herself. Somebody wrote the wrong date on a cheque and now she was a criminal. She hadn't felt like one before; in fact, she had got so accustomed to what she was doing that it had long ago lost its fizz. She thought of her desk at work: its partition stuck with postcards. Already it had the elegiac quality of an old photograph, of an existence taken for granted but now gone for ever.

Natalie stood in the bathroom, brushing her teeth. Her hand was shaking; the toothpaste smeared on her lip. Where was her mother, now she needed her? And where was Colin—her simple, decent husband whom she had hurt so deeply?

She saw him down in the garden. He hadn't gone to work; he must have phoned in sick. It was still raining. Head bowed, he tramped through the mud.

She ran downstairs and followed Colin into the big new shed she had bought him. He was feeding his cane toads. *Watch them!* he had told her once. *Look at them, the fat greedy whatsits, they'll eat anything—bread, cheese, the kitchen sink.* Today he just tipped in a carton of crickets, then turned away, listlessly, and looked at her.

Colin didn't move. The only sound was the trill-phone warbling of the crickets. She remembered larking around. *Hello, this is Natalie speaking, how may I help you?* Today she said nothing. In the tank there was a flurry of activity; one by one, the crickets were silenced.

Natalie took her husband's hand. For the first time, oddly enough, she felt truly married to him.

Colin followed as she led him upstairs. In the

186

bedroom, she took off his woolly hat and unzipped his anorak. She lifted the duvet and they climbed into bed. It was still warm.

Fully clothed, Colin lay down beside her. She pulled up the duvet up over them. 'Our tortoise shell,' she whispered. 'Nobody can get at us now.'

Colin lay flat on his back. She turned to him and stroked his cheek; it was as plump and smooth as a child's—just a faint sandpapering of stubble round the chin. Was he going to be able to cope with this?

She wrapped her arms around him and held him tight. 'I need you, Stumpy,' she said. 'Don't leave me.'

*   *   *

So Colin stood by her. He was a loyal young man and he loved her deeply. Her crime bemused him; it was beyond his comprehension. What could have caused her to cheat, so continuously and on such an umimaginable scale? As the weekend passed, however, he started to accept it simply as a part of her personality. He was a rock-climber; he saw it as a fault-line in otherwise solid granite, a stratum of something soft and treacherous like chalk.

But who cared? He rallied. In fact, he felt a stirring of pride, that he could adapt to these new circumstances with such fortitude. *For better or worse.* Wasn't that the point of the marriage vows— that they were tested?

Besides, he had benefited from her criminal activity; they were in it together. He thought, guiltily, of the ease that money had brought to their lives—not just a house, but a lack of hesitation in gratifying their desires: a Sony wide-screen TV, a new washing-machine for his mother. Over the months he had started to take things for granted— that they would fill up the tank instead of buying only ten pounds' worth of petrol; that if something broke down they needn't worry, they could get it mended or buy another one. None of this had bothered him once; he had lived frugally enough and been perfectly content. Now he felt tainted by his raised expectations; he deserved to be punished. Would somebody take it all away from them—the house, the items they had bought? More to the point, what was going to happen to Natalie? Would they take her away too? He didn't say the word *prison* even to himself, he couldn't bring himself to think about it.

Her betrayal of him, of course, had wounded him deeply. However, she had been so loving towards him since then—more loving than he had ever known her—that at times he was almost grateful for this crisis which had flung them together.

For they were very close now, the two of them clinging to each other in the midst of a hostile world. At last Natalie needed him. How helpless she was, with nobody else to care for her! His protective instincts had usually been frustrated, for she was a feisty young woman. Now, however, they blossomed. He looked after her as if she were an invalid. A few people phoned—a girl from the office, the man called Phillip from the personnel department—but, gratifyingly, she didn't want to speak to them. 'Get rid of them,' she whispered.

Later, Colin remembered that weekend with great tenderness. *Nothing can take that away*, Natalie had said. Amidst all the fear and anxiety he felt true happiness. Soon the outside world would know—reporters, his mother—but just for now normal life was suspended, it was just himself and Natalie, alone. And to no one else, except her solicitor, had she confided her guilt.

They went out together into the countryside. She even accompanied him on his trip to catch meadow plankton, a nutritious fresh food for small lizards and frogs. He gave her a butterfly net and watched her as she swept it through the weeds. For the first time in their marriage she helped him, putting the bags of insects in the fridge until, stunned by the cold, they were ready to be dispensed.

He took her up on the moors, far north, up to Wensleydale. He showed her the ruins of his grandfather's farmhouse and the fields his family had toiled in all their lives. On the fells above, a satellite mast had been erected. It shocked him by its size. Maybe NuLine, the wrecker of Natalie's life, had put it there, but even that failed to blight their time together.

For he was happy. High up in the sky a lark sang, as if flung there by a fist. It was the most secret of holidays, the honeymoon they had never had. Holding hands like sweethearts, they walked until they were exhausted. The windswept, uncaring hills comforted him. They knew that this was a trifling matter and that love would endure, as they had, beyond the pettiness of the present. Natalie trotted beside him in her silly shoes; she was all his, undistracted by her normal, baffling preoccupations. It would be months before the trial but already he felt the possible loss of her. It was in the balmy air, like the scent of autumn.

'Wear what you wore when you came to tea with my mam,' Colin said. 'You looked really nice then.'

Natalie laughed.

'I don't mean—' he stumbled 'I mean, course you look nice, normally . . .' He meant demure and respectable. He hadn't seen those clothes on her since then, in fact.

She ruffled his hair. 'It's OK.'

Natalie looked remarkably calm. He was already perspiring in his white shirt and tie. They were due at the Magistrates' Court at ten. Mr Wigton was meeting them there. *It's only a formality*, he had said. *Nothing to be nervous about.* To Mr Wigton, of course, it was all in a day's work.

Natalie dressed in the pale suit she had worn to Farida's wedding, and pushed back her hair with the velvet band. She looked unfamiliar to him, elegant and yet vulnerable. He wondered at her variety. She was a chameleon, changing her colour according to circumstances. Of course, chameleons also had the ability to rotate their eyes in different directions. He thought: Criminals can do that too. They could talk to someone's mother whilst eyeing the family silver. Despite their closeness, Natalie unsettled him. All these months, while seemingly focused on him, she had in fact been leading a secret life. Another man might have gone back over the past, re-examining events and searching for clues—when had she lied?—but Colin wasn't the type. He trusted her; he had to trust her. It was as simple as that.

He drove her to the court. There was no sign of his mother, thank goodness; he'd feared she had got wind of it. People sat in the lobby, waiting for their cases to be called. Criminals through and through, they sat smoking under the THANK YOU FOR NOT SMOKING sign. They looked both defiant and defeated, the way people do when they expect to be found guilty. He had seen that look on his mates at school. By contrast, Natalie radiated an innocent sort of energy. Colin marvelled at her dewy skin and bright eyes. She would give the law a run for its money!

Oh, but it was painful to surrender her up. She was led away from him; a door clicked behind her. The next time he saw her she was being escorted into the dock. How small she looked! She glanced up at the public gallery, which was nearly empty, and searched along the rows. She didn't seem to see Colin, however; her eyes stopped at somebody else. Colin turned; he recognized the person—it was the man called Phillip, from her office.

She was sworn in and the clerk read out the charge.

'You have been brought here today on a charge of fraud, handling and deception . . .' Colin flinched.

The magistrate was a severe-looking woman. While the clerk spoke, she gazed at Natalie over her glasses. Everyone else, whoever they were, looked casual—even cheerful. Didn't they realize the momentousness of this moment? They looked like old friends, with his wife an irrelevance. He longed to rush across and take her in his arms.

The clerk addressed Natalie. 'How do you plead, guilty or not guilty?'

'Not guilty!' called out Natalie, loud and clear.

'You shall be summoned to a Crown Court,' said

191

the clerk, 'to appear at a future date, and time, to be set . . .'

The magistrate beckoned to Mr Wigton; they spoke together in lowered voices. He nodded twice.

The magistrate turned again to Natalie. 'I shall set bail at five thousand pounds.'

Colin's mouth dropped open. Bail? And then Natalie was whisked away and another person stood in her place.

Colin returned to the lobby. A man approached him, with a notebook.

'Are you Mr Taylor?'

Colin, distracted, nodded.

'This must be a big shock for you.'

Colin nodded. 'It is that.'

'Are you going to stand by your wife?'

'Course,' said Colin. 'She needs me and I need her.'

Natalie hurried up. 'Fuck off!' she said to the man.

'Natalie—'

'He's a reporter, can't you see? A fucking reptile.'

'Reptile?' Colin turned to the man. 'She didn't mean it badly—see, I keep reptiles, I'm a herpetologist.'

'How do you spell that?' asked the man.

'H-e-r-p—'

'I said fuck off.' Natalie pulled Colin away. 'Oh Colin, what'll I do with you?'

Colin's head spun. Could nobody be trusted?

Mr Wigton was waiting for them in a side room. 'I must admit, I wasn't expecting them to set bail at that sort of sum.'

'She was a woman,' replied Natalie. 'She didn't

like me, the old bat.' She pulled off her hairband and rubbed her forehead. 'She thinks I can't be trusted.'

*　　　*　　　*

Back home Natalie mixed Colin a gin and tonic. Never in his life had he drunk a gin and tonic in the middle of the day; in fact, he seldom drank at all.

'How much money have we got?' he asked.

'Not as much as that. Not even half.' She kicked off her shoes, flung herself on the settee and closed her eyes. 'Not a quarter.'

They wouldn't need it, of course. She wasn't going to run away. But they needed money for legal fees—was she going to get Legal Aid? Colin's head spun, he couldn't remember. And she had no wages coming in. They needed money simply to carry on.

'You haven't got . . . ?' He stopped.

She opened one eye. 'What?'

'Any more money anywhere?'

'Any more? What do you mean?'

'Nothing.'

'We've spent it all. Amazing how quickly it goes.' She flung back her head. 'Oh shit shit shit.'

'We'll manage, Nat.'

She didn't seem to be listening. 'Christ, what a fucking mess.'

There was a silence.

He heard her taking a breath. She didn't turn, however; she addressed the ceiling. 'I'm so sorry, Colin.'

'Don't be sorry, love. We'll see it through, things'll work out fine—'

193

But she hadn't heard him. 'I'm so terribly sorry,' she said.

*   *   *

When Colin was out, Natalie phoned the solicitor.

'This business about changing your name,' she said. 'Its being easy. It's all very well, but say—just say, for example—that a person wanted to start another job. What about National Insurance?'

'Piece of cake.' Mr Wigton chuckled. 'Just what are you planning to do, Natalie?'

'Nothing. I'm just interested.'

'You can do what a client of mine did. He visited the Registrar of Births and Deaths, paid a small fee and looked up the files for a male around his age. Found a name, wrote to the DHSS in Newcastle under that name saying that he'd lost his National Insurance card and he couldn't remember the number.'

'What did they do?'

'They sent it. Won't do it over the phone. So there he was—new name, new National Insurance number.' He chuckled again. 'You're not getting any ideas, are you, my dear? If I may be so bold, you're deep enough in the brown and smellies as it is.'

Thoughtfully, Natalie put down the phone.

*   *   *

The next day it was in the local paper. PHONE GIRL CHARGED WITH FRAUD. Colin couldn't bear to read it, though his eye was caught by HERP-HOBBY-HUBBY SAYS: 'I'LL STAND BY

194

MY WOMAN.'

'Herp-hobby!' snorted Dezza. 'You poor sod. Want to keep it?'

Colin shook his head; he pushed away the newspaper as if it were contaminated. Dezza was a big-time breeder, known throughout the north. His premises was three converted lorry containers within earshot of the M1, Junction 37.

Colin could hardly breathe. His python was clamped around him, in the most loving of embraces. She knew what was happening. She didn't want to leave him. He could feel her tightening her hold.

'A thousand quid cash,' said Dezza. 'I'll be making no profit, but a pal in need . . .'

Colin eased the python off himself, unwinding her vice-like grip from around his chest. She had put on weight since April. 'She's in perfect condition,' he said. Her small, shapely head turned away.

Dezza peeled off the notes. Colin lowered the python into a box. Dezza had already found a buyer, a sultan of some sort. Pythons were big in Saudi.

Colin walked away from the box. He didn't look back. It broke his heart, to sell his retic, but there was no alternative. He remembered Natalie laughing as she unzipped his fly. *Got a nice big one in here?*

He walked across to his van. Faintly, he heard the hum of the motorway. Cypress trees stood in a stiff black row; they reminded him of the crematorium where he had left his dad.

He drove home through the drizzle. Colour had drained from the world, leaving it monochrome.

He told himself: Stop blubbing, Colin. It's only a snake.

I'll take Natalie up to the Cross Keys, he thought, up on Ilkley Moor. We'll have a bite of lunch. She didn't know about the python; she would feel terrible if she did. Luckily, however, she seldom went into his sheds.

It was only a matter of time before his mother found out. A neighbour would show her the newspaper. *Why didn't you tell me?* she would say. She would be upset, of course, but underneath there would be a small sigh of satisfaction. *I told you so.* She wouldn't know about Natalie marrying him for his name, the humiliation of it, but this would be bad enough. *I always said there was something about that girl . . . Never trusted her . . .*

He drove down their street. Natalie's car—her brand-new Prelude—had gone. Maybe she had fled the phone calls. Now the news was out, it would spread like wildfire. On the other hand, maybe their friends would melt away, horrified. Would they believe her, when she protested her innocence?

Colin parked the van and let himself into the house.

'Nat?' he called, just in case.

No reply. He went into the kitchen to make himself a cup of tea. An envelope was propped against the microwave: COLIN.

He had no premonition; nothing. Later he realized that he should have guessed something was up. It was odd, that she had used an envelope. He still presumed, however, that he would find a normal note inside. GONE SHOPPING, BACK LATER, something like that. He even filled the kettle before he opened it.

Finally, however, he did. He slit open the envelope with the kitchen knife and pulled out a note.

Dear Colin, it began. *I'm so sorry . . .*

It ended: *It's best this way. I want to spare you the aggro.*

CHAPTER FIVE

Sheila was spending longer and longer in the bath. Befuddled with Valium she lay submerged, yet somehow floating like a hologram above her useless body. She had long ago used up Chloe's bath gels. It soothed her, to be closed away in this room, silent except for the dripping tap. In the cabinet her pills waited in their little bottle. They were her only allies now; they understood. She lay there, drugged by the water.

Chloe used to drive them mad with her baths, hours with the door locked, six different towels on the go, damp footprints on the carpet back to her bedroom. She existed in her absence, for everywhere she went she left reminders of herself—sticky rings on the kitchen table, globs of yoghurt in the sink. And always the caps loose— jars, bottles. Sheila had once drawn a picture of a toothpaste tube calling out to its cap, *'Come back, all is forgiven!'*

There had been no damp footprints now for months. Three months, two weeks and six days. Chloe's bedroom door remained closed. During the day Sheila sleepwalked, half-conscious; during the night she lay awake. In either state she sometimes heard, when she passed the door, a sound inside. Later she realized she dreamed it, for it was unhearable—the sound of Chloe concentrating as she gazed at the page of a magazine, of Chloe just existing.

One night, however, she opened the door and saw David sitting on the bed.

Sheila jumped. He sat so still, as if he had been motionless for hours. She hesitated; then she went in and sat down beside him. She wanted to take his hand—they hadn't touched for weeks—but his body radiated such isolation that it would give her an electric shock.

'Let's go away,' she said. 'A week somewhere. Let's have a holiday.'

He didn't reply. She smelt the cigarettes in his clothes, in his hair. He didn't shave nowadays for days on end. This alarmed her. Nor did he seem to be washing any more. They seemed to have changed places; she had become the clean person now.

'Speak to me.'

'The brewery phoned today. They've been looking at the figures. Twenty per cent down on spirits last month, fifteen on beer.'

'Speak to me, David.'

'They want to discuss the future of the business.'

'They don't care, do they?' The wardrobe walls were stuck with photos from magazines. Gaps showed now, where some of them had fallen off. 'We'll manage. We'll manage it somehow, if we stick together.' Suddenly she laughed. 'I've always wanted to be a hairdresser.'

'What?'

'Highlights, perms . . . *so what are you doing for Christmas?*'

'Sheila—'

She laughed louder. 'Oh my my, look at all these split ends.'

'You taking your pills?'

'You could renovate old MGs. Remember yours, when I broke the gearbox? You said it was a collector's item.'

'Listen, I think you should—'

'And we could move to Devon. That lovely red earth.'

There was a silence. Her laughter stopped. The digital clock flashed 00:00, pulsing on and off. Somebody must have disconnected the plug. Maybe herself, when she had hoovered the room.

Downstairs, they heard a thud. David jumped up, as if released, and hurried out.

Down below, in the function room, a piece of ceiling had fallen to the floor. Water trickled through the light fixture. 'Oh blast,' she said, 'that's my bath.' She had forgotten to turn it off.

David thundered upstairs. Sheila, overcome by fatigue, sat down on the floor. The streetlamp glowed through the window. Paper chains were still strung across the wall: HAPPY BIRTHDAY CLIFFORD. When had the room last been used? Months ago. The street outside was quiet; it must be very late.

That evening Sheila moved into Chloe's room. From that night onwards she lay under the pansy-patterned duvet, gazing at the last things Chloe saw each night before she finally closed her eyes.

*   *   *

199

Their friends the Willetts dropped by. David stood, glazed and unsteady, behind the bar. There was nobody else there except Paddy, an old alcoholic.

'How are things?' asked Marjorie Willett. 'Where's Sheila?'

'Asleep,' replied David.

Marjorie glanced at her husband. He looked at his shoes. 'We heard that things . . . well . . . we just wondered if there's anything we could do.'

'Yes!' said David. 'Have a drink!' There was a manic gleam in his eyes. 'Bell's for you, right, Don? And a gin and lemon for you, isn't it? Sit down!' he shouted. 'There's plenty of seats to choose from!'

They made their excuses and left.

*   *   *

In the function room, the man was plastering the ceiling. Sheila had asked his name, she was sure, at some point. He had a big bottom.

'How peaceful it must be, your job,' she said. 'No worries, just slap slap and then, hey presto! All smooth, as if nothing has happened.' She could stand there watching him all day. '*Making good.* Isn't that a nice expression? Making good.'

She watched, mesmerized, as he flicked his wrist—slap slap with the palette knife and then slicing off the edges like pastry. He stood on a plank, supported by two ladders.

'Do you remember your dreams?' she asked.

'What's that?'

'I said, would you like a cup of tea?'

He must have said yes because here she was, upstairs in the flat, opening the fridge to get the milk—one sugar or two, did he say? There, in the fridge, was a mug of tea.

She felt it; still warm. She had already made him one! Wasn't she silly? And why on earth had she put it in the fridge?

Slowly she filled the kettle, all over again. What an effort it was . . . lifting it and putting it in the sink, turning on the tap. Everything weighed so heavily.

She wanted to go back to bed. She lifted her leaden wrist and looked at her watch. It was only five o'clock.

She went downstairs. The plasterer climbed down his step-ladder and took the mug. They stood there for a moment. The chairs around the wall were grey with dust.

'My daughter died,' she said. 'Her twenty-second birthday has come and gone.'

'I'm sorry.' He fumbled in his pocket.

'The bouncer cried. He cried more than my own husband.'

The plasterer put down his mug, to roll a cigarette. Sheila took advantage of this, and put her arms around him. She held herself tightly against his big stomach. Then she hurried out.

*   *   *

Lying, night after night, in Chloe's bed, Sheila willed the dreams to come. But her daughter refused to return to her, even in sleep.

Sheila dreamed of her own youth, in altered houses. The rooms were too large, and filled with unfamiliar furniture. Water lapped at the front door. Her mother, when she turned round, had the face of old Mrs Skinner, who used to run the post office. *'Want your letters?'* she asked, baring her gums. *'There's a whole lot arrived but I seem to have mislaid them.'*

When Sheila woke she was drenched in sweat.

*   *   *

One afternoon in September a car stopped outside and a man came into the bar. He was wizened, with a jockey's bowed legs.

'Minicab for Milner,' he said.

'You've taken your time,' said David, who had trouble standing upright. He held on to the counter.

'I beg your pardon?' said the man.

'Where is she? What took you so long?'

David squinted across the room, trying to focus on the door. Should he greet his daughter as if nothing had happened? *Where've you been? That must've been quite a party.* David's head swam. *Mum's tidied your room.*

David tried to concentrate. A wasp buzzed around his hair and settled on a puddle of beer. He really must wipe down this counter.

'Minicab for Mrs Milner.' The man frowned, puzzled.

There was a noise on the stairs: a heavy, dragging sound, then a thump, like a coffin. David tried to collect his wits.

And then the door opened and Sheila appeared, dragging a suitcase. She wore her coat.

'Mrs Milner?' said the driver.

'Take this to the car,' she said in a flat voice. 'And wait for me there.'

The driver heaved the suitcase out. Sheila looked across at her husband. The bar was empty.

'I'm going to live with Fiona,' she said.

'In Florida?'

'With Fiona.'

Who was Fiona? David had to work it out.

'I'm so sorry.' Sheila leaned against a table for support. 'You won't talk to me. It's the only way we could get through this, but how can we when you won't talk?' She started crying. 'I'm afraid of what I'm becoming, I'm afraid I'm going mad, and I hate myself for hating people just because they're alive and she's dead. And I don't know if you're feeling this because I don't know what you're thinking.'

She sat down heavily. He sat next to her.

'I don't know what you're feeling,' she said.

'Don't go.'

'I'm so sorry, Dave—'

'Stay here.'

'I'm so sorry for everything. But we just couldn't manage it, could we?'

She turned and kissed him clumsily, on the side of his forehead. She seemed to have even lost the knack of doing this.

Then she got to her feet and left.

*   *   *

As she sat in the minicab Sheila thought: Where have all the words gone? There was so much to say and yet, now the end had arrived, nothing to say at all. It filled her with panic, that after twenty-eight years this was all that was left.

Oh, there were things she could have told him. How she had never wanted to run a pub with him, she had other dreams for her life, but she wanted to be a supportive wife. How she had felt controlled by him, how at the beginning there had been an erotic charge to this but how it had eventually drained her. How she had felt hurt that he had never, once, complimented her about her cooking. She wanted to ask him what went on inside his furious head. Whether it had upset him, that she could have no more children. Whether his memory settled on the same moments of joy as hers did. So many things. What *had* they talked about, all those years?

David had become as unknowable to her as if they had only just met. This filled her with terror. Did other couples feel this, when they broke up? She had no comparison, because no other marriage had been torn apart in the way theirs had been. She and David were set aside from the world, alone.

And now there was nothing left. It was as if the stage set of their life had been dismantled and all that was left, cruelly exposed to the cold light of day, were bits of cardboard. That was all there had been, all the time.

Her heart was breaking. She grieved for him, and for herself.

As she got out at the railway station, she thought of her sister's words: *Do you blame him?*

PART FOUR

CHAPTER ONE

Natalie liked living above a Thai restaurant. She liked the smell of the food. Her father, she presumed, was eating Thai meals all the time. He too had bailed out, it was in their genes. They were close in this respect. She sometimes wondered about him. For all she knew he was living in a concrete apartment block, jammed up against another one, but in her daydreams he was lounging on a beach—oblivious to her, maybe, but living the sort of existence she had imagined for herself, for weren't they two of a kind?

This hadn't quite happened yet: the sand, the cocktails. She was living in Finsbury Park, fearful of a ring at her bell. The future always shunted itself further away, like a person afraid to be touched. She didn't mind. She had to lie low for a while. She knew nobody in London, not really, just a few acquaintances but she was in no position to make contact. She had sloughed off the past. She had cropped her hair and dyed it blonde; it still gave her a jolt, after three weeks, to catch sight of her reflection in a shop window. Nobody knew where she was, not a soul. When Colin rang her mobile she switched it off. He hadn't rung now for some time.

She was sorry about Colin, of course, but she'd had no alternative. There was no way she could stand trial; they would find her guilty. She knew it; her solicitor knew it. The evidence against her was overwhelming. Colin had to understand that it was a matter of survival. He was a reptile breeder, after all. Look at his lizards, snapping at flies, crunching up crickets. They were doing the same thing, struggling to live, and see how he loved them.

And she was fine, absolutely fine. Leeds had been too small for her grand plans. In her heart she had always been a big-city girl—the hum and fizz of it, the sheer size that swallowed up a person and set them free.

Besides, who needed friends? Stacey had phoned, on the mobile. 'Natalie! Where are you? I went to see Colin and he was in such a state.' Her voice had become wary and formal. 'You didn't do it, did you? All those months, when we were working together . . . It's just that—you know—skipping bail, it does make you look a bit dodgy.'

Natalie got a new mobile number. She had moved on from all that, it was consigned to the past. In fact, she could hardly remember what she and Stacey had ever talked about. It was like her car. She thought she had loved her Civic but back in July she had replaced it with a new Honda, a gleaming, metallic Prelude 2000 Sport. The day she bought the new one her previous car had vanished from her mind as if it had never existed. Who cared?

September was unusually hot. Global warming, whatever. Natalie kept her windows open, breathing in the spicy aromas from downstairs. The pavements gave off the heat of a foreign city. She was jumpy, of course. Who wouldn't be, in her position? She froze when a police car drove down her street but it never stopped at her door. At the back of her mind she knew that they must be searching for her. After all, she was wanted for a major fraud; she was a criminal on the run. When she applied the words to herself they unnerved her. She couldn't fit them to her own life—going shopping in Oxford Street, buying a takeaway.

She was alert, of course, her senses as sharp as an animal's. Men had always looked at her but now she interpreted it differently; the old sexual frisson had gone. That bloke eating sushi along the counter, was he a detective? Was he somebody Colin knew, who would follow her back to the flat and tell Colin where she lived and the next morning he would arrive and batter down the door? For all she knew, Colin was capable of violence. Like her car, she could hardly remember him now. Images occasionally resurfaced—a dumpy bloke in a woolly hat, wearing tracksuit bottoms with a white stripe down them, the Colin she had first met—but she could no longer summon up the sensation of living with him. He had slipped in and out of her life in such unusual circumstances that he himself had become unreal.

They wouldn't find her. A month had passed and nothing had happened. How many people lived in London—eight million? She was lost in the seethe of it. This didn't unnerve her—why should it? She was fine. Blondes have more fun, she told herself. Soon she would.

Meanwhile Natalie stayed in her flat. It consisted of two rooms, sparsely furnished from IKEA—she could recognize IKEA now—and various oddments belonging to her landlord, a Greek Cypriot she had never met. The place had no phone, which suited her—what would she do if it rang?—but she had found a *Yellow Pages* in the cupboard. During those hot days she sat there, leafing through it. She was looking for a job.

For she had discovered, to her frustration, that she had suprisingly little ready cash. As luck would have it, the account that the police had discovered—and of course closed, pending investigations—had by far the largest amount of money in it. In the other three building societies, she had deposited most of the cash into high-interest accounts that tied it up, out of reach. To withdraw it would not just mean paying a penalty; it would mean correspondence, and for all she knew the police had traced the accounts and were waiting for her to make contact. And she had spent a lot of cash over the past six months—new car, stuff, things.

So she leafed through the *Yellow Pages* and wrote a list. As she did so, her stomach fluttered.

* * *

L. M. Plant and Tool Hire was situated in a warehouse in Hoxton. Men in overalls straightened up and gazed at Natalie as she made her way to the office. LM was sewn across their hearts.

Bob's your uncle. Anybody can have any name they want.

'Yes?' said a girl.

'I'm Lorraine Middleton,' said Natalie. 'I phoned about a job.'

The girl pressed a buzzer on her phone. 'I've got a . . .' She looked up. 'What was the name again?'

'Lorraine Masterson—' Natalie corrected herself. 'Middleton.'

The girl frowned. Why did she look at her like that? She pressed the buzzer again. It was a direct line to the police station. *I've found her, Officer.*

She's right here, standing in front of me.

'You can go in,' said the girl. 'He'll see you now.'

The room blazed with lights. Behind the desk sat a bald man. Through the window, in a yard beyond, stood a schoolgirl. She leaned against the wall, a cello case propped beside her.

'So you're Lorraine,' said the man.

'Yes.'

'What little birdie told you our secret?' His eyes narrowed, like the girl's.

'What secret?' she asked. *Keep your wits, Natalie.*

'How did you know that Samantha was leaving and we have a vacancy, mmm? When we hadn't even advertised yet.'

'I've been going through the *Yellow Pages* and phoning people up, on the off-chance.' This was the truth.

'I see.' His eyes brightened. 'A girl with initiative.'

'And when I got to you, somebody said there might be something.' Thirty phone calls she must have made.

'Tell me about yourself, Lorraine. What previous experience have you had?'

Outside, the schoolgirl shot them a glance, loaded her cello case on to her back and walked away.

*   *   *

There were three empty shops opposite Natalie's flat. One still bore its name: H. White and Son, Fishmongers. Graffiti was sprayed on to its shutters. Something would replace it; a lick of paint, a new name. Only the previous week an NT

211

phone shop had opened on the corner, next to Finsbury Park tube station. Places re-invented themselves here, like people, and nobody asked any questions. Makeovers, the TV was full of them.

By the end of September she had created three new identities: Lorraine; Sylvia Mullen (when she was interviewed by S.M. Office Supplies); and Mary Wright (M.W. Catering Equipment). As Mr Wigton had suggested, she had simply gone to the Registrar and chosen the names. She was an actress, auditioning for a part. Which one would she land? As Sylvia she was a shy young girl in a fluffy jumper, alone in the big city. Mary was livelier; she had experience in the catering business, she told them, and had come down to London to live with her sister, whose kiddies she adored. These new young women accompanied Natalie, waiting to be given the kiss of life.

One of these outfits, the office supplies place, offered her a job. The trouble was, the business was too small. She had realized that when she arrived. She needed to work in the sort of organization that had a large accounts department, the sort of place in which she would be one of many. Lost in the crowd.

And she was. Nobody noticed her. One night she ate in the Thai restaurant downstairs, sitting alone next to the toilets. The owners had no idea she lived above them. At the next table a girl fed her boyfriend forkfuls of stir-fry, like a thrush feeding her chick. Natalie propped her *Evening Standard* against the candlestick and read the same paragraph several times. Outside in the street a man bellowed; there was the sound of smashing glass. She thought: I could fall down dead and nobody would have a clue who I am. Nobody would know that I had a brilliant idea and made a small fortune, that I married a man who kept tortoise eggs in the airing cupboard. I could raise a few eyebrows; even a few laughs. And—look!—I've got away with it. Who says crime doesn't pay?

For the first time in her life she had difficulty sleeping. She told herself it was the busy road, the foreignness of it all. *I care for nobody, no not I, and nobody cares for me*. Where had she heard that— *Sesame Street*? She had watched it alone, waiting for the key in the lock. She could tell, by the length of time it took to get the door open, in what state her mother would arrive.

Natalie had pains in her chest. She told herself: I mustn't be ill, because I can't go to a doctor.

*   *   *

At the end of September the weather broke. Natalie drove through torrential rain to Brentford. She was going to a job interview. Her windscreen wipers sluiced to and fro; people scuttled across the road; she slammed on her brakes. London was seized by its Friday-afternoon frenzy; people hurried back to a warm house, with dinner waiting. On the news a voice said: *'A twenty-eight-year-old man has been arrested and charged with a series of rapes in the Shepherd's Bush area . . .'*

Natalie shivered. But she was all right, wasn't she? Her top-of-the-range Prelude had central locking, ECU engine immobilizer and remote keyless entry. Not to mention ABS anti-lock brakes, side-impact protection bars and SRS airbags. She remembered her dream of the night

213

before, when she had finally fallen asleep. Colin laid her on the grass and pulled off strips of her skin, chanting, *'She loves me, she loves me not . . .'* like someone plucking petals off a daisy. Her skin tearing off, and she hadn't felt a thing.

T. B. Computer Services was an office building slap up against the raised section of the M4. Natalie sat in the lobby, facing clocks that showed the time in Tokyo and New York. Outside rose giant legs, supporting the motorway. No rain fell there. Nor could the traffic be heard; the lobby was sealed off behind double glazing. Nothing could touch Natalie, for she had a charmed life.

'Miss Batsford?'

Somewhere in Leeds they were banging at the window but they couldn't reach her, she was miles away.

'Tracey Batsford?'

Natalie swung round. The receptionist was addressing her. Watch out, Natalie!

T.B. Computer Services sold hardware, software, whatever. It was huge and, according to the personnel manager, expanding fast. There was a vacancy in Accounts.

'Tell me about your previous experience, Miss Batsford.' The man was Indian, and wore a purple tie that clashed with his sports jacket.

She rolled off the list of her more suitable past jobs—receptionist at a health club, secretary at a firm of accountants. Like all good liars, she knew when to tell the truth.

'And then I worked in the accounts department of a telecommunications company for two and a half years.'

'And why did you leave?'

214

'I wanted to come to London. It's a bigger challenge.'

His window was up on the seventh floor, on a level with the motorway. Traffic was heavy, leaving London for the weekend. It passed soundlessly—a Sainsbury's lorry, a tow-truck carrying a bulldozer. The man said he would set her some simple tests—numeracy, problem-solving—and asked what software she had used.

'I seem to have no address for you,' he said.

'I'm between flats at the moment.' Natalie gave him her mobile number.

*　　　*　　　*

On Monday he called and said she had performed excellently in the test, her CV looked satisfactory, all he needed now was a reference from her last place of employment.

That night she phoned Phillip Tomlinson from a call-box. In the distance she could hear a child crying.

'I want you to write me a reference,' she said. 'To whom it may concern, one of those.'

'Where are you?' he hissed.

'I'm going to give you a box number. Got a pen? Send it there.'

'Natalie!'

'Write it for Tracey Batsford, that's Tracey with an e.'

'But Natalie—'

'Don't ask any questions. And if you don't send it, I'll tell your wife about us.'

There was a silence. Then the line went dead.

A moment later she phoned again. 'A good

reference, of course. *Glowing*. Bye!'

*   *   *

Two weeks later she started work. *Bob's your uncle*, as Mr Wigton said, for just as she hoped, not everyone bothered to write 'T.B. Computer Services' on their cheques. Lazy sods.

This time, however, the stakes were higher. Not just for obvious reasons, like maybe the police were catching up on her. As there were no large accounts to absorb the deficit, there was a greater risk of discovery.

Who cares? thought Natalie, tossing her blonde hair. If they discover something wrong, I'll just disappear. I've done it before and I can do it again. Tracey Batsford will vanish, as if she never existed. Who cares what happens to the real one, my shadowy double, wherever she is?

She gazed at the cheque in her hand. It was for £1,220. I won't do it often, she thought, I'm not greedy. Once a month, maybe. After all, a girl's got to live.

It was a large, airy room, glass on all sides. There were six other people there, gazing at their screens. She didn't know their names; they had hardly spoken, except to say 'hello' and 'goodbye'. In this place, there was none of the camaraderie of NuLine. That was fine. That was the last thing she wanted.

Outside, startlingly close, the cars sped past. An airbus headed towards Heathrow. Ten minutes along the M4 and she too could be at the airport, flying off to a new life—Rome, Melbourne, Johannesburg. None of them sounded real, but then nothing seemed real any more.

Copper-coloured clouds were heaped up; they glowed from beneath, as if the city were on fire. Natalie gazed at the cheque and took out her biro.

She had done it before, often enough. She could do it again. Why, then, was her heart hammering?

CHAPTER TWO

'I don't believe it,' said David. 'What have you been *doing*?'

'I do appreciate your frustration,' said Detective-Superintendent Cobb.

'Frustration?' David stared at him.

'But, as I told you last week . . .' And the week before, and the week before that. The man wouldn't leave them alone. 'We're following up every lead, there have been several new developments, promising ones.' He had a headache; the room was stifling. Tragedy catapulted strangers into his life with a terrible intimacy. This particular case had affected him deeply, he could admit it. He was weary with the sorrow of it. He had lied: they had no new leads. DNA tests on known offenders had all proved negative. How he longed for Sunday, when he would see the eager, lit faces of his grandchildren. 'We'll keep you informed, you can be sure of that.' If he got up to open the window, maybe David Milner would take the hint and leave.

'He's there somewhere,' said David. 'He's out there somewhere. Christ, he must be laughing at us.'

'I don't think—'

'Leave it to me and *I* could find him.'

David got up abruptly and left.

The detective turned to his colleague, Angela. 'Wonder how his wife's coping,' he said.

'All that rage,' she replied. 'And nowhere for it to explode.'

'Except here.'

She gazed at the open door. Far down the corridor, they heard another door slam. 'There goes a man who's capable of murder,' she said.

*   *   *

David had been given notice to quit. This was inevitable. He had felt no surprise when the men from the brewery had walked in and laid their briefcases on the table.

'We are aware of your family circumstances and have taken them into account; we offer you our sympathy, but you must also be aware that we cannot support a business that has been constantly failing. Besides which, the tenancy agreement is for a couple, and now that you're on your own . . .'

They hadn't added anything about drinking during working hours, an occupational hazard but one which the brewery took seriously. This had already been the subject of two phone calls and a warning e-mail from divisional office.

It wasn't true, of course. David had conducted himself with perfect propriety but he hadn't the will to argue. On 5 October they were closing the pub for renovations; they planned to gut the place and theme it, some Frog and Filkin garbage but he hadn't listened, it was no longer a concern of his.

This part of his life was over and he just needed to concentrate on packing up and getting the hell out of there.

So much rubbish—bags and bags of it. Dismantling a home seemed to spawn the stuff. He remembered his sixth-form Macbeth: *Who would have thought the old man had so much blood in him?* It was not as if they owned any furniture; they had always lived in rented premises.

'You've got a good pair of lungs on you,' he told Paddy, dumping down a pile of LPs. 'Buddy Holly, Van Morrison, take your pick, take the lot!' David sprang upstairs, two at a time, and fetched some more. Staggering under the weight of them, all those stupid songs, he carried them downstairs. But Paddy had gone.

Sheila appeared from nowhere. Had she phoned? Her mouth looked pinched, as if she had been sucking something bitter. *Blow-job lips*, David had once called them. With mild surprise, he realized that in the early years she used to suck his cock on a regular basis. She took it tenderly in her mouth, cupping his balls in her hand.

'What did you say?' She looked at him oddly. Had he spoken out loud?

Sheila laid her hand briefly on his shoulder, like a sorrowing schoolteacher with a disappointing pupil, and disappeared into Chloe's room. A while later she came out, dragging yet more plastic sacks.

'I'm giving her things to Kayleigh,' she said. 'I hope that's all right.'

Who the hell was Kayleigh?

'My niece,' she replied.

He must have spoken out loud again. Or maybe she was a mind-reader.

219

'What about the photos in the bathroom?' she asked. 'The collage.'

'Take them.'

'You can look at them whenever you want. All the photos. You can have anything you want.'

'I don't want anything,' said David.

They stood there in the corridor. It seemed too narrow for them both.

'I'm worried about you,' she said.

'I'm fine. I'll drive the stuff there tomorrow.' Her brother Terence had offered his garage for storage. 'Some day you'll have a house, you'll find somebody else.'

'David!'

'Plenty more *fritto misto* in the sea.'

'*Fritto misto?*'

'Fried fish—Venice, remember? The waiter looked like that actor, in that TV thing, the thing with the vet . . .' He ran out of steam.

'What are you going to do, David? Why're you getting rid of all your stuff?'

'Don't worry about me.'

There was a pause. Down in the street a lorry blared its horn. 'I think you should see someone,' she said. 'Just to talk.'

He looked at her. 'What've you done to your hair?'

She made a small noise in her throat and turned away. Her hair was darker, and cut shorter. Less grey in it. He could see her neck.

'Know something?' David said. 'We should have gone on more holidays.' But it was too late, because just then her sister arrived to take her away.

220

When on earth had they used the tea cups? They had been left to Sheila by her Aunty something-or-other, cups and saucers patterned with roses. Throughout their marriage the tea service had accompanied them from home to home—the early years in Morecambe when he was involved in that doomed enterprise, band management and when Chloe had had a plastic beaker, with a spout. Later years in Manchester, first at the Bull and Bush and then at the Queen's Head. Unused, the cups and saucers existed in a parallel, ghostly universe where guests arrived for Battenberg cake and Chloe, slim and pretty, had passed eight O levels.

David wrapped up the cups and put them in a cardboard box. He put his mind to it, concentrating on the task. One sheet of newspaper per cup, folded double exactly down the centre, then scrunched into the cup and the whole thing rolled in another sheet. Finally the ends had to be tucked in. It was important to get it right. If he folded the paper slightly off-centre then the ends didn't align and he could feel the panic rising, heating up his face.

Half an hour had passed and he had done nothing. David roused himself and picked up another sheet of newspaper. It was an old copy of the *Yorkshire Post*. Spreading it out, words caught his eye. *Phone Girl Charged with Fraud*.

Later he wondered: Why did he notice it? Was it the word *phone*? Or was it just that he didn't have the energy to carry on? *Thirty-two-year-old Natalie Taylor, of Heron Drive, Selby Road, Leeds, appeared at Leeds Magistrates Court yesterday charged with*

221

fraud, deception and handling. An employee of NuLine Telecommunications, it was alleged that she had altered payment cheques by substituting her own name. A NuLine spokesman said, 'As a precautionary measure, it has always been our policy to urge customers to write out our full name on cheques when paying their phone bills, or if possible use direct debit.'

*   *   *

Sheila could make no sense of the phone call. David must have been drunk.

'Don't you understand?' His voice rose in his excitement. 'That was why we were cut off! Don't you see, Sheila?' She knew that hectoring tone so well. He started babbling about some woman who lived in Leeds. 'It was her!'

'Who?'

He said he had rung NuLine but they wouldn't talk to him. 'I said I was a customer and all I got was fucking Vangelis. I said I wanted to talk to someone but all I got was fucking *I'm Sheila, how can I help you?*'

'*I'm* Sheila.'

'I said I was the father of the murdered girl.'

The murdered girl. David had never said the words before. Sheila gazed through the window. A gale was blowing; out in the garden, Fiona's weeping willow swayed like weeds in a river.

'David,' she said, 'you're talking gibberish.' Fiona came in from the kitchen, drying her hands, and raised her eyebrows. 'I don't understand what you're saying.'

'It was her fault!' shouted David's voice. 'She

stole my cheque. That's why we were cut off. It was her fault that it happened.'

*   *   *

The next day, Saturday, David drove to Leeds. It only took an hour from Manchester but when he arrived, and drove out east on the Selby Road, he couldn't find the street. Heron Drive wasn't on the map. He stopped at a newsagent's. The man didn't recognize the name but a customer buying some fags said: 'It's that new, up-its-own-arse estate. Son of a bloke I know, he's bought a condo there.'

He gave David directions. David arrived there, and drove along the toytown streets of the housing development. A man pushed a little girl, wearing a silver crown, on her trike.

The Sales Office was a Portakabin draped with a banner: PHASE TWO NOW AVAILABLE. Flags hung limply from a row of poles. David went inside. The office was empty, though a phone was ringing on the desk. It rang and rang—a low, insistent warble.

When he was a boy he was given a toy phone: red plastic, with a string connecting the two parts.

'*Ring ring,*' he said, and passed the receiver to his mother. '*It's for you.*'

'*Who is it?*' his mother asked.

'*I don't know.*'

'*What should I say?*' She gazed at the receiver in her hand.

He gave up. '*I don't know!*'

Suddenly he realized what it was: a piece of plastic, with no voice inside at all.

The phone was still ringing. It must be a matter

223

of urgency but nobody arrived to answer it. *Wherever you are, whatever the time . . .* David gave up and went outside. Across the street, a man was washing his car.

'Can you help me, mate?' asked David. 'Know where a Natalie Taylor lives? I know it's Heron Drive but I don't know the number.'

'Can't help you.' The man shook his head. 'I'm new.'

David walked down Heron Drive. It was yet another row of raw brick houses. He longed for a drink. His body felt loose along the seams; only a Scotch would tighten it up and return him to himself.

'Bang bang! You're dead.'

A little boy sat in a doorway. The barrel of his machine-gun was levelled at David.

'I'm dead already,' said David. 'Look.' He spread out his hands. His fingers trembled; he noticed this with vague interest.

'Fall down then,' said the boy.

David asked him where Natalie Taylor lived.

'She lives here, next door to me,' replied the child. 'She lives with the murderer.'

*   *   *

A stocky young man opened the door.

'Hello,' he said. 'Nobody phoned me, but never mind.'

'No, I didn't phone,' said David.

'Come in anyway.' He stood aside, to let David through. 'That's the lounge.' He pointed.

David went into the room. He paused for a moment, and then sat down.

The young man stood in the doorway. 'Nice room,' he said, and gestured round. 'Built-in shelving, built it myself . . . Feature fireplace.'

There was a pause. 'Is that a phone ringing?' asked David.

The bloke shook his head. 'Crickets.'

He remained standing in the doorway, his large hands hanging at his sides. David became conscious of a curious smell in the house.

'Want to see the other rooms, then?' asked the young bloke.

'Why?'

'Most people do.'

There was a pause. 'Sorry, I haven't explained myself,' said David. 'I'm looking for a Natalie Taylor.'

'Natalie?' The bloke stared at him. 'What do you want with her?'

'I just need to speak to her.'

'I thought you'd come about the house.'

'What?'

The bloke pointed out of the window. There was a FOR SALE sign outside.

'Oh,' said David. 'I didn't notice. Mind if I smoke?'

The young man brought him an ashtray. 'You from the police then?'

'No.'

'She's gone away.' He sat down heavily. 'Two months she's been gone.'

'Where?'

'Why do you want her?'

'Just—unfinished business.'

The bloke stood up. 'Want a cup of tea?'

David followed him into the kitchen. It was

225

stacked with empty cardboard boxes. 'Getting them ready for hibernation,' said his host, filling the kettle. 'Put 'em in, take 'em out, put 'em in, take 'em out . . . sometimes, know something, er—'

'David.'

'Colin.' He shook his hand. 'Sometimes I've been thinking: what's the ruddy point?'

Colin fell into a reverie. A tupperware box stood on the draining board. Inside, its contents were heaving.

'Would you be wanting a biscuit with your tea?'

David shook his head. The kettle boiled but Colin took no notice. He seemed to have run out of energy, too. They stood there for a moment, lost in thought.

'She cheated on you too?'

'In a manner of speaking,' said David.

'You an old boyfriend or something?' he asked bitterly.

'No. Nothing like that. Where did she go?'

'London.'

'London?'

'Leeds was too small for my Nat. She had bigger fish to fry.'

'*Fritto misto*,' said David vaguely.

'Nobody'll find her, she's too darned clever. She'll always be one step ahead, will Nat. Know why? Because she looks after number one. That always came first with her, number one.' Colin gazed at the Fairy Liquid bottle. 'Shouldn't be telling you this. Thing is, I got nobody to talk to. They'd all say *I told you so*. Specially my mam. Even if they don't say it, they're thinking it, and that's just as bad.' His eyes filled with tears.

'I read about her in the paper.'

'She was in all the papers. The local ones.'

'She altered cheques?'

Colin nodded. 'Altered them to Taylor and pocketed the money. See, she only married me because . . .' He broke into sobs.

David's eyes filled too. This startled him. He gazed at the steaming spout of the kettle. 'You don't happen to have anything to drink in the house, do you?'

Colin fetched a half-empty bottle of gin. 'This is hers. Didn't touch the stuff, till I met her.' He poured the gin into tumblers. Five measures each, at least, David noticed.

'Got any tonic?'

Colin shook his head. 'It's dog eat dog in this world,' he said, taking a gulp.

'And you didn't realize?'

Colin shook his head again.

David doused his cigarette under the tap. 'I presume the police are after her.'

Colin nodded.

'They don't have any leads?'

'They know she's gone to London but I could've told them that. She paid by credit card on the motorway. Bought some petrol.'

'They're useless,' said David.

'Trail's gone cold since then.'

'Bloody useless.'

Colin drained his glass. 'When I heard her putting away the pots and pans, making the kitchen into a home, I thought: I'm the happiest man alive. I pinched myself to see if I was dreaming.' He turned his streaming face to David. 'I thought— one day I'll wake up and she'll be gone. The house will be empty, like she's never been.'

David paused. He knew he should feel sorry for Colin, in fact he could feel a stir of sympathy, but he hadn't the energy for it. 'What does she look like?'

'She's got these freckles . . . all on her shoulders and all d-d-down her front . . .'

'I'm not going to be looking down her front.'

'She's just so p-pretty,' he sobbed. 'She's like . . . the prettiest lass you ever saw.'

'What sort of places would she go to?'

'She liked shopping,' he said. 'And clubbing.'

'She got any friends in London, anybody she could be staying with?'

Colin shook his head. 'Not that I know.' He wiped his nose with his huge hand.

David, who had been propped against the kitchen unit, eased himself into a standing position. 'I'll find her.'

'What, in London?'

'I'll track her down. I've got nothing to lose.' They had finished the bottle of gin, he noticed. 'I'm out of a job next week, got nowhere else to go.'

'You'll never find her.'

'Give me a photo.'

They stumbled out of the kitchen, knocking over the cardboard boxes. Everybody seems to be packing up, thought David. What had the bloke meant by hibernation? It sounded a sensible idea to him.

Colin, gripping the banister for support, went upstairs. David followed him. The trilling phones grew louder.

Chloe! Where are you?

Pixies. Can you come and collect me?

The smell was more powerful up here—a

228

pungent, corrupt odour.

Come and fetch me, Dad.

Colin led him into the bedroom. 'Bit cluttered,' he said, 'but now she's gone I can bring them inside and keep an eye on them.'

The smell clogged David's nostrils. He felt sick.

You can't just sit here, rotting away . . .

David sat down on the bed. He gazed at some boxes, filled with straw.

'Something fell on them in the hold,' said Colin. 'Half of them, their shells are cracked. Imagine anyone doing that to poor defenceless tortoises. It's murder, that's what it is.'

Rotting away.

He looked at David. 'You all right?'

David didn't reply. There was a silence.

'Some of them, they'll recover, honest. A little TLC and they'll be as good as new.' Colin rummaged in a drawer. 'Most folk, they're not like you, they don't get upset. They think, ugh, creepy slimy things, which is just plain wrong. Slimy's the last thing they are, in fact their skin's drier than our skin is . . .' He took out a photo and looked at it. 'This is her and me in Paris. We went on a weekend break, a Japanese bloke took it.' He carried it over to the bed. 'Feeling better?'

David pointed to a poster on the wall. 'My daughter liked them too.'

Colin followed his gaze. 'Oh, O-Zone. Nat was their biggest fan, got all their records, once she went all the way to London when they did a gig.'

'She was crazy about the lead singer, what's-his-name . . .'

'Yeah, but I bet she grew out of it,' said Colin. 'Natalie never did.'

229

David got to his feet. 'No, she never grew out of it.' He took the photo and put it in his wallet.

'Good luck,' said Colin. 'You need it.'

One after the other, they filed down the narrow staircase. 'If I find her, what do you want me to do?' asked David. 'You want her back?'

Colin opened the front door and shook his head. 'She's dead to me now,' he said. 'Dead and gone.'

CHAPTER THREE

I'm walking the streets, looking for you. It's funny, I never get tired though I walk all day, and when darkness falls, which it does early now, I'm still walking. Along Oxford Street the shops are lit, bright lights, and there are girls in there just like you, they're standing at the racks of clothes, their heads tilted, considering. They pull off their gloves, because it's chilly now, sometimes they take them off with their teeth, and they stretch out their hands and feel the blouses. They turn and laugh soundlessly to each other, I see them through the glass.

I could stand there for hours. 'What's your problem?' a voice once said. Thought I was a Peeping Tom.

Sometimes it's a girl alone and she selects items and lays them over her arm and on the way to the changing room she hesitates. I know what she's thinking because you thought it too: Am I too big? Will somebody love me one day? I feel close to these girls, through them I'm closer to you because their dreams are your dreams, they're living your life, the life you should be living now.

I know where you'd go, all the kids go there—Covent Garden, Soho, streets where girls like you walk arm-in-arm, knots of men eyeing you and you're tossing your heads pretending to ignore them but that's why you're out on the town, you're there to be watched. And sometimes you wear such thin clothes, on these cold nights, that I want to be a father again . . . 'Wrap up or you'll catch your death.' I want to tell you to be careful, it's a wicked world out there in the shadows where I'm watching you, biding my time for however long it takes.

In Old Compton Street, despite the cold, you spill out from the pubs on to the pavement, and suddenly I catch sight of a profile and my heart leaps but it's always the wrong girl. Once I heard your name called and I swung round but she wasn't you, she wasn't anything like you. There are these Japanese eating places now, they must be new, I haven't been to London for years, the kids like them, rows of kids sitting at long wooden tables shovelling in the noodles. I thought I saw you then, at the far end of a table, but this big bloke blocked the doorway and wouldn't let me in.

'Hey, pal,' I said, 'I'm just looking for a girl.'

Who did he think I was? I'm just a person, I've got as much right to be there as anybody.

Then there's another voice behind me. 'You want a girl?' it said. 'I can find you a girl, no problem.'

I cross and re-cross the heart of London, I must have walked hundreds of miles by now though the city feels no more familiar to me than when I began. I see nothing, that's why. I'm just looking for your face.

Sometimes I sit in a pub, I've become one of those sad bastards I used to serve. I sit there with the Evening Standard *and watch the door, willing it to open and for you to come in. It's only a matter of time, you see, sooner or later our paths will cross. Somewhere—in the street, in a club—I'll find you. I don't care how long it takes, like I told Colin I've got nowhere else to go, all I possess is locked in the boot of my car. I haven't even unpacked and put it in my room, that's how rootless I am in this city. I'm just a pair of eyes and a pair of legs.*

It may take months, it may take years, but time means nothing to me any more; the clock stopped one night in April. I'm looking for you and sooner or later I'll find you. Then we'll talk. For now, at last, I have so much to say.

CHAPTER FOUR

In January, David's money ran out. He got a job as a barman in a pub off Leicester Square. It was a great barn of a place owned by Allied Breweries. In the future, however, he would remember little about it. In fact, ten years later he walked past the place having forgotten that he had ever worked there at all. For during those dark winter weeks he absorbed little, performing his duties as if wound up like clockwork. That the job was too menial for a man of his age and experience scarcely registered. He was civil to the other staff and to the hordes of strangers who crammed the place in the evenings, out on the town for a night Up West, out to get slaughtered. He was alert to only one thing. The chances might be one in millions but he had to believe in it, otherwise . . . otherwise it didn't bear thinking about.

Nor could he remember, in later years, any other life beyond walking and working. *You're such an obsessive*, Sheila had once said—Sheila his wife, whose face he could scarcely remember. He planned his walks with the thoroughness of a general plotting a campaign. Dividing the Inner City by postal districts, he marked a grid on his *A–Z* map and patrolled the designated streets, not stopping until he had covered his allotted route. Hammersmith Broadway to Shepherd's Bush, Kensal Rise to Kilburn . . . He walked fast, a man with a purpose, the photo of a laughing girl in his wallet. If for some reason he didn't complete the route he returned at the earliest opportunity and finished it before embarking on the next. This gave him a small feeling of satisfaction.

Of course he was aware that this plan had no logic to it, he wasn't stupid, for why should she be in one place rather than another? That wasn't the point. And as there was nobody to argue with him, it hardly mattered, did it?

Nor was he entirely inflexible. Some days he rang the changes, transferring his attentions to the underground. This was more a freewheeling kind of thing. He simply consulted his tube map and rode round and round on the Circle Line or took the Northern or District to its final destination— High Barnet, Upminster. He sat there, watching the faces, ready to pounce. Sooner or later, he believed it in his bones, sooner or later he would spot her. He sat there, biding his time like a murderer.

And he wasn't obsessive. He did other things. He must have done, because when it happened he was walking home from the cinema. That's life, isn't it? You plan something and get nowhere; you forget about it and there, on the wall, is the poster.

What was the film he had been watching? He couldn't remember, because when he saw the poster it was wiped from his mind.

O-Zone. One Nite Only.

David stood there in the rain, the traffic hissing past. It was a cold night in February. The poster was stuck on to an empty shop window in the Elephant and Castle, just a few yards from his room. He hadn't noticed it before.

O-Zone plus Support, Single UK Appearance, The Forum, Kentish Town. The date was the following Friday.

*   *   *

I'm going down to London, Dad. Can you lend me the fare for the coach?

Why are you going?

O-Zone are playing. I've never seen them live.

You mean you've only seen them dead?

Dad! That's not funny!

Please Dad, I'll be all right. Rowena and Tim, that's her boyfriend, they're going too, Mum says I can go, I've got my phone with me, I'll be fine . . . please, Dad, you said I shouldn't rot away here . . .

Please please! They're wicked. Please, Dad, I'll be gutted.

How do you speak? I can no longer remember your voice, the tone of it. When I talk to you, in my head, I can no longer find the right age for you. You're too

234

young; it's as if I haven't caught up with your last age. And you don't sound quite right either, I can't catch your tone. What did you sound like?

I turn the dial, searching for you, but your voice has disappeared from the airwaves.

*   *   *

She was here; he felt it. O-Zone stood up on the stage, doing their stuff—not his kind of music, not hardcore enough for him, all that bass couldn't disguise the sogginess at its centre, its girliness—they pounded it out and the audience swayed and jiggled, packed close. So many girls gazing at the lead singer, whatever his name was, ponceing around, prowling the stage with the mike in his hand, jumping and landing with his thighs apart, real bathroom-mirror stuff. He, David, should know.

She was here, in this place with him, singing along to the words he knew so well through her bedroom wall. *Turn that rubbbish down!* Why did she have no taste? He had tried to introduce her to the greats—Cooder, Springsteen, the Grateful Dead—but she had shuddered. Ugh, it was sad old dads' music, music for people who were past it, practically dead.

But David was alive, he had outlived her, a balding man amongst a load of kids, a sad bastard maybe, a groper, maybe they were thinking this if they noticed him at all. No doubt he was as invisible as his own daughter. She should have been there; she would have loved it. The other girl had taken her place.

This was how it felt. For once, David was sober.

235

He held a plastic glass of lager but his head was clear. The other girl, she was living Chloe's life, the cuckoo in his daughter's nest. He knew her face so well, fixed smiling in the photo; he knew every detail whilst Chloe's face had become blurred and all but disappeared. Wasn't that the strangest thing? That by now this other girl, the girl he wanted to punish for what she'd done, she was more real to him than his own daughter. *Nat was their biggest fan . . . she went all the way to London when they did a gig.* Wherever she lived in this vast city, she had been drawn here tonight, pulled by the magnet of the music. He was convinced of it. He had to be, for it was his only chance.

But where, amongst these hundreds of kids? He eased his way through the Forum, nudging past the bodies; he looked at the girls' faces. As time passed, however, his hope drained away. How could he find her? Freckles didn't help; it was too dark to see. How tall was she? He had no idea. Her hair might be shorter or longer.

His earlier euphoria vanished. The whole thing suddenly struck him as insane, as insane as spending the past three months walking the streets.

'This one's for Rachel, wherever you are,' murmured the singer into the mike. The girls near David moaned. O-Zone played their last number, as familiar to David as the beat of his own heart. *Chloe, you staying in your room all day? . . . Chloe, for Christ's sake, get a life!*

And then it was over and the crowd, great hefty girls jostling him, stampeded towards the exit. David struggled to get through. He had meant to leave first and wait outside, watching them one by one as they emerged, but his mind had wandered.

236

Now his exit was blocked and by the time he fought his way outside the kids were already dispersing, walking down the street, their chattering voices drowned by the traffic. Clots of them gathered at the bus stop.

This one's for Sheila.

He had played a few gigs after they had met. Singling out her face in the crowd, he had smiled down at her. And afterwards, at the stage door, she had been waiting shyly, a little apart.

The stage door.

David stood, frozen.

He barged through a group of kids—'Hey, mister, watch it!'—and ran around the corner. Down the side of the building was an alleyway, with the Stage Door sign at the end of it. But already a limo was driving towards him, fast. He had to press himself against the wall.

A pack of kids chased the car but now it was pulling out into the street and in a moment it was gone. Exhaust fumes filled the air.

The kids ran after it. 'Damon!' they yelled. From what David could see, in the darkness, they were very young. And then they were gone too.

*   *   *

Back in his room, David sat at the window. As the night wore on he smoked one cigarette after another. On the other side of the road was a garden centre. Bags of compost were heaped up, one on top of the other; they gleamed in the street light.

It had been hopeless. He knew it all along. Even if this Natalie had been there she was a mirage, as insubstantial as his own daughter. He had fixed his hopes on her, as he had fixed them on Chloe, and created a girl who didn't exist. And now she was lost to him, too. He was crazy to think he could find her. Maybe she wasn't even living in London, she had gone somewhere else. Abroad, anywhere. And what on earth was the point? It wouldn't bring his daughter back.

David drank steadily, with a cold, hard despair. He gazed out of the window. Beyond the slumped sacks rose a block of flats. As time passed the lights were extinguished, all except one. The window was up on the sixth floor. Every night, whatever the time, that one light shone. When David lay on the bed, his legs aching from walking, that light was his only companion. Who lived in that room—a man like himself, sitting there alone while the city slumbered?

Maybe it was a mother, like Sheila, kept awake by a fretful baby. In the early months Chloe had nearly driven them insane. She had cried all night, piercing screams. Dry-eyed, she had cried with a terrible desolation, as if she knew. The only way David could pacify her was to put her crib in the back of the car and drive her round the streets of Morecambe. Round and round he drove, through dark streets empty of cars, until finally she was silenced.

*   *   *

When David woke, he was lying fully clothed on the bed. His head throbbed and his mouth was filled with ash. It was raining. He thought: What do I do now? He had reached rock-bottom, for there

238

was no hope left. He wondered if Sheila ever thought about him. She had no idea where he was; like the girl, Natalie, he had vanished off the radar screen.

He switched on the TV. The breakfast show was on. A man, who looked familiar, was being interviewed. He wore a purple leather jacket and slicked back his hair with his hand.

'Yeah, I'm real excited about our latest single.'

It was the singer from O-Zone.

* * *

Within minutes, David was down in the street, fumbling with the lock of his car. He finally got the door open, flung himself in and started the engine.

It was Saturday morning; there was little traffic about. He drove fast, accelerating through traffic lights as they changed to red. It was only a mile from his room in the Elephant and Castle to the South Bank. He knew the LWT studios; years ago, in his real life, he had taken his family to watch a show there. One of his customers had given him the tickets.

He drove past Waterloo Station and swerved around a double-parked van. He circled the roundabout and turned right. Driving down a side street, he stopped outside the LWT building.

* * *

David got out of his car and strolled over. Fans waited beside a limo. They huddled, herd-like, in the rain. There was something heroic about them, something stoic and resigned, as if they had waited there all week. Thirty of them, maybe more, mostly young girls. He couldn't recognize her, but then most of their faces were turned towards the lobby doors. Besides, during the past night Natalie's face had blurred into something generalized, a hundred girls superimposed upon each other until the features had become meaningless.

The doors opened. A man came out, but it wasn't him. The crowd subsided.

She wasn't here. He had simply made himself believe she would come, it had nothing to do with her, whoever she was. She was in Australia. Anywhere.

And then the doors opened and the lead singer came out, accompanied by a minder.

'Damon!'

The kids surged forward. Somebody held an umbrella over Damon's head as he signed autographs. It was all over quickly—a flurry of paper, some chatter, and then he was getting into the car. The driver started the engine.

'Damon!'

A young woman stepped forward. Furry brown coat, leather boots, beret.

'Damon, remember me?'

He looked at her. 'Hi.'

'Don't you recognize me?' she asked.

'Sure . . .' He gazed at her, frowning.

'Kensington Hilton, remember?'

He paused. Then he grinned. 'Hey, yeah . . .' he paused. 'It's . . .'

The minder touched his arm. 'We've gotta go, sir.'

'You do remember, don't you?' she said.

'Sure I do! It's . . .' He stopped. 'Mary?'

'No, not Mary.'

'Come on, sir.' The minder looked at his watch.

'I'll get it . . .' said Damon, thinking hard. 'It's
. . .' He gave up.

'It's Natalie,' she said.

*   *   *

Luck was on David's side. No lorries blocked his
way, no traffic lights held him up. Natalie's car was
a sporty-looking Honda, metallic-green. He kept it
in sight across Waterloo Bridge, down through the
underpass and up through Camden Town where,
without indicating, it turned right. London was
eerily quiet; all he could hear was his hammering
heart.

Natalie drove fast. Why had Chloe never learnt
to drive? Maybe it stemmed from fear. All those
unknown dangers, all those accidents waiting to
happen. But they didn't happen, did they? Not the
way you expected.

Natalie looked older than he had imagined; in
his mind, she and Chloe had merged into the same
age. This woman was in her early thirties, of
course, he had read it in the paper. And he hadn't
reckoned on the blonde hair or, somehow, the
beret. She was smaller, too, and more vulnerable.
'Hey babe, you take care then,' said Damon, before
he drove away.

David followed the car up Seven Sisters Road. It
was interesting, how much you could learn about a
person from the way they drove. At a pedestrian
crossing, a hesitant little family stepped off the
pavement but the Honda accelerated across and
they jumped back again. It was David who had to

241

stop. Natalie drove skilfully but with no thought for others; he suspected that she never looked in her rear-view mirror—an advantage, in this case.

Chloe *had* learnt to drive. He remembered it now. They had sent her to a driving school because neither he nor Sheila had trusted themselves to give her lessons, it would all have ended in tears. However, she had failed her test. In fact, she had pressed the wrong pedal and ended up on the pavement, wedged against a post box.

All those school lessons; all that homework. Chloe used to weep before history tests, she could never remember dates. The dread of the dentist; those painful fillings. She needn't have bothered, need she? Stuffing her head with facts, getting her teeth drilled. If she had known, she could have saved herself the trouble.

Suddenly, the car stopped without warning. David jammed on his brakes. Natalie left the car double-parked and went into a dry cleaner's. He waited, the engine idling. It was ten fifteen; the street was already busy. Shoppers crowded round a West Indian greengrocer's; they rifled through fabric at a pavement stall. It was a normal Saturday morning in Finsbury Park.

Up the road stood the Astoria. David had seen the Beatles perform there. I was their biggest fan, he thought, I came all the way down to London when they did a gig. How old was he—fifteen? 'Love Me Do' was at number one, and back home in his bedroom in Southport he practised the chord changes over and over on his guitar. *'What a racket!'* said his mother, who loved the Fab Four. *'You're murderering it.'* And somewhere in America a boy was growing up who would shoot John

Lennon dead. All those unwritten songs, thought David. Did John Lennon know the dates of the kings of England too?

The rain had stopped. Natalie emerged, clothes over her arm. Sunlight shone on their plastic wrapping. She flung them into the passenger seat and drove off.

Further up the street she double-parked again and went into a chemist's shop. David felt strangely intimate with her, following her as she did her errands. What was she buying in the chemist's—make-up, shampoo?

Why doesn't she make an effort? he asked his wife. *Why doesn't she do something about her hair? It just sort of hangs.*

Natalie came out, carrying a plastic bag. Colin was right; she was very pretty. Even at this distance he could see that. She stopped outside a halal butcher. Carcasses hung in its window. David could tell, however, by the way she stood that she wasn't looking at the meat. She was checking her reflection in the glass. Men—a Rastafarian, another black guy in a tracksuit—looked at her.

She could be pretty if she lost some weight.

Wisps of hair were visible under her beret. It looked blonder than in the photo. She hurried over to her car; a traffic warden stood there, opening his notebook. She said something to him; he laughed. David watched her smiling at him, flirting with him. He felt a pain beneath his ribcage. *Get a life*, he'd said to Chloe. This young woman, she went shopping, she charmed traffic wardens. No doubt she had a job and a boyfriend.

She got into her car. He drove behind her as she turned left at the tube station and speeded up a

243

one-way street. He had to accelerate, to keep up. It was ten thirty. He was due at the pub at eleven but that was irrelevant now. He would never go back. Pubs were used to unreliable bar staff, here today, gone tomorrow. She turned right, again without indicating, and drove along a street of shuttered-up shops. The sun shone on the grimy brickwork of the houses.

She stopped again, suddenly. He nearly crashed into her car. He braked, reversed and drove around her, keeping his head averted. Further up the street he pulled in and looked into his rear-view mirror. She was backing her car into a parking space.

David switched off the engine and sat there. His heart raced; he longed for a smoke. In the mirror he saw her taking out her bags and dry cleaning. She slammed the door shut and pressed a remote; the car lights flashed as she immobilized it.

She walked up to a side door, next to a restaurant, and rummaged for her keys. Her dry cleaning slid on to the pavement; she picked it up. Then she let herself in through the door, awkwardly, sideways, the stuff over her arm, and went into the house.

He had her. David sat in his car, unable to move. His triumph exhausted him. Like a murderer, he had tracked down his victim. He could kill her now.

For that was how he felt. He had a strong desire to kill her—not for what she had done, which was bad enough, but for what she was: alive, and beautiful, and living the life his daughter should have been living, had she shown any inclination to do so.

He felt terribly tired. It took a superhuman effort just to start the engine. He drove back to the

Elephant and Castle, back to his room. Fully clothed, he lay down on his bed and slept like the dead.

CHAPTER FIVE

Sunday dawned with a cold, hard light. David didn't return to Finsbury Park. Instead he drove to Greenwich, through canyon-streets that blinded him with their glare and then plunged him into shadow. They flickered in his eyes like a black-and-white film. Church bells rang. He felt alert, the blood singing in his veins.

He walked on to the top of Greenwich Park and sat there, gazing over the city. Now London had delivered Natalie up to him he felt released; he knew what he had to do and there was a certain luxury in delaying it. Natalie was his, and her ignorance of this made him, just for a moment, feel protective towards her. And then the anger surged up again.

How fair was the city, spread out in the sunshine! It looked so blameless. Distance had dissolved the banal acts of evil that must be taking place even as he looked. David sat on a bench, the winter sunshine warming his face. He had stepped from one part of his life into another; the excitement quickened his heart.

He got up and walked through the park. The air cut into his lungs. His senses were so sharp that he could feel each blade of grass, crushed by his shoes. The bare tree trunks caught the sun. He suddenly remembered a poem written by a long-ago girlfriend, Bea.

The tall trees, through understanding grieving
Their long black branches weaving
A dream, across the lonely sky
Dreamt in the substance of the wind's soft sigh . . .

What had either of them known of grief, then?
This dream is the web of God, and I, the fly.

Sometimes words chased ahead of you; they waited, patiently, for you to catch up with them.

What had happened to Bea, with her hippy plaits? When they broke up she disappeared to Ireland. He had thought at the time: no sorrow can be worse than this.

When darkness fell he went back to his digs and packed his bag. The shower, down the corridor, was broken. He shaved at his basin and changed into fresh clothes. As he picked up his car keys he looked around the room for the last time. It was seven o'clock. In the flats opposite, the lights were lit. It was Sunday evening, the slackest night of the week in the pub trade. Despite the lure of pub quizzes and karaoke nights, people stayed in, closed off from the world; families drew together in front of the telly. He looked up at the sixth-floor window, where the unknown person had kept vigil with him, through so many nights. For once, the window was dark.

*   *   *

David parked, switched off the engine and sat there for a while. The terrace glowed dully in the sodium light. The Blue Elephant restaurant was closed.

246

There were three floors above it, but only one set of windows was illuminated. He willed them to be hers.

He got out of the car and walked across the street. There were two names beside the doorbells: Brandon and T. Ongali. The third was a blank. He pressed that one.

Nothing happened. He waited a while and pressed the bell again. Upstairs, he heard a window slide open.

'Yes? Who is it?' A head looked down; it was her.

He looked up. 'Natalie Taylor?'

'Who are you?'

'David Milner.'

'What do you want?'

'I just want to talk.'

'Sorry, she's not here.'

The window slid down. He rang again; no reply.

Down the street, diagonally opposite, stood a pub. David decided to wait it out; he couldn't think what else to do. He crossed the road and went inside. A few old boozers sat around, their faces lifted to the TV that hung from the ceiling. *They might be old lags, but they're our old lags.* He suddenly missed Sheila with such force that it took his breath away. The place was barely ticking over; the moment he stepped through a door he could sense a failing pub. Behind the bar stood the landlord: blazer, tie, inflamed complexion. He stood ramrod-straight; there was an ex-army look to him.

David ordered a double Bell's and sat beside the window. He lit a cigarette and waited.

Time passed. An old girl came in and ordered a

Guinness. 'Went to Epsom,' she said. 'Nana took me.'

The publican muttered something. He was older than David and had lost even more hair; the shape of his skull was visible under his skin.

David kept his eyes on the street. An hour had passed. He thought: I've waited all these months, I'm not going to give up now. Three youths danced sideways along the pavement, kicking a can.

He remembered another old girlfriend, Leah. She had a twelve-string guitar; they used to play bottleneck blues together . . . *Been down so long, got nowhere to go but up,* they sang in Mississippi Delta voices. She had got pregnant. If she had gone through with it, how old would his child have been? David worked it out: thirty-three. An almost middle-aged person, walking the earth.

'How's the leg bearing up?' asked the landlord.

The old woman told him. David's mind wandered. Where was Leah now, the girl with whom he had, briefly, created a child? He hadn't thought about her for years. How strange it was, how girls surfaced in one's life. For weeks or months their daily life was as familiar as his own—doctor's appointments, quarrels with their parents. And then they submerged, back into the place from where they came, Morecambe or Southport, back into their former lives, never to be seen again.

Out in the street the door opened. Natalie came out. David had imagined this happening so many times that for a moment he thought it was an illusion. He drained his drink and stood up. Through the window he saw her walk down the street and disappear into the one shop that was open, an off-licence.

He left the pub and crossed the road. A white van, Self-Drive Rental, was parked near her front door. He hid behind it.

Carrying a plastic bag, she emerged from the shop. When she reached her doorway David stepped out.

'Listen,' he said, 'I need to talk to you.'

'Go away, whoever you are,' she said, and tried to put her key into the lock.

'I'm not from the police, I'm not anything to do with your husband.'

'Fuck off—' Her hand was shaking; she couldn't get the key in.

'But I did see Colin.'

She swung round. 'Does he know where I live?'

David shook his head. 'He was really upset, though.'

'Who are you?'

'My name's David Milner. Do you recognize it?'

'Why should I?'

'It was written on a cheque.'

'A cheque?'

'Mr and Mrs D. Milner.'

She gazed at him, puzzled. 'What on earth are you talking about?'

'One of those cheques you stole, it was mine.'

She stared at him, her face blanched in the sodium light.

'It's all right,' he said. 'I'm not asking for my money back.' He smiled at her. It was so long since he had smiled that his skin felt stretched.

'What do you want, then?'

'Let me buy you a drink,' he said.

With some reluctance, she followed him across the road and into the pub. He sat her down at the table by the window and fetched them drinks: a gin and tonic for her and a ginger ale for himself; he had to keep his mind clear.

'I still don't understand,' she said. A roar of laughter came from the TV.

'It was a final demand, I remember paying it. I know I paid it. My wife said I didn't, but I remember posting it. I'm not barking mad.' He smiled again. He tried to keep his tone light. 'And you stole it.'

'But how did you know?' She stopped; her eyes narrowed. 'Anyway, I didn't do it.'

'Oh come on, Natalie. Of course you did. See, my phone was cut off.'

'But nobody knew—'

'What do you mean?'

'The payments went through, that's what was so clever—' She stopped.

'It's OK, I won't tell anybody. That's not why I'm here.'

'Why are you here, then? You want your money back?'

'Last orders!' called the landlord, and rang a bell.

'I don't give a damn about the money,' David said.

'Because nobody lost out, not the way I did it, only the big outfits, and who gives a fuck about them?'

'It's not the money.'

'Last orders, ladies and gentlemen, please!'

David said: 'My daughter died.'

*   *   *

250

'It's Chilean Merlot.' Natalie took a bottle out of her plastic bag. 'That OK?'

She uncorked the wine and fetched two glasses. She wore a fluffy jumper and black leggings; he hadn't really looked at her until now. They were up in her flat. There was a temporary feel to the place—mismatched furniture, marks on the walls where other people's pictures had hung. It looked as if she were just passing through, as he had done.

'So, what happened?' she asked, passing him a glass of wine.

He told her about the club, how Chloe went there for a party.

'I know Pixies,' Natalie said. 'I've been there.'

'I'd promised to collect her, whatever the time. That was our deal. But when she phoned, she couldn't get through. The line was dead.' He gazed out of the window; one by one, the lights in the pub were extinguished. 'She couldn't get a minicab, they were all booked up, so she decided to walk.' Speaking it aloud, after the months of silence, was not the relief he had thought it would be. He stopped.

'She was that girl . . .' Natalie looked at him wonderingly. 'I read about it in the papers.'

He looked her in the eye. 'She died because of your greed. How much was it—a hundred pounds? A hundred and fifty? I can't remember. She died because of your pissy little fraud.'

'Don't blame me—'

'It was all your fault.'

'Don't be daft!' Her eyes blazed. 'Look, I'm sorry for what happened, it must be terrible, but why blame me? Why don't you blame the person who took the minicab your daughter could've

251

taken? Or the person who maybe was in the loo, so your daughter had to wait, so she was five minutes later and that meant she was walking down the wrong street at the wrong time, just when a car—'

'Don't!'

'Blame the buses for not running all night, blame Manchester bloody public transport. Blame your daughter for not asking someone there for a lift, oh I don't know!' Natalie stopped, breathing heavily. 'You're just trying to make sense of it but there isn't any sense, it's all a bloody lottery, haven't you realized that yet? It's like, you put a pin in a map. That's all it is, no more and no less. Don't you understand?' She stubbed out her cigarette in a saucer. 'Just because you've got to dump it somewhere, don't dump it all on me. You don't even know me.'

There was a silence. David suddenly felt weary.

She drained her glass. 'Blame the man who murdered her.'

Down in the street a car hooted. A door slammed; somebody roared with laughter. Then the car drove away and there was silence.

David got to his feet. 'Can I have a bath?'

*   *   *

He lay submerged in the foam. He had poured in Lime and Geranium Bath Gel. The shelf was crowded with girlie things: perfume, a bottle of cleanser, a pack of Go-Blonde Hair Lightener. There was a grubby make-up bag and a bottle of Pantene Soft'n'Easy Conditioner, the sort Chloe used to buy. Natalie, too, had left the lid off.

David lay there until the water grew tepid; he

might as well do this as anything else.

Love, oh love oh careless love ... his daughter used to sing. How did the rest go?

Taught me to weep, it taught me to moan, it taught me to lose my happy home. Such a pure, true voice she had.

Through the wall he heard a tuneless singing as Natalie rattled around in the kitchen. Maybe she was fixing herself some dinner, though it must have been way past midnight. He felt the faint stirrings of hunger; he hadn't eaten all day.

What was he going to do now? The expected scene—remorse, tears—had failed to materialize. She was too tough for him. *She'll always be one step ahead, will Nat. Know why? Because she looks after number one.*

He picked up a towel from the floor. It was damp; Natalie wasn't the most diligent hostess. Though it was dark green, there were pale patches on it: peroxide. He recognized the signs from a few years earlier, when Sheila had briefly and disastrously dyed her hair blonde. 'I look like Barbara Windsor on a bad day,' she had said.

What was she doing now? Maybe she had set up a hairdressing salon in Hebden Bridge. Twenty-eight years of marriage and she had submerged too, back into the unknown. When they had first met they couldn't keep their hands off each other. He had recorded compilation tapes for her, three of them, they had taken weeks—stopping and starting the numbers, timing them and re-recording the ones that overran. A labour of love.

David dressed and went back into the living room. Natalie turned down the sound on the TV and pointed to a plate.

'You like taramasalata?' She had spread it on crackers.

David took a bite but the cracker disintegrated, drily, and clogged his throat. Natalie uncorked the second bottle of wine and passed him a glass.

'I know who we can blame,' she said. 'The bastard who broke into my car. That's when I got the idea, when I saw a cheque for the cost of an alarm. Funny, isn't it, how one idea leads to another. Let's say the whole thing's his fault.' She laughed briefly. 'Turned out he committed a bigger crime than he thought.'

There was a silence. David swallowed a mouthful of wine. Finally he asked: 'Want to know what it's like?'

'What what's like?'

'She'd be going clubbing, like you do. She'd be washing her hair and meeting people and laughing.'

'I don't go clubbing, not any more.' Natalie put down her half-eaten cracker. 'Shall I tell you something? I'm in this great big city and I don't know anybody. I stay here in this room and watch TV.'

'To tell the truth, she didn't go out much.'

'I don't dare talk to anybody in case they find out who I am,' she said. 'It's like I'm in prison already.'

'I wanted her to go out and have a good time. Trouble was, she'd put on weight, she didn't look like you.'

'Think that makes a difference?'

'She used to be slim and quite pretty really. I was so proud of her—I used to be a good photographer, I used to take her photo—'

'Tell me about it. I knew this photographer once, said he'd get me into modelling—'

'But I stopped. When she was a teenager I stopped because . . . I don't know . . .'

'Last I heard, he was doing nine years.'

'I *do* know,' said David. 'I stopped and now I've got nothing to remember her by.'

'At least she *had* a father,' said Natalie. 'She had you.'

'But I never told her the important things.' Suddenly the words poured out. 'I just shouted at her about her room and all the things that irritated me and really it was because I loved her and I couldn't bear her not to make the best of herself.'

'She had *you*.' Natalie glared at him. 'Aren't you listening? My dad couldn't be arsed, he just buggered off, and know what my mum's like? I bet your wife's nice.'

'My wife's left me.'

'She used to leave me alone all night when I was six—'

'She left me because I wouldn't talk to her.'

'I used to lie in bed and think she must've died and then who would take care of me? And then I'd hear the door slam and her laughing and some bloke laughing, both of them pissed, and she didn't even come in and see if I was all right.' Natalie had finished her cigarettes. She took one from his packet. 'I saw things no child should see. I saw things and I heard things. And we moved from place to place so I didn't have any friends, and sometimes the blokes would come and live with us and once, one of them . . .' She poured more wine into their glasses; it spilt on to the table. 'Maybe you should blame her, for making me what I was.

255

But then she'd had a tough time when she was little, so maybe you should blame them, *her* parents—oh I give up.' She pushed back the hair from her face.

'But you're alive,' David said.

It was chilly. The central heating must have switched itself off. Natalie sat, hunched in her sweater, and stared at the floor.

'When she left,' said David, 'I just said *Got your keys?* I didn't even say goodbye.'

She looked up. 'Don't blame yourself.'

The table had burn-marks along the edge, from some past tenant's cigarettes. He said: 'After it happened, I used to drive round, in the night. I used to drive along the streets she must have walked on her way home. I wanted to be near where she was. I tried to make it all all right, that she wasn't frightened, that she was happy because she'd enjoyed herself at the party . . .'

'She probably had.'

'Some nights I'd park the car where she was found—'

'Where *was* she found?' Natalie looked at him eagerly. After all, this was a murder story, like in the papers. 'I don't remember where it was.'

'Whitworth Street.'

'Where's that?'

'Just near the station. Piccadilly Station. There's a patch of waste ground there.' He stopped. There was a slope, behind a hoarding saying FOR SALE: DEVELOPMENT LAND. People tipped rubbish down it. There was a row of old buildings: Follies Disco, Yellow Cabs, a health club. A few feet away, traffic thundered past. He said: 'Some people had put flowers there, bunches of them with cards.'

'Did you?'

He shook his head. 'I sat there and willed myself to feel something but I couldn't connect it to her . . . that place.' The slope was steep; at the bottom lay a broken pushchair and a filing cabinet. 'They had taken her away by then. I couldn't believe she had been there. People coming and going at the station, everything going on around her as if nothing had happened. It didn't hit me at the right moment, see. It happened just when I wasn't prepared for it.' He paused. 'I like to be prepared.'

They drank in silence for a while.

He said: 'I wasn't prepared for the pain. The physical pain of it.'

Natalie asked: 'Why didn't you talk to your wife? Why are you here, for Christ's sake? You don't even know me.'

Gazing down at his feet, he noticed how scuffed his shoes were. It was all that walking. He used to take care of his clothes, he used to keep himself in trim. He thought of the landlord in the pub across the road; how he had stood rigidly in his smart jacket, with his face like a skull. 'I keep thinking of all the things she's missed, since then, and some of them I'm glad about.'

'What do you mean?'

'I'm glad about them, for her sake. Like that shooting in that American school. I think—at least she's been spared that. It came and went without her worrying about it—if she *would* have worried about it, and then I realize I didn't know her well enough to know if she would've been that upset.' He found he was crying. It was such an unfamiliar sensation that it took him by surprise. 'I never got to know her, see, once she'd grown up. Somehow

257

there wasn't the time.' He looked up. 'Can you put on the bloody heating?'

Natalie got up and went into the hall. He watched her fiddling with the thermostat.

'I'm glad she missed it,' he said, 'and all the stuff about the dying planet, things like that, because now I don't have to worry about it either, things like surveillance cameras everywhere and old dears being mugged. I mean, what sort of world is it? What's the point of it all? But I don't have to worry about it for her, that she's got to grow up and find that out.'

Natalie came back into the room and sat, splay-legged, at his feet.

David said: 'She was alone. I wasn't there to help her.'

Natalie's eyes filled with tears. She took his hand.

'I'm so sorry,' she said.

He pulled her head to his chest. It was a clumsy gesture; she had to shift forward and he felt he was hurting her neck. But she was all he had.

'She wasn't even robbed,' he said. 'There was still eight pounds in her wallet. The minicab fare.'

Outside, a car alarm started wailing.

'I haven't told anybody this,' he said.

She muttered into his jacket: 'What can I do?'

'Do what I came here for.'

Her head jerked back. She stared up at him, her freckles vivid against her white skin. 'What did you come here for?'

'Come back with me.'

'What?'

'Come back to Leeds and give yourself up. Nothing will get my daughter back but—don't you see? Justice will be done.'

'Come back with you?' Her mouth hung open.

He laughed a thin laugh. 'Call it my final demand. Otherwise, nothing makes any sense.' She had shifted away from him; they both found it embarrassing, clasped together like that. 'We've got nothing to lose, either of us. Please, Natalie.'

There was a faint gurgling sound. It was the water in the radiator, heating up.

'They'll find you sooner or later,' he said.

'I know,' she replied.

'It's only a matter of time.'

She sighed, and wiped her nose on her sleeve. 'It hasn't been so much fun, this time around.'

'Do this for me,' he said urgently. 'For Chloe. Please!'

She got to her feet gracefully, in one movement, like a ballet dancer. He thought of his daughter's fat thighs. *She waddles*. Did he say it aloud, to Sheila?

'All right,' said Natalie. 'Give me five minutes. I'll go and pack.' She went into the bedroom and closed the door.

He sat there, on the hard dining chair. She had agreed! For a moment he could hardly believe it.

There was still some wine left, in the second bottle, but he thought: I've got to drive. Even in his state, he thought that.

He spoke aloud to the closed bedroom door: 'It was me, really, who was to blame.'

There, he had said it.

His back ached. Sitting on the hard chair, he felt that he was sitting in judgement. But who was he to judge? That was why he had been unable to speak to Sheila. On the long drive north, through the

259

night, he would tell Natalie this. He was as guilty as she; they were in it together. Now the words had been loosed there was a flood of them, they would gush out, all the things he would tell this girl who until tonight had been unknown to him.

He would tell her about his youth, those heady years when anything had been possible. How he'd had a talent, a true talent like his daughter did, but that life had extinguished it. How all his hopes had been pinned on his daughter, to do what he had failed to do and to redeem him.

He felt sanity returning, warmth filling him like the heat in the radiator. He would go back and deliver Natalie up to the police. He would give up smoking; he would go on the wagon and sort out the rest of his life. A small shift would restore some balance to the world; some kind of justice would be achieved.

He looked at his watch; it was three in the morning. What a long, strange night it had been . . . It seemed to have lasted weeks. Peace flooded through him. With surprise, he realized that his rage was gone. He had lived with it so long that it took him a moment to identify the sensation. It was like the silence when you discover that, some time ago, the rain has stopped. The stillness and then the first, tentative birdsong, ringing through the air.

He gazed at the bedroom door. There were pricks in the paintwork. Some past occupant had pinned up pictures, like Chloe used to do: a party polaroid, a photo of a baby tiger. Behind the door his surrogate daughter was packing. Such was his gratitude to her, now that she had surrendered, that he did indeed think of Natalie warmly, like an alternative child—prettier and more adventurous than Chloe had ever been. The sort of girl he had tried to bully Chloe into becoming. Who knows? They might even stay friends, he might even visit her if she went to prison.

Later he realized how odd it was, to think this way—proof, if proof were needed, that he hadn't yet regained his sanity. But that was how he felt. He was drunk, after all.

Half an hour had passed. David got up and tapped on the door.

'Natalie? We should get moving.'

There was no reply.

Perhaps she was having second thoughts. She was sitting on the bed, her face grim. *Push off and leave me alone.*

He tapped again. Silence.

Finally he opened the door and went in.

Natalie lay on the bed, unconscious. Beside her, on the floor, was an empty bottle of pills.

*   *   *

David stood there, frozen.

'Natalie!'

He lunged towards the bed and shook her.

'Natalie, wake up!'

She was so frail. He could feel her thin shoulder blades beneath her sweater. Gripping her in both hands, he lowered his face to hers. She was still alive; he could feel her breath, soft against his lips. He cupped his hand under her breast; her heart was beating.

'Natalie, don't do this.' A stupid thing to say, but still.

There was no phone beside the bed. David got

to his feet and stumbled into the living room. On the shelf was a volume of the *Yellow Pages* but he could see no phone there either.

A mobile. She must have a mobile. He went back into the bedroom. Natalie looked smaller somehow, diminished already. Her blonde hair, spread out on the pillow, showed its dark roots. Transfixed, he stood there. He could almost see the life in her ebbing away.

She was still breathing. He could see the mauve mohair of her chest gently rising and falling. 'Please don't die,' he said, his voice oddly conversational. 'I'm going to call for help. You've got a mobile, haven't you? Everyone's got a mobile. Chloe's got one though she's always losing it.'

Natalie's bag sat on the floor. He turned it upside down and shook the contents on to the carpet.

'Or else the batteries would be flat,' he said. 'I'd hear her voice breaking up, fainter and fainter, and then she'd be gone.'

He spotted the mobile. It was right there on the bedside table, in front of his eyes. He was too flustered to think straight.

'Stupid me,' he said. You had to keep talking to coma victims. In fact, it came naturally. It kept him calm, too. 'Now, I'm going to dial 999. You'll be fine . . . they'll look after you, might need a stomach pump or whatever but don't worry, nobody'll know what's happened, you needn't come back to Leeds, I promise . . .' His hand was trembling; he could hardly hold the phone. Squinting at the buttons—he was getting shortsighted—he said: 'Now how do I work this thing, eh? Chloe's is different.' He pressed the red button. Nothing happened. 'Shit.' He peered closer. Yes, that was the *On* button. He pressed it again. The tiny screen stayed dark.

'Oh help me, please,' he said. The battery must be flat. But even if it was flat, surely the light would come on?

Frantically he pressed the buttons but the phone was dead.

He climbed to his feet. 'I'm going to get help. Wait here.' This was a daft thing to say—was she going anywhere? 'Bloody phones, never work when you need them.' He touched her foot, in its thick stripy sock. 'Please don't die, Natalie, it wasn't that bad, what you did. I didn't mean it—it was all my fault, you were right, I just needed someone to blame.' He gazed at her closed eyes, the fringed lashes against her skin. 'It only makes it worse. Don't you see?' He urged her, with all his heart, to wake up. 'Don't you see? It makes my daughter a murderer too.'

He looked at her one last time. Then he hurried out of the flat, leaving the door ajar, and thundered down the stairs. He left the front door on the latch, stepped backwards into the street and looked up. The other windows of her building were still dark.

Up the road, in the distance, he saw a call-box. He ran there, fumbling in his pocket for change. Did you need coins for 999?

It makes my daughter a murderer. What did he mean? Surely what he meant was *It makes me a murderer.*

The booth had been vandalized. Somebody had wrenched out the phone; loose wires dangled down.

David stared at it. Not again, he thought. Please

263

God, don't let it happen a second time.

Wherever you are, whatever the time . . . just phone.

The tube station. There must be a phone there. He turned right and ran up the street. It had started to rain. It seemed to take an age before he reached the main road. A taxi approached, its sign illuminated.

'Taxi!' Waving his arms, David stepped into the street. 'Hey, stop!'

The taxi drove on. Just another drunk, the driver was thinking.

Finsbury Park station was closed but there were two phone booths beside the entrance. David went into one, lifted the phone and dialled 999.

A voice answered. What service did he require?

'Ambulance,' he gasped, and gave the address.

And then he was pounding back down the street, past rows of rubbish bags left out for the morning, back to Natalie's flat.

He pushed open the door and rushed upstairs, to the first floor. Natalie's door was still ajar.

'It's all right, I'm back,' he called, like a husband returning from a day's work. 'They're coming.'

He went into the bedroom.

The bed was empty. She had gone.

CHAPTER SIX

'Don't mess with me, baby . . .'

Damon's voice blasted out. Natalie drove fast, through the empty streets. The windscreen wipers sluiced to and fro.

The boldness of what she had done—look, she had got away with it, yet again, she was a cat with nine lives!—the sheer boldness set her heart hammering.

It wasn't that bad, what you did, he had said.

The poor bloke. She was sorry for him, truly she was. The way he'd talked to her, pouring out his heart, it touched her. And his distress, when she lay on the bed . . . she'd had a strong desire to sit up and say, *Just kidding*.

It must be terrible to have a daughter die. Raped and strangled, too. She remembered shivering when she'd heard it on the news. It must be the worst thing that could happen. Poor David. But she couldn't help him; nobody could. Nobody could bring his daughter back; the pain was something he had to work through, by himself.

What a weird night it had been . . . one of the weirdest of her life. Who would have guessed the long chain of events that had resulted from one little cheque. There had been two others, she remembered them now—it was the day the computers were down. She hadn't thought of that; what had happened to the other people?

It was over now, over and done with. Soon it would be a new day. She must pick herself up, dust herself down and start again. A girl had to survive. Did he really think she would give herself up to the police? Was she mad?

She was driving through Hackney. BLACKWALL TUNNEL. The sign loomed up through the rain. She had a plan, of sorts. Her Aunt Judy lived in Folkestone. Judy had a history of mental problems and wouldn't be overly curious about Natalie's appearance on her doorstep. They had kept vaguely in touch over the years—the odd Christmas card—but she hadn't turned up at Natalie's wedding and she would know nothing about her arrest. Natalie would lie low in Judy's bungalow for a few days while she decided what to do next. France was a possibility; her friend Melinda worked in a sports shop in Rouen. Natalie had plenty of ready cash—eight thousand pounds at the last count—and it was high time she disappeared from T.B. Computer Services. She was surprised they hadn't yet twigged that something was going on.

'*Got that lovin' feeling, all over again,*' sang Damon. It was O-Zone's latest single; Natalie sang along, loudly. It was reassuring to hear her own voice, keeping herself company.

In one respect she had spoken the truth. These past months had been miserable, she could admit it now. She had never been so lonely in all her life. She had even missed Colin, that was how desperate she had been.

Never mind. '*Hold me tight, baby!*' she sang as she drove under a flyover.

BLACKWALL TUNNEL. M20 FOLKESTONE said the sign. Too late.

'Shit!' She had missed the slip road that led up to the motorway. In a moment she emerged from the underpass, the rain battering again at her windscreen.

That was OK; she would just have to find her way back. Slewing the car to a halt, Natalie reversed on to the pavement and turned round. All she had to do was return the way she had come, drive under the flyover, do a U-turn and get on to the slip-road.

Except that she seemed to be swept up into a one-way system. It swung her round to the left and suddenly she found herself in an industrial wasteland. Large buildings loomed up on either side. An illuminated sign blazed: ACORN STORAGE.

Damon's voice seemed to be getting fainter. She turned up the volume, but it didn't seem to make a difference. She looked at the dashboard. Was it her imagination, or were the lights dimmer?

'Gimme love, gimme love!' she sang, urging Damon to stay with her, but he was fading. She could hardly hear him now.

It was then that she realized the car was slowing down. She pressed her foot on the pedal but there was no answering surge. She slammed it on the floor but nothing happened.

Natalie peered through the windscreen. The headlights were getting fainter. She kept singing but soon she realized that she was singing alone. Damon had gone. She stopped; silence filled the car.

And then the lights on the dashboard went out completely. The engine cut out and the car drifted to a standstill.

*   *   *

The electrics must have packed up. She was alone, in the middle of nowhere. The rain drummed down. She was sitting in a dual carriageway, with low buildings either side. She could hardly see out, now, with the windscreen wipers stopped, but she dimly glimpsed headlights approaching from the other direction.

A car slowed down, as it passed her, and then accelerated. She turned, and watched its tail lights.

Its brake lights came on, dazzling red in the darkness. The car veered to the left and drove across the central reservation. It was doing a U-turn. The headlights swung round, in her direction.

Wasn't it strange? She knew it would do that. She rummaged in her bag and pulled out her mobile phone. Holding it up to her face, in the darkness, she punched the *On* button.

Nothing happened. She stared at it, in her hand.

'Fuck. Fuckfuckfuck.' She remembered. Back in the flat she had pulled out its SIM card, so David couldn't use it. She had left the card under her pillow.

Natalie flung the phone on to the seat. She grabbed her bag and leapt out of the car. Down the road, the headlights approached.

Natalie ran away, fast. She ran for her life.

CHAPTER SEVEN

Natalie's boots pounded along the pavement. She was a fast runner, but a car was faster. She could hear it approaching behind her. She ran past a closed gate, and then a fence. There was nowhere to hide. GUARD DOGS PATROLLING said a sign. Ahead of her was a side street. She reached it, swerved right and ran down it. Clutching her bag to her chest, she put on speed. As she ran, she searched for a gap, but walls rose up on either side.

Faintly, she could hear the sound of the car. It

had turned down the side street too; the noise of its engine echoed against the walls. It was getting closer.

Behind her, the car's headlights lit a sign: UNITS 12–22. Ahead was a T-junction. Natalie darted left and ran down the road. Behind her, the noise of the car engine grew louder.

It wasn't David. She knew that; how could he possibly have followed her? It was someone else. *There has been an alarming rise in the number of unsolved crimes against women. The police have warned that women at night should be vigilant at all times.*

And then she saw a gap between the buildings— just a slit, bathed in the light from a streetlamp. She ran down it and found herself in an alleyway. It was heaped with rubbish; she swerved around the bags, skidding on the wet ground. On one side loomed up a blank wall; on the other side lay a car park filled with bulldozers. Natalie stumbled over a mattress.

Her lungs were bursting. She leaned against the wall, gasping for breath. *Raped and strangled.* Which happened first? Which gave him the most pleasure?

Why didn't David's daughter use her mobile phone—did it all happen too fast? The car juddering to a halt beside her, hands grabbing her coat and pulling her in. A hand pressed against her mouth.

Sodden in the rain, Natalie stood propped against the wall. She gulped the air, trying to force it into her lungs.

Excuse me, could you tell me the way to Piccadilly Station? Maybe he had said that, leaning out, the door already ajar.

You shouldn't be out alone, haven't you read the newspapers?

The other girl paused—just for a split second. One second too long.

Pop in.

Natalie felt sick. She pushed herself away from the wall and ran on, the breath bursting her lungs. The alley ended in a parking lot. TEXAS HOMECARE. She jumped over a barrier and ran across the expanse of tarmac. Ahead, sheltering under the eaves of the store, stood a row of phone booths.

Maybe the girl's mobile didn't work. Heart hammering, she pressed the button but the battery was dead. It had packed up like Natalie's, a dead thing in her hand.

Hey, want a lift? The door swinging open, wide. The man's face in the street light.

Natalie's heart hurt. Her legs were leaden as she stumbled across the car park. It seemed to take for ever. There was no sound of a car, nothing.

Maybe I'm imagining it. Maybe the girl thought that. *The sound of a car, it's all in my head. Fear does that to you.*

At the far end of the car park, headlights appeared. The car slowed to a halt and waited for her.

Natalie squeezed her eyes shut and opened them. The tarmac was empty. Somewhere, far off, a dog barked.

She was standing in a booth now. Its light was blinding; she felt exposed on all sides, naked. She punched in 999.

'What service do you require?' said a woman's

voice.

'Police,' Natalie gasped.

'Name?'

Natalie paused. What name should she give?

Chloe Milner, she thought. Just tonight, they were together.

She tried to gather her wits. She wasn't thinking straight—had she imagined the car? Maybe nobody had been following her at all. She had become another girl. *That* girl. Any girl.

'Are you there?'

Her head swam. Lorraine, she thought. Tracey Batsford.

'Are you there?' asked the voice. 'Can you give your name?'

She took a breath, and finally spoke the truth. 'Natalie Taylor,' she said.

CHAPTER EIGHT

Leeds Crown Court is a modern, heavy, redbrick building. Inside it is airless and windowless. In Court Number 4 the judge sits in front of pleated beige curtains; this gives him a theatrical look, as if he is just the prologue and soon the curtains will open and the real show begin.

The public sits behind panels of tinted glass; when they turn to look at the person in the dock, they see their own faces reflected. Beyond, the other people—the accused, the jury—are only dimly visible, as if seen in a dream.

One person will never stand in the dock, for he has never been found. Maybe, at this moment, he is helping his daughter with her homework. He leans over her, his arm resting on her shoulder. As he gazes at the exercise book the sums dance in front of his eyes. They make no sense, for his mind is elsewhere. He smells the scent of his daughter, the breathing life of her. Maybe she leaves the top off the ketchup bottle and this annoys him, but only in the way that all fathers are annoyed. He wants the best for her; he fears for her, as all fathers must, in this brutal world. Absent-mindedly, he strokes her slender neck.

Or maybe he lives alone and is sitting in front of the TV, knocking ash into a takeaway pizza box. He's never any trouble, his landlady remarks. Keeps himself to himself. Maybe he has a birthmark down the side of his face, a big beetroot stain, but nobody has lived to report it.

Because—who knows?—maybe he has done this thing more than once. Nobody will ever find out, not in this case. He will take his secret to the grave.

It is not a murderer who sits in the dock. It is Natalie. Dressed in black, she looks small and defiant. Her eyes challenge the jury, who listen with varying degrees of attention to the prosecution witness. It is an afternoon in October, the second day of the trial. Their eyes are drawn to her. It is hard to connect this young woman with crime, she looks so thin and defenceless. Her blonde hair is neatly brushed. The evidence against her seems overwhelming but many people in the jury are secretly on her side. After all, she hasn't murdered anybody. Her crime is a bloodless one, just figures on pieces of paper. Bloody clever, in fact. Maybe, if they had thought of it themselves ... just maybe ...

Nobody came to any harm and they too resent these big corporations, fat-cat payouts, the staggering greed of it, the contempt for ordinary folk. They too have been driven mad by mornings wasted trying to reach a human being and only getting 'Greensleeves'. They too have shivered on a station platform, waiting two hours for a train that never arrives, while the Railtrack chief gets a million-pound bonus. Just thinking about it makes them enraged. She looks so small in this room which is heavy with the weight of the law.

The public gallery is only half-full. After all, this isn't a murder case, it's nothing sensational. Amongst the people sits David, ramrod-straight. He's dressed smartly in a suit, white shirt and tie, as if it is he himself who has been accused, and is trying to impress the judge with his respectability. His eyes are fixed on Natalie.

Voices drone on—Phillip Tomlinson is in the witness stand, he's saying, 'She phoned me at my home and told me to write her a reference under an assumed name . . .'

David's eyes, however, don't move from Natalie's face.

Colin sits behind him, in the public gallery. He too is looking at Natalie. She glances up; she looks at him, briefly, and then turns her head away. Beside Colin sits Stacey—dumpy, plain Stacey from NuLine. Her hand slips into his.

'Terrible, isn't it?' she whispers.

Derek is history now. Stacey has been a supportive friend to Colin during the past months. On many occasions she has fed him cake at her flat and listened to his woes; they have gone rock-climbing together. She loves rock-climbing, she says. In a few weeks his divorce will be finalized.

'You all right, Stumpy?' she whispers, gazing at him through her glasses. He nods.

I never liked Natalie, she thinks. Always thought she was better than us. Prettier, brighter, slimmer legs. And now—see—there is some justice in the world.

When she's at work she doodles dreamily on her jotter. Stacey Taylor... MRS S. TAYLOR...

She settles back. This is better than going to the cinema. She gives Colin's hand another squeeze.

The minutes tick by. The courtroom is stuffy; some members of the jury struggle against drowsiness. David, however, stays wide awake. His eyes don't leave Natalie's face; there is a fierce concentration to him. He hasn't seen her for eight months; his last image of her is lying on a bed in Finsbury Park. Around him, people shift on the seats. They might leave, soon, for a cup of tea.

Another witness is called: some NT book-keeper who starts itemizing the allegedly stolen cheques. Somebody coughs, a rattly, smoker's cough; it is Natalie's mother. Her purple hair is startling amongst the drab browns. A fly buzzes around David's face.

And then Natalie looks at him. Across the room, through the darkness of the tinted glass, her eyes meet his.

'... cheque for the sum of a hundred and twenty-three pounds, fifty-nine pence, dated the eleventh of February...'

The voice drones on. The fly buzzes around his ear.

'... cheque for the sum of a hundred and forty-four pounds, fifty pence, dated the twentieth of

February . . .'

Some of the jury members, following her gaze, turn and look at David. The minutes tick past. Through his own face, reflected in the glass, David looks at her. He knows, now, that he is capable of murder. He thought he had died, that night in April, but there was still life in him. Enough, anyway, to be finally extinguished in Finsbury Park. *Nothing will get my daughter back but . . . justice will be done* . . . Evil, however, has finally triumphed, and the next time, if he can get his hands on Natalie, it will be he himself who stands in the dock. What will be his plea? That the world is senseless?

Natalie looks at Colin. She is not listening to what is being said. She turns away; more minutes pass.

What is going through her mind? Why does she choose this moment? Later, David will ask himself this question over and over. He will never meet her again; he will never learn the answer.

In the days that follow, Colin, too, will ask himself a similar question. Nobody will ever know; only Natalie, in her heart.

For at that moment something snaps. Something that she has resisted, all these months of stubborn self-justification. These moments cannot be forced by others, like an injection to trigger the birth of a child. She has arrived alone, after a long journey that has brought her to this place, and to David's face. Looking at him, she finally understands.

Or maybe she just realizes that the case against her is overwhelming.

Natalie stands up and turns to the judge. The witness falters, and stops speaking.

She holds up her hand—a quaint gesture, as if she is stopping traffic. The room is silent.

She addresses the judge in a loud, clear voice. 'Excuse me,' she says, 'but I want to change my plea.'

The judge starts to speak; Natalie's counsel jumps up.

But Natalie carries on talking. 'I want to change it to guilty.'